FORBIDDEN
THE CAMPBELL FAMILY SAGA 1

GLORIA DAVEN

PROLOGUE

JARRED

Jarred trotted into Sean's office as ordered.

This past weekend had been one of the best he'd had in a long time. Mentally, he was still in Verbier with Rose, careening down the steep slopes. She was the woman of his dreams—there was no other way of putting it.

Jarred knocked on Sean's office door and waited for his gruff "Come in." This time, he found his brother standing at the window rather than enthroned behind his desk. Jarred walked to the middle of the room and stopped, waiting.

"How was your weekend?" Sean turned to look at Jarred. His expression was perfectly neutral, with no indication either way of whether he knew where Jarred had spent the past few days—or, more importantly, with whom.

"Good."

"That's good." Sean regarded Jarred intently for a moment before continuing. "I'm dissolving your department. It hasn't been economically viable in years. Go ahead and start assembling a team for Manchester. We'll be leasing a space downtown, so find yourself an apartment around there."

Wait, what? Sean wanted him to *move* to Manchester?? What the hell?! Jarred fought back a rush of anger. Sean obviously hadn't just come up with this idea today. So first he'd insisted Jarred return to London, only to refuse to give Jarred his old job back. Then he'd been mad about Jarred selling his condo so he could renovate his late mother's house. And now Sean was just dissolving Jarred's entire department here in London? And shipping him off to Manchester? Was this some kind of prank?

"How long have you been cooking this up?" Jarred sniffed. "How come I had a choice before, but not now? You *know* I'm planning to buy Mom's house and renovate it to live in, so *now* you're sending me to Manchester? What gives?"

"Restructuring has been on the table for a while now. Clever little monkey like you can probably put the rest together."

"What the hell is that supposed to mean—was bringing me back here just some kind of game? And what about Rose? Why would you bother promoting her if you were just going to eliminate the department?" He wondered if he'd be able to take her to Manchester with him.

"The promotion was only ever temporary, and she knows that. I was originally planning on waiting a bit longer, but given the circumstances, I think it's time to move forward."

"Given what circumstances?"

Sean scowled at him furiously. Several long seconds of tense silence ticked by. "Don't play stupid," he finally snarled. "I warned you, Jarred. Keep your goddamn paws to yourself. Which part of that was so hard to understand?"

So Sean *did* know about him and Rose. Dammit.

"You have exactly two options here: stay away from Rose, or get the hell out. You think I'm going to let a little shit like you bring down the whole fucking company? YOU GOT THAT?" Sean had worked himself up into a frenzy. He clenched his fists, seemingly itching to hammer his point home. Literally.

Jarred bit his tongue to keep himself from saying anything rash. Where did Sean get off, treating Jarred like this? Their dad was still the primary shareholder. Then again, Dad probably wasn't likely to contradict Sean.

Jarred wasn't necessarily worried about his own fate, but Rose didn't deserve to be out on the street. Especially not on Jarred's account. He knew there was no point wondering whether she'd come with him to Manchester. Giving her up was out of the question... but Manchester wasn't exactly the other side of the world. They could still get together on weekends.

Unless...

"You're letting her go?"

It was more of a realization than a question.

"The team in Frankfurt needs reinforcements."

Frankfurt in Germany? Rose wasn't about to move away from England. She was always talking about how much she liked it here. "She'd never agree to leave the country."

"It's that or find another job."

"Then I'll quit instead."

Sean scoffed. "Don't make a fool of yourself."

"What, you'd *still* fire her?"

"Spending time abroad looks good on a resume. Rose would be stupid not to take the offer."

Silently, Jarred turned to leave.

"I want a list of names for your team by the end of the week," Sean called when Jarred was at the door. "The new office will be move in-ready next Monday."

Rose was going to hate him. He'd raised the stakes too far, and now he'd lost everything.

CHAPTER 1

Five weeks earlier

F

JARRED

Ace-jack of hearts in the hole. Pot at $32,000. Queen, queen, jack on the flop—the first three community cards the dealer laid out—so Jarred already had two pair: queens and jacks. The cowboy across the table, eyes hidden behind mirrored sunglasses, drummed the first two fingers of his right hand on the table.

Jarred focused on keeping his poker face even though his mind was all over the place. He was really craving a drink. Just enough to take the edge off, calm his nerves again. Once this game was in the bag, he could hit the bar.

The cowboy was the last one still in the game; the other three were sipping their drinks nearby, chatting quietly as they watched. Waiters moved with silken grace through the small crowd clustered around their table.

The cowboy sure didn't seem to be in any hurry to decide.

Jarred loved Texas Hold'em. A thrill that grew with every card the dealer revealed. Even once all five cards were out, it might still be anyone's game—if you knew how to read the table and calculate your odds. And bluff at the right moments, of course.

He wasn't even supposed to be in Vegas right now. He'd been on his way to L. A., to meet his sister Alice. The second anniversary of their mother's death was coming up, and he sure as hell didn't want to spend it alone. He knew he'd just fall into another deep hole and end up doing something stupid that he couldn't remember afterward.

Jarred took a long, slow breath and told himself to get a grip. He wished he didn't miss her so damn much. This had to get easier eventually, right? *Focus, dammit. Too much on the line here.*

The cowboy finally decided to call Jarred's bet, which grew the pot to $37,000. The dealer laid out the fourth card, the turn. King of hearts. If the cowboy was holding a king, his two pair would beat Jarred's; with a queen or a pair of jacks, he'd win with three of a kind. Check, bet, or fold? Jarred felt his chances slipping away.

But there was still one community card to go. Another jack or a third queen would give Jarred a full house: two of one kind, three of another.

Jarred wanted to win. Not even for himself. Nobody in his family knew that he always donated his winnings. He had to consider his next move carefully. Gut check time. He ran through several different potential outcomes in his mind... and felt like kicking himself when he realized the screamingly obvious: two hearts in the hole, two hearts on the table. He was one card away from a flush, and he was so damn distracted that it hadn't even *registered* with him. Jesus. Jarred slid another five grand into the center of the table.

The cowboy took just as much time with his own hand. He rotated two chips in his hand, back and forth, back and forth. It was maddening. Neither of them said a word; time seemed to stand still.

Finally, the cowboy called.

The dealer flipped over the last community card, the river. Eight of hearts. He'd hit the flush! *Okay, be cool, be cool.* The cowboy's nose wrinkled almost imperceptibly when he saw the eight. Chips still rotating in his hand, he stared at the cards. Or seemed to, anyway—Jarred couldn't see his eyes, which was always a disadvantage. Jarred remind himself to keep a straight face, to swallow the eager anticipation already rising within him.

Jarred went all in. Another $15,000. The cowboy called the bet with unnerving speed. Sweat trickled down Jarred's back, causing his shirt to cling uncomfortably. Had he read the cowboy wrong? Maybe the nose thing was a bluff. Did he have the full house after all? Dammit! Come on, luck, just one more time. Come on. Come on.

He flipped over his ace-jack, and a murmur rippled through the crowd. Jarred's heart hammered against his ribcage.

The cowboy slammed his cards down and left the room. Queen-ten of diamonds. A weight fell from Jarred's heart. He'd won! He'd actually won! The crowd seemed to breathe a collective sigh before breaking out in animated chatter—who they'd thought was holding what, how they'd have played which hands.

Jarred signaled to the dealer that he'd had enough, and scooped up his chips so that he could cash them in near the casino entrance. He'd take the winnings straight back to the safe in his hotel room—just a ten-minute walk away, but it seemed like a good night to splurge on a taxi. Having all these eyes on him was already making him uncomfortable enough; walking down the Strip with a giant wad of cash would probably give him a full-blown panic attack.

He knew he probably ought to be used to attracting attention by now, seeing as how he'd been doing it all his life. He was a Campbell, the son of one of Britain's most influential real estate moguls, and all five of them—

Jarred, his sister, and their three half-brothers— were all naturally charismatic as well. Though they had four different mothers, the Campbell children looked remarkably similar: tall, dark-haired, athletic build. Only their eye color varied. Blue, green, gray, brown, the whole spectrum.

The British press had long written Jarred off as a spoiled playboy, while somehow also declaring him one of the country's most eligible bachelors in the same breath—more nonsense that merely encouraged him to stay the hell away from London. There was no winning that war; they'd put him in a box and locked it. Only once in his adult life had he felt there was any hope of reshaping his public image: back when he'd still worked for his dad, he'd closed a couple of genuinely great deals, and people started thinking of him as an up-and-coming young business leader instead of a superficial rich kid.

Well, those days were over, but having a no-limit credit card in their father's name meant he could live just fine without a job. He'd thrown in the towel at twenty-seven. Now he was nearly twenty-nine. His old friends were presumably still working diligently on their careers and thinking about stuff like family planning.

Family planning. Right. He'd get around to that just as soon as he found the right woman, which at this rate would be a quarter to never. All five Campbell kids were equally useless where relationships were concerned. Any armchair psychologist would probably point to their bizarre family dynamic as the problem. Five kids, six stepmothers, one serial-monogamist father. At nearly seventy years old, Dad had recently married yet again; the happy couple was currently honeymooning somewhere in the Indian Ocean.

Though Jarred was a long way from needing a honeymoon, he still had an island paradise in his immediate future: he was planning a trip back to the past, and it involved flying to the South Seas with his sister.

On a whim, Jarred whipped out his phone and tapped her number.

"Hey, how's it going? Need me to save you from the clutches of another level-ten clinger?" Alice giggled. He could picture the teasing twinkle in her eyes.

"Not this time, no." Alice had helped him escape more than a few awkward situations. She had a thing for wigs, so sometimes at parties, people wouldn't even recognize her as his sister. Her emergency rescue plan involved putting on a foreign accent and throwing her arms around his neck effusively; then all he'd have to do was gaze affectionately at her and whisper something in her ear to make her laugh, and every woman within ten feet would run for the hills.

"You talked to Dad?" she asked. "That last party was too wild even by your standards. I can't imagine he's just going to let it slide."

"He's on his tropical-island honeymoon with Marlene. Pretty sure I'm the *last* person he wants to hear from." Marlene: stepmom number six. He barely knew her, seeing as she and Dad had only dated for a year before tying the knot. It was weird knowing that a total stranger was now living at his childhood home in Kensington.

His family had drifted apart over the years; they barely even called each other to say happy birthday anymore, nor did they get together during the holidays. His dad had even bought a chalet in Verbier, hoping their mutual love of skiing would provide common ground, but they rarely used it as a group—everyone just did their own thing.

"Okay, well, I'm sure he'll want to speak to you as soon as he's back in London. They're flying home the day after tomorrow."

Had Alice talked to Dad already or something? The two of them had always had a special bond; they called each other all the time. Maybe Alice knew something Jarred didn't.

"I was just calling to make sure everything was still on," he said, trying to sound cheerful. "I'm landing in L. A. at about nine that night; let's just meet right at the departure gate for Papeete. You got the ticket confirmation, right?"

"Yeah. You know I don't have to fly first-class," Alice said.

"Non-negotiable, sorry."

Alice was the most down-to-earth member of the Campbell clan. She loved her independence, and she was the only one of the five kids without an AmEx Black card tied to Dad's account. She worked hard at her job, as a tax accountant for a company with over ten thousand employees worldwide.

"So what are you doing in L. A.?" he asked.

"Sitting in a bikini on Manhattan Beach. Thinking about the miserable London weather I left behind, I can't believe it took me this long to pack my bags."

"Just wait till you get to the South Seas, you'll never want to leave," Jarred replied. Hearing himself say it out loud, it was suddenly a pretty tempting thought.

CHAPTER 2

ROSE

Today was a big day. Rose felt it in every fiber of her being. Once she'd locked the front door behind herself, she paused for a moment, sweeping her gaze from the overcast sky to the gray-green arm of the Thames, and then to the colorful residential buildings dotting the street. She wished she had time for a stroll through the Royal Observatory Garden—her favorite spot in all of London, just a few minutes from her apartment. The Observatory was situated in the middle of expansive Greenwich Park, surrounded by old chestnut trees; being up there made her feel like she could touch the sky. The breathtaking view of Canary Wharf and the distant financial district always filled her with pride, since she worked for a company that made those architectural masterpieces possible in the first place. At age thirty, having climbed the corporate ladder steadily for several years, Rose now headed up a small team at Campbell Investments. Residential projects were her bread-and-butter, but they occasionally called her in to help with the big skyscrapers as well.

The wind tugged at her wool coat; Rose hoped her freshly styled hair would survive the short walk to the train station unscathed. Her curls were practically impossible to control, and as much as she loved a nice breeze, she was trying to avoid showing up to work with a giant bird's nest on her head. The rest of the office would probably die laughing. Not that Rose minded having a laugh at her own expense or anything, but preferably not today. The "crown prince"—Sean Campbell, the oldest son of the owner of Campbell Investments—was stopping by this afternoon.

Sean did his best to speak to every Campbell employee in person at least once a year, though his busy schedule made it a nigh-impossible task. Sometimes he even invited random staffers out to lunch. Rose figured even sitting across from him would make her too nervous to eat a single bite. And God help her if she knocked a glass over or dropped food on her blouse. She'd probably just die right then and there.

She'd been surprised to receive her own meeting

invitation last night. The subject line was certainly plenty vague:

From: Sean Arthur Campbell
To: Rose Murphy
Re: Outstanding issues

Good morning Rose,
I have a couple of things I'd like to discuss with you. Conference room Sky Garden is reserved for tomorrow, Thursday, at 4 PM.

Best regards,
Sean Campbell
CEO, Campbell Investments

Rose had read the brief message over and over, but she couldn't begin to guess what those "outstanding issues" might be. Maybe he wanted to talk about an ongoing project in more detail, or maybe he wanted her to be involved on some new endeavor, or maybe she was getting a new boss, or... was he giving her new responsibilities? Merging departments? Promoting her? Laying her off? Every time she thought about the upcoming meeting, Rose's imagination ran away with her all over again.

She was tempted to call Mandy, but it was probably still too early. Her best friend had left London a few years ago and moved back to Watford, a town of about eighty thousand people that was mostly known for printing presses and automobile plants. Rose and Mandy had grown up there, about an hour's drive from Greenwich; their parents were best friends, so the girls had known each other all their lives. Rose's parents still lived in Watford, while her two older brothers had since moved to Liverpool and Manchester.

Though Rose and her brothers spoke fluent German thanks to their Swiss-born mother, they all considered England home. Rose didn't talk to her brothers very often—they'd never had much in common, even as children, and she'd always felt like they saw her as an annoying little brat. But she had Mandy, and she had a job she loved, so all was well.

She finally arrived at the cable car station. The view over the Thames would be a good distraction. Rose loved London, but there was no way she could afford the rent around London City. Greenwich was a good compromise: it was reasonably close to the financial district, which meant her commute was surprisingly short, but there was still plenty of green space. Plus a cable car! What more could she possibly want?

Well, besides a partner, but she knew she'd meet someone eventually. New year, new opportunities, new leaf. It had been more than a year since her last relationship; Aaron had been totally out of her life for months now, but it had taken her that long to get over him. Probably because her friends had all thought of them as practically married; her mom had even called him the son she'd never had. Aaron could charm the pants off a donkey.

Which was the whole problem.

Not literally, of course, but God only knew where she'd be now if she hadn't just *happened* to discover that she wasn't Aaron's only girlfriend. He'd denied everything until the end, but every inconsistency brought to light had eroded her trust a little more. Rose still didn't know for sure whether she'd been unfair to Aaron, whether she'd jumped to conclusions too quickly, but there was no going back either way. Aaron had moved to the US, and Rose was focusing on the future.

Well, right now, she was *mostly* focused on that 4 PM with Sean…

"I can't believe you drove all the way into the city just to have lunch with me!" Rose flung her arms around Mandy in the Campbell Investments lobby.

"You sounded like you needed a friend," Mandy smiled. "And my parents were excited to have Ella for the afternoon. Ella was a little disappointed, though —she was dying to see you."

Rose was the godmother to Mandy's four-year-old daughter.

"Just tell me when you want me to take her for the weekend. We'll have a blast!"

They strode through the glass doors and started down the exterior escalator. The building entrance was technically on the fourth floor; the front courtyard was covered, forming a giant atrium with columns supporting the hundred-foot-tall ceiling. The building's all-glass exterior created a prism effect; it was only a few years old, and it reflected Campbell Investments' company values: modern, innovative, sustainable.

"Ella's been talking about wanting to visit you for days. She can't wait."

The weather was still stormy. Mandy tucked her blond ponytail inside her coat and took Rose's arm, and they hurried down the narrow sidewalk to their favorite Italian place, which was tucked away on a side street.

"And Rob? He looking forward to getting away?"

Mandy sighed. "I think so? He's super stressed again." Her gray eyes took on a look of worry. Mandy and Rob had met at work; now that Mandy had decided to stay home with Ella, Rob seemed to think he needed to try twice as hard at the office. Mandy, meanwhile, was slowly but surely making a name for herself as a children's book author. She wasn't making anywhere near her old salary, of course, but she was a lot happier now.

"A weekend away will be good for you guys," Rose said. "I'm just glad I can help out."

Mandy, seemingly lost in thought, didn't respond. They walked the rest of the way in silence.

The restaurant welcomed them with the intoxicating scent of fresh bread and herbs. Rose and Mandy grabbed a two-person table near the window; after a cursory glance at the menu, they both ordered the linguini with prawns and zucchini. The restaurant was small but incredibly cozy, with just five tables in the main dining room and then two side rooms reserved for groups. At least one of those rooms was booked this afternoon, judging from the loud conversation and laughter drifting out. The area around the front entrance had a bar and a few extra tables. The walls were decorated with wine bottles and photos of Tuscany. Just walking into the place felt like stepping into a different world; Rose always came away feeling like she'd just been on vacation.

"So have you figured out what Sean wants?" Mandy asked. "Man, what a catch, right? He's so charismatic, and based on how well Campbell Investments is doing, he must have a decent head on his shoulders."

"Course he does, he's the CEO. Which is intimidating enough as it is."

"Sure, I guess... God, that whole family is hotter than hell, aren't they? I don't even think I could pick a favorite." Mandy grinned. "Sounds like they all really get around, though, if what the gossip rags say is true."

"I wouldn't believe everything you read in those,"

Rose said with a dismissive wave. "The headline and the article don't even go together half the time." Anyway, Rose only had eyes for one of the Campbells, and he'd left the company years ago.

"I wonder if Sean's going to promote you. I mean, they let your last boss go, right?"

"Yeah. It's weird how high the turnover in our department's been since Jarred disappeared off the face of the earth."

"Right? I'm seriously starting to wonder what's up with your personnel department. Maybe you should tell Sean about all the weird bullshit that went on this past year. You had the one boss lose a huge contract for you, and then the next treated your office like a dating website... you should have reported them both."

"Maybe, but that's all water under the bridge now." Not that those hadn't been awkward experiences, but at least both of those idiots had been replaced quickly. The constant flux was making the rest of the office skittish, though. Downsizing and restructuring rumors had started making the rounds almost immediately after Jarred's disappearance—along with endless crazy theories as to why he'd left. The most popular was that Sean and Jarred had had a blow-up argument because Jarred was the more successful of the two. Rose wasn't so sure: their sales numbers had been going up steadily since his departure. She suspected he'd left for personal reasons, which made it none of her business.

"I bet it's either a promotion, or he's got a big project in the pipeline. Unless you think you're in trouble for working for me on the side?"

Mandy had a way of drawing completely random conclusions. Her leaps of logic was enough to make Rose dizzy. "I doubt they're going to call illustrating children's books working for the competition."

"But theoretically you should still have gotten permission from your employer before starting a second job."

Rose knew Mandy was right. But Jarred was gone, and she didn't feel like bothering his successor with something so trivial. She liked drawing, that was all. Illustrating was her dream job. Or would be, if she weren't averse to starving to death. To keep the two worlds separate, Mandy published Rose's illustrations under a pseudonym, which Rose figured meant there was no way anyone at the company would ever catch wind of her little side hustle.

"My money's on a promotion, then. Sean's probably heard that your department's had way too much staff turnover since Jarred left, and now he's going to offer you the job, since you've got seniority. Which is saying something at your tender age," Mandy added with a note of pride in her voice.

Their food arrived, and they exchanged a delighted look from across their steaming plates of pasta. They sighed in perfect unison when they took their first bite, and then hurried to swallow before dissolving into giggles.

After they'd finished eating, Mandy surprised Rose with one final guess: "You know what else it could mean? Jarred's coming back."

A highly unlikely scenario, but the one Rose would have liked best of all.

The afternoon flew by; next thing Rose knew, it was nearly four o'clock. Campbell Investments was mostly tightly packed open-plan offices, so there was very little privacy anywhere; even the small conference rooms had glass walls. Two years ago, they'd taken the company paperless and converted to hot-desking—so arriving late meant you might miss your chance at a desk and get stuck in one of the "pods," which reminded Rose of restaurant booths. The lockers available for personal items were just big enough for a pair of shoes and a purse. At least the floor-to-ceiling windows provided plenty of natural light. Unless the weather was bad... which it usually was. The bright red pods were the only splash of color amid the myriad shades of gray: gray desks, gray carpet, gray lockers. Illustrator Rose technically knew what all those different grays were called, but Campbell Rose thought it wise to keep that information to herself.

Having arrived extra-early as usual, Rose had had her choice of work areas that morning. She'd picked a spot that gave her a good view of the entrance to the open-plan office, so she saw her boss even before he swiped to open the furthermost glass door. Sean Campbell had always struck Rose as the approachable type, and apparently she wasn't the only one: two or three of her coworkers approached him to chat before he even finished stepping inside.

Rose picked up a pen and a notebook and headed toward the conference room. When Sean saw her coming, he excused himself from the others—handshakes all around—and hurried over to meet her. A friendly smile played on his full lips, softening the hardness of his angular features and the coldness his blue eyes seemed to radiate in photos. He was practically a caricature of London's "new generation" of CEOs: athletic, elegant, slightly too smooth. Rose usually went for the edgier type, but she couldn't deny that Sean was pretty damn cute. When Mandy was right, she was right.

Sean held the conference room door for her with a gallant flourish. "After you, Rose."

Rose didn't mind people calling her by her first name at work, though her Swiss side felt that it expressed a certain intimacy that sometimes made it harder to maintain professional distance. *Speaking of distance*, she thought as they entered the tiny conference room, which barely offered space for four chairs. And the Campbells were a tall bunch; Rose put Sean at around six-three. She wasn't exactly short herself—five-seven, and usually in heels—but next to him, she felt like a garden gnome.

Sean gestured for Rose to sit before taking the

chair opposite hers. They didn't bother with coffee, and Sean snuck a peek at his watch in a way that suggested he might not even be staying for the entire half-hour he'd booked the room. Well, if it meant he'd get straight to the point, all the better. Sitting so close to him wasn't really helping her concentration, and—*dammit, Rose, this is the CEO, act professional.* Not that she was interested in him... but what if their knees accidentally touched?

"Rose. How do you like working at Campbell Investments?" Though Sean's eyes seemed to burn straight into her soul, his tone was perfectly neutral, which made it easier for her to focus. Rose hesitated, trying to figure out if the question was a trap. Okay, probably best to say something super enthusiastic. Knock his socks off with her dedication to the Campbell Investments cause.

She was sure she'd think of the perfect response.

...Any minute now.

"It's good. Really good. Um, why? Have there been complaints?" She twirled her pen nervously. *Yep, great work, Rose, knocked that one out of the park.* She'd even followed it with a self-deprecating question, put herself down at the first available opportunity. Such a girl thing to do. She squared her shoulders—hopefully without making it too obvious—and straightened up a little in her chair.

"No, no complaints. The department's inefficient. Has been for a long time."

Oh, of course. Ever since Jarred left and they'd brought those losers in to take his place.

Rose bit her tongue to keep herself from saying any of that out loud.

"Which means that I'll be downsizing a bit," Sean went on, "but first we'll need to do some restructuring. I'd like to make you the interim department head; if you're amenable, I'll freeze your current position."

Rose blinked at him in surprise.

Sean took a breath to say something else, but then seemed to change his mind. He waited a moment, and then raised a questioning eyebrow when she didn't respond. "Any questions?" The moment the words left his mouth, he let out a short laugh and shook his head. "Oh, well, of course you'd have questions. I'll send you the job description. You'll have to submit an official application, but if you want the job, it's yours. You've been with the company for a long time, and you have a good eye for lucrative investment opportunities. We need that around here."

"Thanks for placing such confidence in me. I'll be happy to look the job description over." See? That wasn't so hard. Rose knew the description by heart already, since it had been posted so often in the past two years. She'd never had the guts to throw her own hat into the ring. Her excitement at the prospect of being promoted was muted only by the realization that it probably meant Jarred wouldn't be returning after all. Not that Rose was about to let a little sentimentality get in the way of her career.

"How long is 'interim'?"

"I'm not sure yet." Sean was already on his feet again. "Assume it will be longer-term." With that, he nodded to her and walked out.

CHAPTER 3

JARRED

Once he'd reached his hotel room and had his winnings—nearly $70,000 in all, though that also included the original buy-in—securely inside the safe, he could breathe again. He knew he should probably try to catch a few hours' sleep, but he was too preoccupied with what Alice had said about their dad. Maybe he ought to call? He'd have done it by now if their relationship were even half as good as it had once been. Jarred stared at his phone, thumb circling the line showing his father's number. To call or not to call? In the end, he just chucked his phone on the bed in frustration, followed by his jacket.

He crossed the room to stand at the floor-to-ceiling window looking directly out over the bright lights of the Strip.

Something told him that he'd gone too far in Atlantic City. None of it had been planned, of course—he wasn't *that* nuts—but once he realized things were getting out of control, he hadn't done anything to stop it.

He should have left as soon as his conquest for the night snapped a photo of him. He avoided cameras like the plague; if he'd wanted his picture plastered all over the place, he could just as well have stayed in London, where everyone and their mother recognized him on sight. But no, he hadn't demanded Tiffany delete the photo, hadn't said a word when she'd posted it to Facebook. Hadn't thrown her friends out when they showed up to his room. Hell, he'd invited the whole group to stay—the room was plenty big, right? They drank, danced, made out. Someone passed a joint. Jarred had felt like he was in college again, back when all was still right with the world.

He'd sobered up instantly the next morning, after jolting awake to find himself alone in the living room of a thoroughly trashed hotel suite.

Jarred's phone vibrated. He went to the bed and glanced at the display, then took the call. "What do you want, Sean?"

"Where are you?"

Why, sure, Sean, let's dispense with the pleasantries. Jarred's oldest brother sounded like he was trying and failing to control his temper.

"Las Vegas, why?" Jarred grunted.

The silence that followed suggested that maybe Sean was even angrier than Jarred first suspected. Oh, right, he'd made that promise to Sean last year... "Listen, Sean, I—"

"No, *you* listen," Sean broke in. "I'm *sick* of this, Jarred. I can't fucking *express* to you how sick of it I am. You've been hiding under a rock for two years, only showing up when you run out of alcohol at home or when you need Dad to clean up another mess of yours. And don't even come at me with some dumbass excuse, I know *exactly* what you've been up to, there's no escaping your goddamn name in the tabloids. Enough is enough! It's been two years since your mom died. It's hard, I get it, but you can't spend the rest of your life dwelling on it. Self-destructing isn't going to bring her back, right? So get your stupid ass home already!"

Jarred was too bewildered to reply. Sean had never been one to put things delicately—not when it was just the two of them, anyway—but he was surprised that Sean would bring up that particular sore subject now. People in his family didn't talk about sensitive topics; they just made them go away.

Once the silence had grown unbearable, Sean continued in a quiet voice: "You loved your job, you loved your life. Why throw it all away?"

Because you can't turn off a guilty conscience, but you sure as hell can numb the pain, Jarred thought. His mother had died of a stroke; she'd only made it to fifty-four. In the years prior, she'd been depressed a lot and drinking too much. After she and Dad split up, she'd started dating younger guys, living wild, neglecting the beauty salon she owned—which had once been among London's finest. She'd gone downhill fast.

Jarred had watched it happen. They'd all watched it happen, but none of them had done anything to stop her. He'd made a few half-hearted attempts to talk sense into her, but Mom had always waved him off, insisting she was fine. And then one day he'd seen a photo of her with a guy young enough to be her son, and he'd told her he was ashamed of her.

Those were the last words Jarred ever said to his mother.

He wished to God he could take them back. Hell, his dad was no different with his girlfriends, and Jarred had never told Dad he was ashamed of him.

If only he could turn back time. He'd have done everything differently.

Sean's last question hung in the air. It was a good one. Why *had* Jarred thrown his life away? Jarred didn't have an answer. Because he couldn't handle pretending that everything was roses and sunshine? Because he wanted to punish himself? Or because it was the easiest and most efficient way of wallowing in self-pity?

"I'm sorry," was all he could come up with. Then he ended the call and switched off his phone. If there was one thing he'd mastered, it was sticking his head in the sand.

CHAPTER 4

JARRED

His flight to L. A. landed right on time. Alice was already waiting at the departure gate for Papeete, of course. She always showed up insanely early for everything. Jarred usually found her engrossed in her laptop, bashing away at the keyboard while taking calls on her headset. Consultant life seemed incredibly stressful—and if you wanted to make partner, you had to start by striking the word "vacation" from your vocabulary. So Jarred was all the more surprised to find Alice reading a paperback. Her purse was beside her. Closed. No sign of her phone anywhere. As he approached, he peeked at the front cover. A romance novel?

"Don't stare, your eyes will freeze like that." Alice smiled affectionately and stood up to give Jarred a proper hello. Though his older sister was nearly five-seven, Jarred was still a full head taller, and Alice was so slim that he was always afraid to squish her when he hugged her.

"I was wondering where Bunny went and what monster was sitting here in her place," he remarked with a teasing wink.

"Gross, you know I can't stand that nickname." Alice pushed him away playfully, but then thought better of it and plucked at his hair. "*Somebody* could use a haircut, I see. And what's with the beard?"

"I'm lazy?"

"Either that or you knew Alice would fix it for free."

"You've been cutting my hair since I was fourteen. Why stop now?"

"I've also been telling you to find another hairdresser since I was eighteen." She rolled her eyes, but Jarred didn't buy it for a second. He knew how much Alice loved trimming hair, dying hair, styling hair… basically anything hair-related.

"Are you boarding the ship as you, or did you pack the wigs?" God only knew what weird flights of imagination Alice was planning on indulging this time.

"No wigs. This trip is me-time."

"Since when do you read romance novels?" He scooped up the book sitting on the hard plastic chair; his extra six inches of reach gave him a few seconds to flip through it before Alice finally managed to snatch it back. "Who's Ryan?" Jarred made a show of peering at the inside cover. "And why does he *hope that destiny brings you together again?*" He smirked. "I didn't know you went for the cheesy type."

Alice turned tomato-red. So she'd met a guy, hm? She shifted her weight and smoothed her dark hair nervously. The two of them looked a lot alike: same dark hair, same light brown eyes, same nose, same chin. Sometimes Jarred was glad that Alice hadn't turned out looking like their mother, who'd had blond hair and blue eyes, a real California girl. Other times, he found himself wishing for a visual reminder of Mom, something to keep her memory alive.

"Ryan was a fling. No more, no less." After packing the book away, Alice flopped down onto the hard chair, arms folded. Like Jarred, she'd worn a T-shirt, jeans, and sneakers. "You're sober," she remarked to change the subject. "Unexpected change of pace."

"I'm in a good phase."

"Even though Sean ripped you a new one?"

"Who told you that?"

Alice laughed.

"I thought you were going no-contact with your 'dumbass freeloading half-brothers,' quote-unquote."

"Oh, well, maybe I was just too stressed out to realize that my dumbass freeloading half-brothers were making an effort. Just because they fail all the time doesn't mean that they're lazy or stupid or only call Dad when they want a handout."

"Sassy." Jarred gave Alice a gentle poke. She got a little self-righteous about at times, but she was the only one of them who still hadn't taken a penny from their dad. She'd even paid her own way through Oxford, completing the degree in record time while working two jobs; Jarred and his older half-brothers, Sean, Henry and Liam, meanwhile, had mainly gone to college for the athletics and the parties. They'd all graduated, of course—Dad had made sure of it—but without his beloved rowing team, Jarred doubted he'd have had the motivation to get up in the morning. He missed it... he missed a lot of things. Even before Sean called to lecture him, he'd already been thinking about flying home.

"Do you think you'll be able to make your peace with the past after this trip?" Alice asked gently.

"I hope so."

"Well, then, come on, Mr. Campbell. The South Pacific awaits." Alice got up and extended a hand. Their flight had just been called, and as first-class passengers, they got to board first. Jarred's spirits began to lift as he presented his boarding pass and followed Alice down the gangway. Surely there was nowhere to go from here but up.

It was an uneventful trip; by the time they approached for landing, the sun was already up. French Polynesia was Paradise. Jarred could hardly wait to dive into the brilliant blue water. As lovely as

Tahiti and the neighboring islands were, Jarred wasn't particularly interested in the waterfalls, or the fern grottos, or the rolling green hills that were perfect for hiking, or the markets, the fresh fish, the delicious French wine, or the black pearls... his one and only goal for this trip was to enjoy the beach. The perfect waves off the Tahitian coast, the azure Pacific, the white beaches on Moorea, the black beaches on Nuku Hiva, the pink beaches on Rangiroa, the coral islands of Bora Bora. Ten days wasn't nearly enough for the South Pacific, now that he thought about it. He'd always wanted to come here.

"You think it's really as nice here as Mom always said?" Alice peered through the window, fascinated.

"Stuff was probably a lot less commercialized when they came here on their honeymoon. It was like thirty years ago. But I bet we'll still have a lot of fun." Most of the time, anyway. The anniversary of their mother's death was coming up. Fortunately, they were spending it in Paradise this year, in hopes of feeling closer to her.

"So am I even going to see you again before the end of the cruise?" Alice narrowed her eyes suspiciously.

"What's that supposed to mean? Your room's right next to mine, so I assume we'll see each other before eight in the morning and after six at night, or whenever it is we have to return to the ship. Otherwise, you're welcome to join me in the water."

"That all sounds awfully tame." She still looked skeptical.

"Nice for a change, don't you think?" Bringing women back to his cabin wasn't even on his agenda. He needed time to himself. He felt freer and more content already, and they hadn't even boarded the cruise ship that would be their home for the next week and a half. Jarred wanted to keep this wonderful feeling of lightness for as long as possible.

ROSE

"You *are* applying, right?" Mandy beamed at Rose through the screen. It was late evening, and they were video-chatting from their respective sofas over a glass of wine.

"Yeah, of course. I don't think he'd say something like that just to set me up to fail. I mean, I'm sure other people will apply, too, but... who knows? Maybe they've got a quota of women to fill. Anyway, the job position even mentions that they've already got a strong candidate. That has to be me, right? Nah, I really can't imagine Sean was just *lying* about me having the job in the bag. He knows I'd probably quit on the spot. And he said himself that he appreciates my work."

"Finding another job might not be easy. Times are still tense in the financial industry, and we still don't know how Brexit's going to affect things. Although I guess you could always apply to places in Germany or Switzerland if worse comes to worst."

"I can't imagine leaving England. I love London."

"Yeah, but Zurich? Go swimming in the lake on your lunch breaks in summer, ski trips every weekend in winter? Sounds like heaven!"

Mandy spent several more minutes painting a cheerful picture of Rose's new theoretical life in Switzerland. She sounded so certain that Rose found herself shifting uncomfortably in her seat.

"Let me live in London a little longer before you send me out into the world," she finally joked. "I feel good about this promotion. I mean, I obviously have no idea what he meant by 'restructuring'… he's not wrong, the department hasn't been living up to its potential lately, but I think I've got what it takes to turn that ship around."

"Of course you do. Wasn't it your big project that your old boss screwed up? …Hey, have you drawn Sean yet? For real, I mean, not as a caricature." Mandy's gray eyes twinkled merrily. With her hair in a braided bun, like it was tonight, she looked like barely twenty. She had one of those naturally kind-seeming faces, and it probably helped her sell kids' books just as much as her talent for funny stories did.

"You know me too well," Rose sighed and got up to fetch her purse. "My notebook's full. Sean's on the last page." She'd already picked up a fresh notebook—she was kicking this year off with a red one.

"Which flower are you starting the next one with?" Mandy raised an eyebrow. Rose always drew a flower on the first page of each notebook, and wrote things that were important to her within the petals so that she'd never lose sight of them.

"I was thinking of a sunflower."

"Your favorite, hm?" Mandy grinned. "Does your name ever bother you, since you don't like roses that much?"

"Oh, it's not that bad. Anyway, that's what pseudonyms are for, right?"

"Becka Pacino," Mandy cackled. "So cute, I can't even *say* it without laughing!"

"Rude!" Rose scoffed theatrically. "But yeah, I love sunflowers. There are so many different kinds... the bicolor ones are my favorite. Anyway, back to Mr. Sean aka Sexy Campbell."

"Just don't let that slip when you're around him."

"If you think that's workplace-inappropriate, don't even ask what I call Jarred."

"Wait, what? Why haven't I heard this? Rose Murphy! I am your best friend! Tell me *this instant!*"

"Let's just say he looks great from the back. Or did." Rose felt herself turn six shades of red.

"So, what, Asstastic Campbell?" Mandy whistled.

Her imagination had regularly run away from her whenever Jarred was anywhere nearby. She'd never thought she'd find herself hanging on someone's every word when they were talking about an investment project, but what could she do? She loved how his whole face would light up as he spoke; sometimes he'd get so worked up that he'd fling his suit jacket aside and roll up his sleeves. Only at team meetings, of course... not when customers were there or anything. She'd felt like a total groupie sometimes, but at least nobody'd ever noticed.

Jarred's last project had been a skyscraper not far from their office. Project Spike, it was called—a reference to the shape of the finished structure. There'd been construction issues from day one; they'd had to revise the plans several times, because the aviation authority had called the original height of over a thousand feet too dangerous for landing aircraft. Things had been shaky on the financial end as well, but then Jarred decided to get involved himself; that was enough to lure additional investors, mostly from oil-rich countries. They'd gotten as far as excavating and finishing the foundation before running into more construction snags, this time for logistical reasons. Though it was probably just a coincidence, it certainly felt like the disaster-cherry on top that Jarred suddenly disappeared the day after construction finally ground to a halt.

Well, not literally, of course—he wasn't kidnapped or anything. After his mother's unexpected death, he'd simply stopped coming to work. After a couple of months, his name had started cropping up in the tabloids. Rose had kept up with the news at first, but eventually she'd stopped paying attention. The guy in those newspaper photos had nothing to do with the person she'd worked for, admired, and probably fallen a tiny bit in love with. His expression was stony, his mouth a tight line; the spark in his light-brown eyes was gone, leaving them cold and hard. He looked like he'd forgotten how to laugh.

A chill ran down Rose's back. She'd actually cried over Jarred back then. Crazy. They'd hardly even known each other.

Rose paged through her notebook until she reached the drawing of Sean, and then held it up to the camera.

"Wow, that's awesome! He looks like a nice guy, and also good enough to eat. I can't believe he's single. He must have them lined up around the block."

"They're all single, I think. Except Arthur Campbell, who's made a hobby out of getting married as often as possible." Rose regarded her own drawing of Sean. He really did have a rakish air about him. The more asymmetrical a face, the more interesting Rose found it. Sean's little flaws weren't immediately obvious, but you could see them when you looked closely. The corners of his mouth weren't level, so he always seemed to be smirking; his nose was a shade too long; his eyebrows weren't perfectly curved. And his hair was apparently just as unruly as Rose's, because no matter how well he combed it, he always had a stray lock or two drooping down his forehead. He was still a good catch, though as far as she knew he'd never been caught by anyone. She'd be interested to see who'd finally land him.

"Show me one of Jarred," Mandy exclaimed. "I know you kept every drawing you've ever done of him, so cough 'em up."

Sighing, Rose got up again to fetch her sketchbook. She'd done dozens, in fact: Jarred laughing, Jarred poker-faced, Jarred hunched pensively over a report. Her favorite one of all showed him standing outside the office, hair whipping in the wind, thousand-watt smile.

"What're you doing there?" Rose had spotted Jarred as soon as she started down the escalator outside Campbell Investments. It was an unusually warm, sunny May day, and Rose was itching to take her sketchbook down to the Thames. She wasn't sure what she wanted to draw; she'd decide once she got there.

"I'm looking at our employees, picturing how someday soon this many people will be streaming out of Spike after work. That building's going to be a masterpiece, Rose, I'm sure of it. I know we've run into a lot of hurdles along the way, but we'll get there."

"You know I don't need convincing, Jarred." Rose grinned at him impishly.

"Yeah, sorry, sorry. I guess I spent so much time fighting for that project that now motivational speeches are my default mode." He smiled bashfully and brushed his

mussed hair out of his face. He looked so kissable. Whoa, where'd that come from? Pull yourself together, Rose.

"Which way you headed?" There was a look in his eyes that she couldn't quite interpret. Her face wasn't somehow broadcasting what she was thinking... right?

"To the Thames. You?"

"City center."

She barely stopped herself from making a disappointed noise, wished him a nice evening, and hurried off. She was a hundred percent sure that he was watching her leave, but she forced herself not to look over her shoulder.

At least now she knew what she wanted to draw.

"You could hang those in a gallery!" Mandy remarked, jolting Rose back to the here and now. "They're so detailed, they're almost like photographs. I wonder if Jarred knew you had a thing for him and did all those drawings of him…"

"I doubt it. Anyway, it was never going to happen. What, you think I'd risk my job just to hook up with the boss?"

"Oh, of course not."

Rose waited for a "but" that didn't come.

They said their goodbyes a few minutes later. Instead of going straight to bed, Rose found herself lingering on the sofa, studying her own sketches.

She wished she knew where Jarred was. And whether he was okay.

CHAPTER 5

JARRED

Nuku Hiva, French Polynesia. Today was the day Jarred had been dreading the most. He'd been sitting on the balcony of his eighth-deck suite since sunrise. The ship would be docking at eight and setting sail again ten hours later. Yesterday had been at sea, and tomorrow would be as well, which meant today was his best chance to stretch his legs. Or to get wasted and hopefully forget that today was the anniversary of his mother's death.

"Hey, how long you been sitting out there?"

"Too long." His voice threatened to break.

"Come on, then, let's grab some breakfast and explore the island. I didn't sign us up for the tour group; I figured we might want to spend today on our own. I've reserved a jeep for the day—and a driver, unless you want to do the driving."

He was grateful that Alice had handled the organizational side of things.

Ten minutes later, they met outside their suites, freshly showered and changed.

Their luxury cruise only had around seven hundred passengers and four hundred personnel, which was nice because the restaurants were never too full. Being in the suites also meant they got VIP service; they could even have meals served in-room by a private butler.

The ship was lavishly decorated from bow to stern: majestic crystal chandeliers, fine porcelain fixtures, silver tableware, hand-painted frescoes in the large dining hall. Supposedly the sommeliers all hailed from traditional vintner families. There were three sit-down restaurants, along with a handful of cafés and bars. Jarred had spent teatime yesterday at the poolside bar, enjoying scones with clotted cream and strawberry jam as a classical string quartet played nearby.

He hadn't yet told Alice that he was flying back to London after the cruise. Well, that's what he'd decided yesterday... he was already starting to second-guess himself. Good Lord, how lost could one person get? He couldn't wallow in self-pity forever. This wasn't living.

All this brooding was killing his appetite, but he followed Alice to the restaurant anyway, where he tossed back two cups of coffee and choked down a few bites of scrambled egg. He was glad when they finally left the ship. As much as he missed being behind the wheel, he decided not to do the driving. He loved driving, but less so when his head felt like it was stuffed with cotton balls.

The two of them clambered into the waiting Jeep. Jarred stared out at the landscape without really registering anything. "Alice, do you ever think... um, do you think we could have prevented it?" He'd never expressed that thought aloud. Not even to Alice, even though she'd always been there for him. Once something like that was out, he couldn't take it back... and what if Alice told him it was his fault? On an intellectual level, he knew he was a grown man who had a hard time accepting consequences, but he *felt* more like a five-year-old boy who was afraid of getting spanked.

"No, of course not, why would you even say that? Wait a minute... you don't think you were somehow responsible for Mom's death, do you?" Alice clapped her hand to her mouth in horror.

He cleared the lump from his throat, unsure how to respond. Maybe this was all just him getting carried away in his grief. "Yeah, I... did think that, anyway. Like, I should have helped her more, I shouldn't have been so focused on my own life." His voice dropped to a whisper. "I shouldn't have told her I was ashamed of her."

"I can't believe I'm hearing this. Jarred! You know that Dad offered to help her out, right? Over and over again, but she never would take it. She just couldn't deal with the fact that he'd stopped loving her, that she was getting older, that her life hadn't gone the way she'd wanted. But that's not your fault! Whenever she called, you always dropped everything and came running, remember?"

"Not always." Near the end, her calls had mostly just annoyed him.

"This might not be the right time to bring it up, but… you should probably get in touch with Dad. He's *furious* about how you stuck him with the bill for that suite you trashed in Atlantic City. Next time maybe *don't* put it in your goddamn *Facebook* that you're having a party at a fancy hotel and have a no-limit credit card?"

"That wasn't me! How dumb do you think I am? I wasn't even planning on having a party. All I was trying to do was bring a girl back to my room, and things just… escalated. She called one of her friends, the friend called another friend, and so on."

"Right. Hundred percent innocent victim." Alice made a skeptical face.

Well, no, obviously not. "I'll call him when we get back, promise."

"I'd do it as soon as possible if I were you."

They rode the rest of the way in silence. Nuku Hiva was nicknamed "the mystical island," and the name really did fit—the whole place had an incredible energy. They were on their way to see the eleven stone tiki statues; they could have gone to the waterfalls instead, but that would have meant joining the guided tour, because most of the journey was by boat. Having a private driver meant they could visit the more remote villages along the eastern coast, and hopefully they'd be able to take a stroll on the beach as well.

"I'm thinking about quitting the consultant business," Alice announced after a while.

"Oh?"

"Yeah… maybe revive Mom's beauty salon, you know? Just an idea I've been turning over for a while."

Jarred shrugged thoughtfully. "If that's what you want to do, I don't see the harm in trying. You've certainly got the business skills… I guess you'll be looking for an investor? Henry can probably help you out." Henry'd made a career out of supporting start-ups, so why not Alice, too? Assuming she didn't want to use their father's money, which she never did, just on principle.

"Yeah, that's a good idea, I'll talk to Henry. Speaking of hair, what do you say I trim that mop of yours when we get back to the ship? Looks like you finally found your razor on your own, at least."

"I could just go to someone on board. I hear the beauty parlor's fantastic."

"You would *dare* turn your back on your stylist after all these years? You're even getting a special rate —those are harder to come by than you realize."

"I've never paid you a cent, Bunny."

"I know," she snickered. "If I'd charged you, I

could retire by now." She sighed theatrically as she twirled one of the long locks falling into his eyes.

"That bad?" Jarred gasped in exaggerated concern.

Alice's expression turned serious. "I can't help wondering how many women's hearts you've broken over the years."

He blinked. "Cutting hair to breaking hearts, that's one way of jumping topics." He clutched his chest theatrically. "Not a single one, I swear it! But what's up with you and the bartender on the ship?"

"If you swear you've never broken a single heart, then I swear nothing's going on between me and the bartender. Surely you wouldn't accuse me of putting a staff member's job at risk." Her eyes twinkled mischievously.

"If you believe me, then I believe you. But you really shouldn't get involved with the staff. That's rule number one: never mix business and pleasure. It's just asking for trouble."

"Never?" Alice echoed, looking innocent.

"*Never*," Jarred replied emphatically.

ROSE

She couldn't believe how much time she'd spent on this application already. Getting the paperwork together hadn't been too bad—she'd remembered where she'd stashed her diploma, and luckily she kept records of past projects and achievements so that she'd be ready for her end-of-year progress meetings —but she was having a hell of a time with the cover letter. Mostly because she wanted it to be absolutely perfect.

After hacking away for a while longer, she threw up her hands. There was no point driving herself crazy. She held her breath and clicked the "Send" button on the application platform.

She received a response the following day. After a psychological test, two long interviews—one with her would-be immediate supervisor, another with the HR department—and a week of anxious waiting, she finally got the call she'd been waiting for. Unbelievable! She'd actually done it!

If they didn't live so far apart, Rose would have invited Mandy out for champagne first thing; calling her was the next best option.

"Congrats, Rose!" Mandy squeaked. "I knew you'd get it."

"Oh, God, I'm so relieved. I was afraid their little psych test would show that I had no leadership potential or something."

"Pff. You've got *all* the leadership potential. You're just too kind and understanding sometimes."

"Yeah, yeah, I hear you. Next time a co-worker tries to pawn his responsibilities off on me, I'll say no."

"Co-worker? More like a member of *your team*. Or a minion, if you prefer."

"Right."

Hammering out the details of her new contract didn't take long, and Rose settled into her new job fairly quickly. It was a lot more work, of course; most days, she found herself dashing from one meeting to the next, sometimes even literally. Administrative nonsense ate up a ton of time, too. She was suddenly handling a flood of vacation requests, holding target-setting meetings, and providing a listening ear when her co-workers—wait, sorry, team members—needed to get something off their chests.

One issue from her "old" job was still weighing on Rose's mind, and she was hell-bent on fixing it herself instead of delegating: one of her old projects was nowhere near up to snuff. Campbell Investments had wanted to build a 100-unit residential building near the city center, in a once-shabby area that had recently gotten hip. They'd finished the first phase of the project. The original plan had been to find a buyer for the complex ASAP and turn the biggest possible profit on the sale, but then Rose had received new orders to focus on selling the penthouse and the luxury condos instead. The smaller units on the lower floors were going to be rentals, targeted at two-income households with one child or less—larger families simply wouldn't have enough space.

They'd managed to rent out the lower floors

completely, but tenant turnover was high; interest in the luxury condos was practically nonexistent. Rose couldn't figure out what the problem was. The apartments were all bright and modern, with decent kitchens and a nice layout. The bedrooms had ample closet space and en-suite bathrooms, and the interior finishes were high-quality, low-maintenance materials. There was just no good explanation for it, and she'd spent so long staring at the data that it was practically burned into her retinas.

She'd probably just have to visit the place in person, Rose thought one evening as she collapsed into bed after work. Eventually, anyway. Once she wasn't running around like a chicken with its head cut off. Right now, she was simply too exhausted to muster up the necessary energy for her apartment-building problem child.

"Why don't you ask them for a personal assistant?" Mandy asked the next time they spoke. "See if you can flip the gender script, find a hot younger guy who can make coffee and take dictation."

Rose had retreated to an empty meeting room. Her desk felt like Grand Central Station these days—she was desperate for some peace and quiet.

"Oh, it'll be okay, things are probably just hectic because it's the start of the year." Rose would be damned if she was going to admit she was struggling already.

"But your old bosses all had help, right? Why shouldn't you?"

"I never really thought about it. Jarred's old assistant got pregnant and quit; the ones after her always left when their bosses did." Rose doodled idly in her notebook: a picture of her dream home out in the countryside, with a treehouse and a veranda.

"Want me to come to town Friday evening? We could go out for your belated birthday celebration. My parents will take Ella... I may or may not have already asked."

Rose grinned. "What about Rob?"

"Business trip to the US. He'll be back next week."

"Okay, but then I'll come to you on the weekend. My mom is always looking for excuses to bake, and I've been missing the country air."

"Deal. And then once Rob gets back, I'll sit him down and demand that we schedule our romantic weekend away. I mean, if I even recognize him at the airport. I might just end up bringing a random stranger home." Mandy giggled.

"Hah! You couldn't miss that blond Hun if you tried."

"No, you're probably right. Okay, see you Friday! Take care of yourself, Becka Pacino."

"Yeah, yeah. You should get cracking on that new book, Becka's getting impatient."

"I can't help it if the Muse refuses to bestow her gifts upon me."

"Well, kick her ass, then!"

A quiet "ahem" made Rose startle up from her sketch. Sean was in the doorway. "Gotta go!" She mashed the end call button and took a deep breath. Oh, Lord, how long had Sean been standing there, how much had he heard? "Sorry, I didn't even hear you come in. Can I help you?" She hurried to smack her notebook shut. Great, personal calls *and* doodling. Cue the lecture on professionalism. Then again, it was well after five, so hardly anybody else was even around.

"Doing okay?" was all Sean asked. His blue eyes regarded her kindly, though he looked as exhausted as she'd been feeling for days. But of course *Sean* was tired—he ran the whole company. No doubt his job was ten times more stressful than hers. Rose's first instinct was to nod eagerly and assure him that everything was peachy, but she forced herself to stop and think carefully about her response.

"Takes a while to find a rhythm with all the paperwork," he continued, never taking his eyes off her. "It'll get easier over time. But I think you could probably use a little help right now. There are a couple of new projects I think you should be a part of."

"Um, o-okay, that sounds good, thanks," Rose stammered.

Sean nodded, wished her a good evening, and slipped away as silently as he'd come.

CHAPTER 6

JARRED

Bora Bora was his personal highlight. He could have easily spent more than two days there: snorkeling, diving, sailing to the coral islands, or just lying on the beach. He'd heard people describe Bora Bora as the most romantic island in the world, and what had sounded to him like a cheap travel brochure line had turned out to be a hundred percent true. Too bad he was here with his sister instead of a wife or girlfriend. Hadn't even met any nice girls on the ship. Which was rare for him, because he definitely enjoyed the company of the opposite sex. This felt like the wrong time to start an affair, though, seeing as he was planning on heading home as soon as they landed in Los Angeles. He was finally ready to go back to his old life.

. . .

Their return flight was uneventful. Alice wanted to stay in Los Angeles a while longer, so he only booked one ticket to London—his own. He wasn't totally comfortable leaving her there by herself.

"Will you quit freaking out? I have another week of vacation, and I'm sure as hell not spending it freezing my ass off in England."

"You're meeting up with the bartender, right?"

"So what if I am? He's nice."

"Nice?" Jarred smirked. "Because he's trying to get in your pants."

Alice snorted in annoyance. "I'm thirty, not sixteen, calm down."

"I just worry sometimes. I'm your brother, I'm allowed." He gave her a playful jab in the side.

"My pain-in-the-ass baby brother," she grumbled.

"You got it," he laughed.

They landed in Los Angeles and headed to the border control checkpoint. It was only eight in the morning, and his connecting flight didn't leave until that afternoon, so he had plenty of time to see her off and then re-check his bag in Terminal 2.

But first they had to waste an hour of their precious lives in passport control. Though he and Alice both had dual citizenship thanks to their American mother, the border guard still looked Jarred up and down carefully, asking polite yet probing questions regarding his travel plans. Maybe he should start putting down a different profession? "Investor" always went over like a lead balloon. *Just be cool, Jarred, keep it friendly.* The whole process was infuriating, but after what felt like days, he was finally able to retrieve his passport and catch up to Alice.

"Why do they always give you the third degree? There must be something suspicious about you. Maybe it's the British accent with the American passport?"

"You have the exact same accent!"

"Then maybe it's because you're dressed like a mob boss."

He glanced down at himself. Balmain trousers, Tom Ford shirt... but L. A. was absolutely crawling with rich and famous types, so what was the problem? *Rich mama's boy,* the devil on his shoulder sneered. "Come on, let's go get our bags," he muttered, pushing Alice toward the baggage carousel. Once he was in the travel lounge, he could relax over a little virtual poker.

Their bags were already waiting for them, so it wasn't long before they were outside the terminal, saying their goodbyes.

"Call me when you land?"

"Of course. And you call me if the bartender starts getting pushy. I'd be happy to come beat his ass for you."

"Shush. Call Dad, don't forget."

They hugged one last time before Alice climbed into a taxi, blowing him a kiss as she rolled away. He waved and watched until she disappeared from sight. Time to begin his real return journey, the one back to his old life. The thought made him uneasy. Nervous, in fact—his hands were already clammy, and his skin was tingling. He took a deep breath and started walking to Terminal 2. It was nice to get a little fresh air, although LAX airport air wasn't quite the same as South Pacific Ocean breeze.

Check-in and security went smoothly; first-class passengers were always treated well. Now *this* was how things were supposed to be; the little episode at the customs checkpoint was soon forgotten.

Jarred went straight upstairs to the lounge. The reception area was small, but modern. The rest of the lounge was all soothing, rounded shapes, with plenty of plush seating and floor-to-ceiling windows providing exceptional light. The walls were mostly white and copper, a stylish contrast to the dark gray, forest green, and burgundy of the upholstery. He fetched himself a coffee and sat down with a satisfied sigh.

Oh, damn, his phone was at twenty percent, how hadn't he noticed that before? No matter, there was a charger in his carry-on, along with his jacket, his wallet, and a pullover.

There was... *supposed* to be, anyway. He rummaged around in the bag some more. Had he put it in his checked bag like an idiot? Or forgotten it on the ship, maybe? Dammit. When had he last seen it? He couldn't remember. He furrowed his brow, trying to decide whether to borrow a charger from the lounge reception desk—assuming they had one, anyway—or to go ahead and buy one. But he'd need one on the flight to London, so... He chugged the coffee, picked up his bag, and headed out the door.

He glanced around when he reached the bottom of the floating staircase. The terminal was fairly small. Smartshop, that sounded promising.

Sure enough, they had the charger. Smiling, he went to the register and presented his credit card. Couple more minutes and he'd be relaxing in the lounge again.

"Sir, your credit card was declined."

"What?"

"Your credit card was declined," the cashier said more slowly, as though Jarred didn't speak English.

"Could you try it again?" Calm, stay calm. This could mean anything. Maybe the magnetic strip was dirty. Or he'd forgotten it was about to expire, and the new one was waiting for him back home.

"I tried twice, and the card was declined both times. Do you have another?"

Um. No? Why would he? This one was unlimited, what would he need a second one for? A line was beginning to form behind him. How awkward.

"We also accept cash."

Cash? He never carried cash! Oh, wait... Vegas! He'd stuck a fifty-dollar-bill somewhere for emergencies... hopefully not in the pants he'd checked? Jarred rummaged frantically through his pockets and bag, but didn't see the money anywhere. Gritting his teeth, he told the cashier he'd be right back, and then ran out of the store as though the Devil himself were chasing him. He wasn't actually planning on returning. Why would he? He was broke. The reality of the situation began to sink in, and he didn't like it one bit. He felt like a leper, like everyone around him was pointing at him and whispering.

Good God, don't freak out. There has to be a rational explanation for this. Some kind of misunderstanding. Maybe he should call the credit card company...? And risk draining the rest of the battery, with no guarantee that he'd be able to borrow a charger in the lounge?

He stood there in the middle of the hallway, paralyzed with overwhelming indecision. Which was beyond pathetic, really. Him, a grown man who'd juggled hundreds of millions of euros on massive international projects, and now one little credit card issue was enough to break him?

Hardly! He knew what he had to do, obviously; he just wasn't sure which order to do it in.

Better text Alice.

Jarred: Credit card not working. Tried to buy a charger, got declined. Don't want to test it at an ATM and risk it getting retained.
Alice: Credit card company?
Jarred: Battery's almost dead.
Alice: Shit. Bad luck. Don't they have one in the lounge you can borrow?
Jarred: Haven't asked yet.
Alice: Well, do that! Did you call Dad yet?
Jarred: No. Why?
Alice: Why don't you ever just do what people tell you to do?
Wait a minute… no, Dad would never do that. Surely.
Jarred: You think he froze the card?
Alice: Could be.

WHAT?! Jarred immediately scrolled to his father's number. He picked up immediately, which both bewildered Jarred and left him temporarily speechless.

"Hello, Jarred, I've been wondering when you'd finally call. Sean's expecting you in London tomorrow; I've heard you're on your way there anyway. Be at the office at ten."

"And if I don't?" Jarred retorted. He'd already been planning on giving Sean a call tomorrow and discussing his eventual return to Campbell Investments, but he wasn't about to admit that to his dad. He was a grown man, and he wasn't about to let his father boss him around.

Grown man? Really? The devil on his shoulder cackled derisively.

"Your credit card is frozen. You'll get your first paycheck in two weeks. Until then, you're very welcome to stop by the house for dinner. Marlene would love to see you."

So Daddy Dearest was cutting him off. He knew full well that all of Jarred's money was tied up in his condo and the sports car he'd rather die than sell. The condo was just an investment, a place to sleep—and not even that for the past two years. Hotel rooms around the world felt more like home than his own four walls. The only problem was that plenty of similarly priced condos were vacant around London, even places with a more breathtaking view of the city. He'd be selling at a huge loss in this market, so that was no option.

Jarred supposed this was what people meant by "having your back to the wall."

"How is my life any of your business? Since when do you suddenly care, anyway?" That wasn't entirely fair, of course—his father had always shown him plenty of attention when they were together. He just hadn't been home all that often, because he was too busy making money. More money than he could ever hope to spend on his own, in fact, though his children were certainly doing their part to help out. But Jarred was way too pissed to keep his tone respectful. Especially because he knew full well that his father had every right to rake him over the coals.

Jarred probably did need to apologize. Sooner or later.

"You'll be working in your old department," his father said, ignoring Jarred's snide remarks.

"So I'm just going to pick right up where I left off two years ago?" Right, because God forbid he report directly to his brother, or—gasp!—have equal footing. Nope, still two or three rungs down the ladder. Grrreat.

"Not quite," his father replied calmly. "You blew Sean off yet again the last time you spoke, so he's given your old job to someone else."

"What the hell is *that* supposed to mean?!" His voice cracked slightly. Other passengers stopped in their tracks and gave him funny looks. He'd completely forgotten he was still standing in the departures hall.

"In this case, it means that the person who got your job is extremely valuable to the company and earned that promotion. But that person could use your help, and you're going to provide it."

"You want me to play assistant? You can't be serious!" Jarred hissed. He should probably take it down a notch. Throwing a tantrum wouldn't help the situation, and he certainly didn't want to draw any more attention than he already had.

"Assistant, right-hand man, consultant, Girl Friday, call it what you want. This is how it's going to be."

Dammit. But there was nothing he could do to

change his father's mind. Long-term, he could start looking around for a new job, but leaving Campbell Investments and working for some random stranger felt wrong even in theory. He wasn't about to use his keen business instincts in service of the competition. Then again, he wasn't sure if he even still had those keen business instincts.

"Listen, I'm... I'm sorry about the thing with Atlantic City. I wasn't trying to... it just got out of hand and... I just wanted to apologize."

Well! That wasn't so hard. He exhaled slowly, waiting for his father's response.

And waiting.

The other end of the line remained silent for so long that Jarred began to wonder if his phone had died. He checked the display. Nope.

"How long are you expecting me to play lackey for this guy, then?" he grunted.

"For as long as Sean and I consider necessary. Jarred. We're doing this to help you, not to punish you. Someday, when you've got kids of your own, you'll understand. Oh, and this 'guy' is a woman. Rose Murphy? Maybe you remember her. Anyway, we're expecting you to keep your relationship *professional*, if you understand my meaning."

Rose Murphy ... The name sounded familiar, but he couldn't place a face. But surely it wouldn't be so bad if he just showed her the ropes, gave her some pointers on how to lead a department successfully.

And hopefully in another few weeks, he'd be the boss again anyway.

His father had already hung up. Jarred realized he'd forgotten to mention that he was definitely going to be late, unless his flight from L. A. to London set a new air-speed record. So much for making a good first impression.

CHAPTER 7

ROSE

What a difference a proper night's sleep could make. Rose stretched languidly before reaching for her cell phone to see how much longer she could relax in bed. After nine? Already?? The problem with blackout curtains was that they... blacked everything out. She turned on the bedside lamp and then hurried to the window. Sure enough, it was light outside. Well, technically it was dark outside, because the sky was completely overcast, and it was raining in sheets. *Shit, shit, not today!* She had an important appointment today at ten—she was meeting her new assistant and showing her the ropes. And then investors were coming by an hour later to explore a potential partnership.

Rose panicked at the realization there was no way in hell she'd arrive on time, and then panicked all over again when she realized that she'd have to take a cab or an Uber unless she wanted to show up looking like a freshly bathed poodle. Chances of finding a cab or an Uber in the next thirty minutes: slim.

Dammit.

Rose dashed to the bathroom, tossing her nightshirt onto the bed as she passed, and took the world's shortest shower. Dry shampoo would have to do today. She gathered her long hair into a tight bun and threw on the outfit she'd laid out the night before: her dark-red suit with a white, high-necked blouse, a plain but elegant "power suit" that gave her an extra boost of confidence when she was due to meet new clients or partners. Pearl earrings, check. High heels in the purse, check. Ugly but impenetrable rain boots for the commute, check. In the meantime, Rose checked and re-checked the Uber app every thirty seconds, until she finally saw a car heading in her direction. Five minutes for make-up. At minimum, she had to cover these dark circles under her eyes—the one good night of sleep hadn't quite gotten rid of them yet. Swipe of mascara, subtle pink lipstick, done.

A car stopped outside Rose's building. Nine thirty-eight! It was at least half an hour to the office, but that was without traffic… something that only happened in London at four in the morning. So embarrassing! She got more and more nervous with every passing minute as the car trundled through the city. She didn't arrive until almost ten-thirty. Yikes.

Hopefully someone had at least offered the new girl a cup of coffee?

Even in her boots, Rose did her best to dodge the puddles on the sidewalk. The umbrella she was clutching did nothing to prevent her coat from soaking through on the short walk, and her face felt damp as well. Impatiently, Rose tromped up the escalator and straight to reception. Luckily, one of the front desk assistants was free.

"Good morning, my name's Rose Murphy. Do you know if anyone's come to collect my ten-o'clock appointment?" She wished she'd gotten a name, at least. Sean had organized everything; all she knew was that she was supposed to be at her desk at ten. Sean hadn't responded to her message about being late. Maybe she ought to just go upstairs and see if anyone was waiting for her. Then again, where would the new girl have waited? Rose didn't have her own desk, either.

"No, he said he would wait in the canteen."

"He?" Rose blurted out.

The receptionist's eyes suddenly widened, fixing on something behind Rose.

"Rose, you're late," a sonorous voice behind her rang out.

The hair on her arms stood up before her conscious brain had finished registering that the voice belonged to a man she hadn't seen in a very long time. Slowly, she turned around—and could barely suppress the urge to throw her arms around his neck, just to make sure he was really there in the flesh. Wow, she had a way bigger crush on him than she'd even realized. Just seeing him was enough to knock her flat.

He looked older, more mature, and as perfectly polished as ever. His brow was furrowed; his hair was shorter, exposing the scar on his forehead—the flaw that made his face more interesting. His features seemed more angular. He looked like he was still in great shape; his tailored navy suit flattered his athletic figure. Her gaze drifted up to meet his light-brown eyes again. He didn't seem happy to see her in the slightest; he regarded her with cool condescension.

"Finished staring yet? Like I said, you're late. Client meeting starts at eleven on the dot. I suggest you duck into that restroom around the corner and make yourself presentable." Jarred's gaze wandered from her practical, but hideous boots to her dripping coat and umbrella before lingering on her face. After a moment, he raised a questioning eyebrow.

How rude! Rose *hated* that. People looking at her like she was dirt on their shoe. But of course he was the boss, and she knew she hardly looked office-ready. Wait a minute, no, she was the boss. Right?

"Good morning, Jarred. Please excuse my late arrival. I'm going to go freshen up; I'll just be a moment." She extended a hand, which he shook firmly. A warm feeling radiated through her. She was reluctant to pull away, but the clock was ticking…

and holding Jarred's hand any longer would probably seem weird.

JARRED

He watched Rose hasten to the restrooms. She looked overworked. What the hell had gotten into him, snapping at her and looking down at her like that? It wasn't *her* he was angry at. It certainly wasn't her fault that his father and half-brother had decided to make him her assistant. Anyway, she'd obviously proven herself valuable to the company, which in itself was enough to earn his respect. He appreciated having hardworking people on his team. Had appreciated. Would appreciate. One of those.

He sighed and checked his watch. It had been a hell of a morning. He hadn't been on time either, of course. Having landed early was the only reason he'd even made it to his place by ten. After fifteen minutes of ignoring how weird it was to be back within his own four walls, he'd left again. But being in the lobby of Campbell Investments again was making him nervous. He could feel the eyes on him, could hear the whispers as people began to recognize him. He didn't even want to *think* about how bad it would get upstairs.

Jarred grew impatient. *She'd better not show up to the next meeting late*, he thought. Ideally, they should have discussed how they were going to approach the meeting. Then again... he could also just keep to the background, let her take the lead. Assuming he could make himself do that. He assumed that neither Sean nor his father had announced that he was returning; otherwise Rose wouldn't have acted so surprised to see him.

Rose finally emerged from the restroom and strode purposefully in Jarred's direction—a sight that briefly took his breath away. Her dark-red pants suit flattered her figure, and those heels made her legs seem endless. She was only half a head shorter than him now. Her lips, now redone to match the outfit, practically demanded to be kissed... which was a completely stupid thing to think.

Oh, yes, he remembered Rose perfectly well. Far too well. He'd have invited her out to dinner years ago if it wasn't for his half-brother Liam.

Back when he'd still been working for Campbell Investments, Liam had fallen in love. Hard. Day and night, all he'd ever talked about was Cheryl, Cheryl, Cheryl. At least she worked in a different department. He'd have probably married her if it hadn't come out that she was only after his money. The discovery left Liam a shell of his former self. In the end, she'd even tried to get him on the hook for child support, claiming she'd been pregnant when they broke up. That part had turned out to be true, actually—just not the part about Liam being the father. Maybe she'd been hoping that roping him into fatherhood would buy her time to convince him that her feelings were genuine...? Anyway, the main result of the whole thing had been a giant tabloid clusterfuck, because Cheryl sold her version of the story to any gossip mag that would listen. Their father had lost his mind, but he'd made it all go away, as always. Liam had been laying low ever since; Jarred assumed he was probably in Verbier, but he didn't know for sure.

Which was why Jarred had set himself an ironclad rule: no mixing business and personal life.

Technically, it was just a principle, though... there was nothing about that in company policy or anything...

"Ready. I really apologize for being late. Maybe we could sit down and discuss a few things after the meeting, if you have time." Rose gave him a friendly smile, diligently ignoring how impolite he'd been earlier.

"Of course." He gestured for her to lead the way to the turnstile. The scent of summer sun hung in the air as he stepped through himself. "I'm happy to let you take the lead during the meeting," he added as they waited impatiently for the elevator.

Rose laughed heartily, a sound that pierced him straight to the heart. "Is that supposed to be a joke, Jarred?" she asked, eyes twinkling.

"It's your show, Rose," he replied with a grin. Saying that out loud felt like his first step toward accepting that London had changed in his absence.

New skyscrapers had cropped up nearby, for starters... just not the one that he'd poured blood, sweat, and tears into. It took him a moment to gather the courage to ask: "So, how come Spike never got finished?"

"Too many complications, and once you left... I dunno, I think you were the one holding it all together."

It was true—he really had been orchestrating the whole process. The memory ignited a brief flicker of Jarred's old passion for the job, something he hadn't felt in a long time... he'd spent the past two years getting his jollies elsewhere. He knew his way around dozens of casinos now, and had a list of charities to support with his winnings. He knew which clubs had the best music, and which had the hottest women. And he knew which friends to call when he needed which varieties of mind-altering substances. *How's that for a pointless existence?* The only reason he could still face himself in the mirror was that at least he'd donated nearly all the proceeds from his gambling hobby—"gambling addiction," some might say. Even he couldn't say for sure why he was suddenly so ashamed of the direction his life had taken. Maybe because Rose seemed to admire him, and it made him uncomfortable.

They got into the elevator and rode to the fortieth floor, to the conference rooms used with clients. The office floor was quiet. Rose deposited her coat and boots in a small kitchen before joining Jarred in the reserved room, where she pulled her laptop and notebook out of her handbag. Did she take her work home with her every night? She'd touched up her makeup, so the circles under her eyes were no longer visible, but she still seemed worn out.

Rose was already taking up way too much space in his head. Just then, he noticed that she was wearing a ring. Probably for the best—that way he wasn't even tempted. To distract himself, Jarred switched on the projector and checked the cold drinks.

Shortly before eleven, he and Rose returned to the 39th-floor lobby to meet their potential new business partners. Seconds later, the elevator doors opened, and three men in dark suits emerged. Jarred knew T&H Invest. They had a reputation for super high-risk investing, so he didn't view them as good candidates for long-term partnership. But Sean had organized this meeting, which suggested that he didn't share that view. Actually, the fact that Mr. By-The-Book had even considered bringing such a shady company on board made Jarred a little uneasy: was Campbell Investments really in such dire straits? *Hey, Sean, a briefing would have been nice...* Oh well, he'd just have to improvise. Wait, no! He was here to observe. Anyway, surely Rose had more information than he did.

As the three men approached, Jarred heard Rose draw in a sharp breath. Um... okay?

CHAPTER 8

ROSE

Oh, dear Jesus, this could not be happening! Was she hallucinating? If only. But no, there she was, with real actual Jarred standing next to her and goddamn *Aaron* smiling and reaching out for a handshake. It took Rose a second to shake off the paralysis.

"Hello, Aaron, when did you get back to town?" She did her best to sound polite, but the question came out sounding snappish even to her own ears.

"Last month, and you look as amazing as ever, Rose," he said in an unabashedly flirtatious tone. Judging from his perfectly confident demeanor, he didn't consider himself even one iota at fault.

Stay professional, she reminded herself. Their past had no business in this room. Rose ignored the compliment and turned to welcome the other two men, who immediately rubbed her the wrong way. Seemingly assuming Rose was Jarred's assistant, they hardly deigned to glance at her, and instead peppered Jarred with questions about when he'd arrived and what his plans were.

Jarred, to his credit, didn't immediately jump at the invitation to the boys' club. "Ms. Murphy will be leading the meeting. If you'll follow me, please?"

The two men—Jones and Newman—seemed only too happy to comply. Their eyes had a greedy luster, as though they were expecting big things from this meeting. Rose felt a headache coming on. So much for that boundless energy she'd felt when she first woke up.

Aaron lagged slightly behind, which meant she felt obligated to do the same, so it wouldn't seem like she was trying to run away from him. "You got married?" he asked quietly.

"None of your business?" she retorted. *Whoa, chill out, Rose.*

"Ouch!"

She and Mandy had exchanged friendship rings a while back, and she was wearing hers today. It was gold, but it certainly didn't look like a wedding ring, at least not to her. But whatever—if that kept Aaron in check, she didn't mind keeping the truth from him. Right, like she would have run off and gotten hitched so soon after they broke up? He never did understand how much he'd meant to her.

Aaron, radiating his usual life-is-a-bowl-of-cherries charm, smiled at Rose like she was his most precious treasure. She was half-expecting him to lace his fingers with hers and lean in for a tender kiss. That was one thing he'd definitely excelled at. Kissing was one of Aaron's specialties. *God, stop it already! Try being a damn professional for once!* She needed to put some distance between them, stat. If this kept up, she'd probably have to hand the meeting off to Jarred and find some quiet corner where she could crush a Valium into her tea or something. No, no, she wasn't about to let Aaron mess with her head. She was the boss! Yeahh!

When they reached the conference room, Jarred started taking care of refreshments. Wow, he really *was* letting her run the show. Rose stared at him for a second in surprise, but quickly composed herself, walked to the head of the table, and sat down. *Okay, lady, head high, shoulders back, don't forget to smile.*

A minute later, Jarred was still posted near the coffee machine, even though everyone was already sipping drinks. "Gentlemen, please, have a seat." Rose's voice was firm and decisive.

Their guests blinked at her in bewilderment. Out of the corner of her eye, she could see that Jarred was struggling to keep himself from laughing—but when Aaron and the other two turned to look at Jarred as though for confirmation, he'd already put on a poker face. He poured two glasses of water and set one beside her before taking a chair as well.

Though he'd left a seat between them so that she

could stay focused—*yeah, good luck with that, Rose*—she still caught a whiff of his wonderfully masculine scent. Did confidence have a smell? If so, this was probably it. "Gentlemen, thank you so much for accepting our invitation. I'd like to lead off with some information about Campbell Investments, and then I'll go into some of the areas where we see potential for collaboration with T&H Invest."

JARRED

They'd scheduled an hour-long meeting, but according to the clock on Rose's laptop, T&H had wasted the first fifteen minutes of it asking Jarred nosy questions, and then it took Rose another five to get their undivided attention. She was nervous, but it couldn't be on account of the presentation—she didn't make a single mistake, and she never looked at her notes once. Probably had to do with the way that Aaron guy was staring at her, like he had a compulsive need to make sure he never missed a single motion she made. His eyes practically devoured her as she took a sip of water and then ran her tongue over her dry lips. The guy didn't even try to hide that he was doing it.

Rose cleared her throat and shot Jarred a quick, uneasy glance, but after he nodded encouragingly, she went on speaking in a firm voice. Jarred had been planning to let Rose run the meeting from beginning to end, but he could tell that she could use a break, so he decided to take over. *How noble of you, Jarred!* Yeah, okay, he was also itching to be part of the discussion. He loved debating, loved convincing other people that he was right.

"So, gentlemen, do you have any questions, or was everything Ms. Murphy said clear?"

He felt her annoyed eyes on him. Well, tough luck.

There was no way in hell that he wanted T&H as business partners. Maybe they seemed like a good fit on paper, but Jarred knew better. Aaron and his colleagues would likely sign any contract Campbell Investments put in front of them. Greed was written all over their faces.

Jarred decided to turn the tables on them: instead of discussing the subject of collaboration from his company's point of view, he asked the T&H guys for their opinions. How did they think they could benefit from working with a strong partner like Campbell? If they'd come prepared, they might have some interesting arguments. He handed off to T&H with an encouraging nod before leaning back in his chair and crossing one leg over the other—a posture signaling rejection, belying his friendly remarks.

Rose, meanwhile, had her notebook open, and sat waiting with pen in hand.

ROSE

The meeting was finally over, thank God. All Rose had to do was say a few friendly goodbyes, and then she could get the hell out of this room and calm down. It was that or strangle Jarred right where he stood. And *Aaron*, ugh, where did he get off, staring at her like that? Remembering that she'd slept with him gave her the creeps now… oh, who was she kidding? She'd been his naïve little girlfriend. How could she have thought *he* was the one? Yikes!

Jarred had already gotten up to lead the way out. She followed hastily so that her ex wouldn't have a chance to rope her into another skeevy exchange, and bid the visitors goodbye with firm handshakes and fake smiles. The very second the elevator closed behind the T&H guys, Rose stomped toward the ladies' room furiously.

"Rose!" Jarred's sharp tone stopped her in her tracks. Slowly, she turned around, doing her level best to keep her rage in check. "Don't start bitching, now. Just tell me, what's the deal with that Aaron guy? Do you know each other?"

"Bitching? Are you out of your mind? If you have a problem reporting to me, maybe you should just tell me now, before you leave me standing there like an idiot again."

"I didn't leave you standing anywhere like an idiot. You looked like you were going to pass out any minute."

"Oh, *my* mistake, so I was supposed to be *grateful* that you were concerned about my *health*. Sorry, uh, you don't know me at all."

"But Aaron does, I guess? Do you two have something going on or what?"

"Mind your own goddamn business, Jarred," Rose snapped before resuming her furious trek to the restroom. She realized she probably ought to go clear her laptop and notebook out of the meeting room in case someone else was using it, but if she didn't get five minutes to herself right now—preferably ten—she was probably going to make a scene.

Hey hey, guess what? You already did! Rose stalked into an empty stall, flipped the toilet lid down, and sat. Yep, she'd done that. She'd screamed at Jarred. The owner's son. Her ex-boss. Crap. Was she going to get fired? *No, no, don't panic.* She could still apologize.

Then again... apologize for what?

JARRED

He watched her go, startled. Great, so, today was getting off to a fabulous start. He'd already managed to piss his boss off how many times now? Better make himself useful just in case she was reporting regularly to Sean or something. He gathered her things from the conference room and headed back to their floor. He needed to ask about getting his own laptop anyway, and getting access to the server again. And then Rose needed to tell him what she wanted help with. Hopefully something more interesting than typing letters.

Of course all the desks were taken. A murmur went through the office as soon as he stepped in. People waved and called out hellos; he nodded in response before making his way to one of the red sofas, depositing Rose's stuff on the nearby table. Hopefully she'd be back soon—he couldn't do a damn thing around here without his own laptop.

A few minutes later, she walked in through the glass doors and strode right up to him. "You don't have to cart my things around, but thank you." Rose set down her coat, boots, and bag, took a seat, and hesitantly retrieved her notebook.

"No problem, and I wasn't snooping or anything."

Did she just breathe a sigh of relief? Wow, she really thought he was capable of that. This was going to be one hell of a working relationship.

"Do I get a laptop, or do you want to explain my responsibilities first, or what? Should I, like, make coffee or something?" He'd meant it as a joke, but it suddenly occurred to him that he wouldn't mind fetching drinks for Rose in the slightest. She looked like she could use something stronger, actually. He was curious whether it was on his account or Aaron's.

ROSE

"How come you didn't call?" The disappointment in Mandy's voice did nothing to improve Rose's mood.

"Didn't have time," Rose yawned.

"That's crazy, that they both showed up again at the same time."

"If I never see Aaron again, it'll be too soon."

"I love that he thinks you're married. I hope it keeps him awake at night, just drives him absolutely batshit that someone else snagged you... although I guess Jarred thinks that too now, so that kind of sucks."

"What do you mean? I couldn't care less what Jarred thinks. As far as I'm concerned, he can go ahead and disappear again."

"You don't really mean that. Jarred is 'brilliant, a visionary, and a fantastic boss,' quote-unquote. You went on about how great he was every damn day."

"That was a long time ago." Today was not exactly her finest hour, and she hated that Jarred had been there to see it. "Maybe I'm really not cut out for this job."

"Bullshit. You're just overworked, you need a break. We're going clubbing Friday night, and by

Saturday morning the world will feel like a brand-new place. Dancing's the best medicine. Next to drawing, in your case. Any new creations today?"

But of course. On her ride home, the pen had practically flown across the paper of its own accord. She opened her notebook and held the phone over it —Mandy would never stop asking otherwise.

"No comment, hm?" She'd been wanting to draw Aaron, or a donkey with Aaron's face, but her hand had had different ideas.

"That's an incredible drawing."

Hm, yeah, it was pretty good. Completely inappropriate—she was still furious at Jarred, furious at how he'd acted today—but pretty good. His visage beamed at her in pure adoration from the page, as though he were about to propose or something. But that was obviously fantasy-Jarred, not real Jarred. He'd been away so long that she'd built him up in her mind, created a version of him that had never existed. Like how some people projected all their romantic fantasies onto singers or movie stars. Reality was almost always completely different.

Still, he *had* been extremely nice and helpful for the rest of the day, and he'd done every little thing she'd asked. That was something.

JARRED

"You going to just sit there chugging beer or you want to tell me what you're doing back in London?"

"Visiting my older brother?"

Henry's laugh was loud and sarcastic. "Yeah, obviously, how could I forget that I'm always your first port of call… I hear Atlantic City was a real rager?"

"Wasn't my fault that the hotel room came out a little worse for wear."

"A little worse for wear! Go blow smoke up someone else's ass. Next time call me so I can be there." Henry drained his pint in one go. "C'mon, let's get some food in us, before you're too wasted to tell me what's really going on."

They were sitting at the counter of the pub nearest their offices. Henry's was just down the road from Campbell Investments, in a Georgian-style building with a doorman and five other tenants. Not a particularly glamorous office, but it was Henry's pride and joy.

They ordered burgers and a second round of beer. It was still early in the evening, so the place was fairly quiet. These days, the air smelled of fried food rather than the cigarette smoke that had always seeped into their hair and clothes.

Their beers arrived quickly, and they clinked their glasses together before taking huge gulps. Then Jarred launched into a long explanation. When he got to the part about his dad and Marlene wanting him to come by for dinner, Henry burst out laughing all over again.

"If I were you, I'd have gone out to dinner with me first, too. Huh! So the old man froze your card. Never would have expected that. You're the first one of us he's cut off. I'd have put my money on Liam. Nobody knows what the hell he does all day... but he doesn't draw any attention to himself, which is clearly where you went wrong." Henry smirked. "So now what? You going to bend to Dad's iron will or dip into your savings?"

"What savings? I sunk almost everything into the condo and the Ferrari."

"What'd you do with your poker winnings? Don't tell me you kept playing until you lost it all again."

"Sometimes."

Henry looked horrified. "Man, you're nuts!"

"Joke! I donated the winnings."

"Oh yeah? To who?"

"Whoever needed it. Nursing homes, orphanages, free clinics, hospices."

"And you didn't tell Dad that?"

"None of his business." He'd sell the condo if he could. Nothing about it felt like home. The whole place was foreign to him. Professionally decorated, pretty to look at, but that was it. It was a decent investment, anyway. Not quite as lucrative as the penthouse would have been, but penthouses didn't mix well with his fear of heights.

"And you're playing second fiddle at work, hm?" Henry snickered. "Never thought I'd see the day."

"Second? Closer to fiftieth. It's maddening."

"Sure, well, you've been putting up with it for a whole *day* already. Oh well, buck up, nothing to be done about it."

"Thanks for that pearl of wisdom, sensei. Never would have figured that out myself."

"Very welcome, grasshopper." Henry bit into his burger.

As they ate, Jarred thought about Rose. Did he owe her an apology? She'd been cool but cordial for the rest of the day, and they hadn't mentioned the little episode outside the elevators again. He decided a clarifying discussion was probably in order tomorrow. And there was no escaping dinner with Dad and Marlene, either...

CHAPTER 9

JARRED

News of his return had spread quickly. Old acquaintances texted and left messages saying that they couldn't wait to see him at the private clubs in Belgravia and South Kensington. Jarred hadn't quite decided whether to hit the town or keep a low profile for a few weeks to placate his father. Having his credit card blocked gave him the sense that he could potentially lose everything. Which was ridiculous, since he was hardly destitute... but for the first time in his life, he felt like he was actually on his own.

He really needed to get out of this negativity spiral. He'd never been the melancholy type before. He'd enjoyed life to the fullest, giving a hundred and ten percent in everything he did. Work had been his elixir of life, while sports—especially motorsports—

had provided the thrills. But after Mom's death, he'd basically crawled under a rock for weeks, because he couldn't stand being around people. When isolation hadn't helped, he'd resorted to narcotics, which was when his life had *really* started to go off the rails. Drugs had a way of making a person forget they were mortal.

The friends he'd surrounded himself with back then had been false friends; his few real friends had given up on him one by one. At the time, he'd snarked to Alice about how he didn't need anybody, and if his friends were willing to drop him like a bad habit, they weren't worth his time anyway. *Wow*, he'd been such an idiot. Rebuilding all of those burned bridges was going to be a lot of work.

After a restless night, Jarred got up at some insanely early hour to jog by the Thames. Nothing but concrete as far as the eye could see. With every step he took, the thought of selling his Barbican Centre condo and finding somewhere new cemented in his mind more and more.

The skyscrapers along the Thames stretched proudly into the heavens. Jarred liked looking at them, and he liked putting Campbell Investments' money toward constructing new ones, but that hardly meant he wanted to live in them. Mostly because the views other people would call spectacular made him break out in a cold sweat. It seemed like an ironic twist of fate that he, of all people, was afraid of heights.

So yes, he needed a new place. But what he needed to do even more urgently was fix his relationship with Rose. He wondered if she'd agree to have lunch with him. Worth a shot, anyway.

It was still dark out when he returned home an hour later. It had been a long time since he'd pushed himself that hard, and he felt incredibly alive, awash in happy hormones. He could hardly wait to put his new plans into action.

ROSE

Rose had been so afraid to oversleep again that she'd barely gotten any rest, even though she'd actually put out a second alarm just in case—the old clock-radio alarm stuffed in her nightstand, with the buzzer loud enough to wake the dead. That's what Aaron had always claimed, anyway, which was why he'd insisted they use his phone. Even after Rose had banished Aaron from her life, she hadn't thought to bring the clock radio out of retirement. Until now.

She'd lain awake until the wee hours of the morning, mentally replaying her conversation with Jarred over and over again. It was definitely time she sat Jarred down and made sure they were on the same page; she had neither the time nor the energy for any more pissing contests. He had to accept that she was the boss. The end. If he couldn't, she could always get

Sean involved. Best not get too obsessive about it though. Actually, she was starting to wonder why she'd been so mad in the first place.

Rose checked her voicemails in the cable car. Mandy and Ella singing "Happy Birthday." Rose was thirty today. She didn't feel a bit different than she had yesterday or the day before.

When Rose walked into the office at seven-thirty, she was astonished to find Jarred working away at a desk near the hallway. She almost never ran into anyone when she came in this early. Her first impulse was to take the workspace furthest from his, near the window. But no, that would be childish—she knew she ought to stay close. After all, Jarred had been gone for two whole years, so he was still remembering the ropes, and he'd probably have questions. And as his boss, she ought to be supportive, right? Which meant not sitting a thousand miles away. Probably. She walked over to one of the desks near his. He went on typing for a while, fully absorbed in his work, but eventually he glanced up and smiled at her. "Good morning, Rose."

He sounded like he genuinely meant it. On closer inspection, in fact, he seemed way more relaxed than he had the day before. Even after she'd returned the greeting and he'd returned to his work, that smile was still playing on his lips; she was half-expecting him to start humming. At least someone here had gotten a proper night's sleep, instead of lying awake for hours brooding over the previous day. It occurred to her that he might be in a good mood because he hadn't been alone in bed—but she drove that thought out of her head immediately. None of her business.

Good Lord, why was he still smiling?

The real question was, when had she become such a grouch? She was a cheerful person... most of the time, anyway.

Rose shrugged off her coat before fetching her heels and writing materials from her cubby. What had put Jarred in such a good mood? But she was probably giving this way too much thought. Coffee, coffee would help. "Jarred?" she called. "You want a coffee?"

He looked up in surprise. "Good idea, I'll come with you." He jumped to his feet and walked over. "... What?" he grinned.

"I, um, I wasn't thinking that you'd come with me."

"Wow, are you always this pleasant to your subordinates?"

"Sorry. I barely slept." Rose rubbed her forehead a little, trying to drive away the exhaustion and kick-start her concentration. Her stomach growled before they'd taken three steps.

"No sleep, no food. Let's go down to the canteen. I

haven't been there in a few years, but I'm hoping Sean hasn't started cutting corners there."

"Oh, no, the canteen's fine. The baked goods are unfortunately still fantastic. I'm addicted to the lemon muffins."

"Yeah? Can't tell by looking at you. I always liked the raspberry ones the best."

Rose couldn't tell by looking at him, either. Jarred's suit fit perfectly, and the tight-fitting shirt beneath did nothing to conceal his muscular figure. His eyes were full of life today, Rose realized as they waited for the elevators. *Quit staring at him already, Rose.* He sure didn't make it easy to look away, though. Certainly not when he had that warm smile on his face. Just the way she'd drawn him.

"Do you do any sports?"

Jarred's question caught her off guard. "Um, I was on the rowing team at university, but these days I don't have time. I walk to work sometimes—well, not the whole way, but the last part. I live in Greenwich. The pedestrian tunnel under the Thames is really cool, isn't it?"

Why was she so hyper?

"I was a rower, too. Which university?"

"Cambridge, you?"

"Oxford. We'll beat you again next time."

"In your dreams. It's eighty-three to eighty for Cambridge, you know."

"The Boat Race," the annual rowing races between Oxford and Cambridge Universities, were legendary.

They'd started in 1829, and they'd been held on the same stretch of river since 1845. Up to a quarter of a million people came to watch every year.

"Wanna bet? Next race is in two months." He held out a hand.

She shook it. "You're on."

"I'll have to think of a good wager." His sly wink made her swallow hard. But surely he wouldn't pick anything too awful…

When the elevator door opened, he moved aside to allow her through first. Rose stepped over to the glass, to watch the skyscrapers around them slowly awaken. It was dawn; the skies glowed in pink and orange, with hardly a cloud in sight. If the weather stayed dry through lunch, she'd have to spend her break drawing by the Thames.

As she gazed out at the panorama before them, she breathed in Jarred's faint scent, wishing she could just close her eyes and daydream; she was almost disappointed when the elevator dinged and Jarred announced, "We're here." They stepped out onto the tenth floor and passed through the swinging wooden doors to the canteen. Clattering and hissing noises drifted from the kitchen. A handful of Campbell employees populated the small tables, either chatting quietly in pairs or alone and engrossed in a newspaper or a phone; Jarred drew a few amazed looks, but didn't seem concerned. He went straight for the cake display and perused the selection with interest. Rose sidled in beside him, curious what his second choice would be since there weren't likely to be fresh raspberry muffins in January.

"What do you want with your muffin?" Jarred glanced at Rose. "Coffee?"

"Green tea with lemon, please."

"You're a real lemon fan. Okay, you want to find us a table? I'll bring everything over."

Rose opened her mouth to tell him that there was no need for him to pay, but what came out was "Thanks! My treat next time, okay?"

"Sure." He seemed like he was actually looking forward to it. Well, good.

Rose picked a spot by the window with a direct view of the forecourt to the neighboring building, which was far more lively than half an hour before. How tiny the people seemed. Rose loved looking down at the city. The higher the platform, the better. She was so fascinated by the comings and goings outside that she didn't hear Jarred approach, and jumped about a foot in the air when she suddenly heard him clear his throat.

CHAPTER 10

JARRED

Jarred reflexively reached for his credit card before he remembered. Not being able to use it was irritating. A lot of people still preferred cash, of course, but he was fresh out of that as well. Before things could get embarrassing, he realized that there might be a few pounds left on his employee card. He handed it to the cashier and exhaled in relief when it worked. Another lucky break.

The next jolt came when he saw that she'd picked a table by the window. Of course she had—everyone liked sitting by the window. It was sunny, and the view was breathtaking. So now what? Ask her if she minded switching tables, or sit beside her instead of opposite so that he wouldn't have an unobstructed view into the abyss? He cleared his throat quietly.

"Oh! Sorry, I never get tired of this view. I'd buy one of those condos at the top of the Shard if I could find enough money in the cushions of my couch. Must feel like you're living in the clouds. Have you been out on the platform?" Her eyes sparkled as she spoke. The platform she was referring to was eight hundred feet up and stretched across several stories. Wild horses couldn't drag Jarred up there.

"No, I'm not big on heights," he replied curtly.

"Oh, that's a shame," Rose blurted out, looking disappointed. "Well, I mean, having both feet firmly on the ground is nice, too."

He didn't like the thought of disappointing Rose, though he wasn't sure why. What difference did her opinion make to him? None, theoretically, but he felt like kind of a loser, and he certainly didn't want that. So he set down the tray and took a seat beside her. Suggesting a table in the middle of the room was suddenly no longer an option.

"Chocolate fan, hm?" Rose took her green tea and lemon muffin from the tray.

"I read somewhere that it's good for your nerves." He hadn't had a chocolate muffin in a million years. At some point, he'd stopped eating sweets entirely. Once upon a time, he'd had the world's biggest sweet tooth, and he'd loved Christmas because it smelled like cookies everywhere. But those days were long over. Besides, it was the middle of January.

"So did you grow up in Greenwich?" Jarred wanted to get to know Rose better. He couldn't remember much about her anymore, except that she was of the quiet, hardworking variety. She was really pretty, in sort of an unobtrusive way. He wondered how she dressed out of the office, whether she wore her dark-blond hair down. It seemed like it might be long, but Rose had it in another tight up-do, apart from a few stubborn wayward strands that framed her heart-shaped face. Her lashes were long and dark, with just a hint of mascara. Jarred had never paid much attention to whether women wore makeup or not, but he decided he liked Rose's natural look a lot.

"No, in Watford—north of London. My parents still live there. How about you? You live in the city?"

"Ten minutes' walk from here."

Rose tore her muffin into pieces before sliding one into her mouth. She sighed happily and then smiled in embarrassment. Jarred was intrigued by the effect she had on him. If she weren't already taken, he'd ask her out. He wondered if she had children. Was that the kind of thing he could just ask without it seeming weird?

Uh, hello? This is your boss we're talking about? Jarred was tempted to ignore the alarm bells blaring in his head. "But you didn't want to move back to Watford? Does your husband work in the city, too?" Jarred's breath caught in his throat. Not exactly his smoothest approach.

Rose nearly choked on her bite of muffin, and hastily sipped her tea to wash it down.

"Sorry, is the thought of living in Watford so

shocking?" Or else she was really that horrified that he'd ask if she was married...?

"No, sorry, question just surprised me. I'm single, never been married."

He glanced at the ring on her left hand.

"Just a friendship ring! My best friend Mandy has one too. Anyway, I've never known for sure where you're supposed to wear which ring. My mom's from Switzerland, so she wears the wedding ring on her left hand and the engagement ring on her right; Mandy wears them both on her left and the friendship ring on her right, and, anyway, no, like I said—" She stopped abruptly, glancing down at the crumbs on her muffin plate. "What about you?" she blurted out. Her cheeks flushed bright red, and she bit her lip in embarrassment.

Jarred grinned. Well, turnabout was fair play. "Neither married nor engaged nor otherwise taken."

She merely nodded. Was that relief on her face? *Good Lord, Jarred, you're not doing yourself any favors thinking about that.*

Jarred finished his muffin in silence. God, delicious, he felt like rolling his eyes in ecstasy. Just one final order of business before they returned to the office. "Listen, I wanted to apologize for yesterday. I really did want to support you—I'm just not used to playing second fiddle. Plus, I never would have invited T&H if it had been up to me. They're not my idea of a proper partner."

"I'm sorry, too. I shouldn't have yelled at you.

That's nice that you wanted to be supportive... maybe next time we should make a game plan in advance."

"As long as you show up on time," he said with a teasing grin.

"That's never happened before." Rose cringed.

"I was late, too," Jarred confessed.

"Oh, well, we're even, then. How long are you sticking around, then?"

"Trying to get rid of me already, hm?" Jarred quipped for lack of a better answer. They were obviously both well aware that he was only playing assistant temporarily, but he wasn't going to be the one to spell it out—that was Sean's territory. Probably time he spoke to his half-brother anyway; he hadn't been available yesterday. Well, why not now?

"Shall we?" he asked, already preoccupied with what he was going to say to Sean.

"Of course." Rose stood up immediately and stacked their empty plates on the tray, which she deposited on the conveyor belt for used dishes.

They returned to the elevator together, but Rose got out at their floor alone; Jarred continued to the top.

His brother had time to see him today. Lovely. It felt like he was there to beg audience from the king—Sean sat in his desk chair as though it were the royal throne, and seemed to look down on Jarred even from below. His office was furnished sparsely, with functionality in mind. Besides Sean's massive desk, it had a pair of dark loveseats around a glass coffee table, a simple kitchenette, and a door leading to a private restroom. Dark gray carpet, like everywhere else in the building. The wall near the door was lined with professional photographs of skyscrapers, but the view behind Sean was far more breathtaking than any photo could ever manage.

Better if Jarred stayed on this side of the desk. Being on the fortieth floor wasn't really helping his nerves.

Sean, dressed in a fine dark suit, eyed him severely. Jarred, not for the first time, wondered if anyone on Earth still wore three-pieces besides his brother.

"Welcome back."

"Thanks."

They'd never had much to say to each other, but so far this barely qualified as a conversation.

"Has Rose gotten you settled in?"

Jarred nodded. "When do I get a real project?" Probably not his most tactful approach, but he wasn't feeling particularly patient at the moment.

"When I think the time is right."

"So, what, you expect me to just sit there waiting for you to decide that I've suffered enough?"

"You're in no position to make demands after the way you screwed up."

"Oh, I can't *wait* to hear *your* opinion about *my* lifestyle again. I *love* how you think it's any of your business."

"Anything that hurts the company is damn well my business."

"Lovely. Thank you for making your priorities clear." AKA, reiterating that Jarred was not among them. He knew Sean couldn't stand him; luckily, he didn't care. Or theoretically didn't, anyway. Having Sean's boot on his professional neck was making it harder than usual to remain indifferent.

"Take a look at the ongoing projects. Give Rose a hand—she's got a lot on her plate. Plenty of fires to put out in your department."

"Hm, why would that be? If I remember correctly, I left everything in pristine condition," Jarred sniffed.

"Wow, stop the presses. You have memories going back two whole years? My mistake, I thought all the coke and booze had taken care of that for you. Oh, well, works out the same in the end."

Ouch.

Jarred turned and walked out of the office before he could say anything too clever, but he still heard Sean's parting "And keep your hands to yourself out there" shot loud and clear.

ROSE

When Jarred returned to his desk, his face was a stone mask; he sat down at his desk and stared at the laptop screen for several long minutes. Rose was about to ask him if he needed help when he turned to tell her that he was going to spend time catching up on their ongoing projects. His eyes were hard and cold, unapproachable—nothing like the Jarred she'd spoken to earlier that morning.

Rose gave him a brief refresher on the various file directories before leaving him to his own devices. Meetings kept her on the go for the rest of the morning; she didn't manage to take a break until one. Jarred was still rooted to the spot, staring at his screen with laser focus, pausing only occasionally to jot something down. His notebook was red like hers, she noticed. The company provided them for free, but she was surprised to see he'd picked the same color. Something else they had in common. And hadn't he been drinking green tea in the cafeteria, too?

Her mind was galloping in a direction she didn't like. Again.

After fetching her coat and hat, she told Jarred she'd see him after lunch. She wasn't even sure he'd heard her. Once she reached street level, Rose took a deep breath of more-or-less fresh air and gazed up at the blue sky, suddenly wildly happy that she had time to walk to the Thames. She headed straight for Tower Hill, buying herself a cup of tomato soup on the way. There was plenty of places to sit around here, and she'd even thought to grab a free daily paper that morning just in case it was wet.

Rose enjoyed the sun and the breeze, but she still

hurried to finish her soup—she didn't want to sit around in the cold for too long, and she definitely wanted to spend a little time drawing. Her hand flew over the paper as she sketched the Tower, and then added a couple standing in front of it, arms wrapped around one another. She'd always been a romantic, but recently almost all of her drawings had featured couples in love... or Jarred.

When it got too cold for her, Rose packed up her things and started for the office. She made a resolution not to obsess too much about the fact that Jarred was back. They were work colleagues, nothing more. He wasn't even a friend. No doubt he'd be taking a position closer to Sean's soon, and then he'd forget all about her. She just had to get her weird crush under control. Couldn't be too hard, right?

On her way back, she stopped to get a caramel macchiato. They only tasted good if you drank them extra-hot. Which Rose was planning to do, because she was freezing. Definitely shouldn't have sat outside for so long. Hopefully the extra sugar in the caramel would help her power through her afternoon meetings. God, she needed some proper sleep.

The thought promptly pushed Jarred to the forefront of her mind again. Rolling her eyes in annoyance at herself, she hastened into the open-plan office, where she found Jarred still staring at his computer with a sour look on his face... and then discovered a giant bouquet of roses on her desk. Baccara roses, judging from the deep red color. Must have cost a fortune. Rose counted thirty. An insanely romantic gesture.

And there was only one man outside her circle of family and friends who knew that today was her birthday.

CHAPTER 11

JARRED

He wasn't sure what irritated him more: the bouquet of flowers or the useless conversation with Sean. Like he'd caused some giant international scandal or something. Ridiculous. Okay, yes, Atlantic City had gotten slightly out of hand, but other than that, he didn't see what the problem was. He didn't even live all that extravagantly. He'd paid for most of his flights with miles, and he hadn't always stayed in first-class hotels... hell, why was he even trying to justify himself? Dad had never complained about his spending, and Sean had no right to be so sanctimonious. He had plenty of expensive hobbies, especially that yacht.

Jarred had spent the whole morning studying the department's current projects like a good little worker bee, but it hadn't done anything to calm him down... and when they'd delivered that enormous bouquet for Rose, it had put him in even lower spirits. Which he didn't understand in the slightest. He wasn't the jealous type, for God's sake. Why would it bother him at all that someone was courting her?

Red roses, too. That wasn't just flirting, that was serious. Well, why had she claimed she was single, then? Had she been lying? Why would she lie about that? And why had he been thinking about this nonstop since the flowers arrived? Maybe he ought to take a break. It was well past lunchtime, and he hadn't eaten a thing, which was probably bad for both his mood and his blood sugar. Ugh, even he couldn't stand himself lately.

Rose returned to the office, derailing Jarred's self-pity train. Huh... shouldn't she be happy to see those? After hesitating briefly, she strode to her desk, set down her cup and reached for the card waiting among the flowers. She read the note, tore the card into about a thousand pieces, grabbed the bouquet, and headed straight for the elevator.

Jarred blinked in confusion, but then hurried to catch up. He caught the elevator just before the doors closed. Rose was staring stubbornly ahead, her lips pressed into a thin line. She got out at the ground floor and went through the turnstile. Jarred stood there for a moment, uncertain. It would be weird of him to just follow her, right? Partly because he hadn't brought a coat and it was barely forty degrees out;

partly because he wasn't trying to look like a complete stalker.

But Rose didn't leave the building. She stopped at the front desk, said something to the receptionist, handed over the roses, and gave the receptionist a quick wave goodbye. Then she returned to the elevator with an expression of obvious relief—which turned to bewilderment when she spotted Jarred.

"Everything okay?" Jarred wanted to know the whole story, of course, but he had to admit that this was exactly none of his business.

"I'm cold," was Rose's surprising response. She looked agitated. He had a sudden urge to put his arms around her, but that would have been even less appropriate than asking what the hell was up with the flowers.

"C'mon, let's go to the canteen, I'm hungry." He winked at her encouragingly, and actually managed to draw a tiny smile out of Rose.

"I don't have much time," Rose mused, but followed him to the elevator anyway. Neither spoke until they reached the cafeteria counter.

"Tea?" Jarred asked. "Hot cocoa? Hot milk with honey?"

"Milk and honey? I'd fall asleep," she said, although her expression suggested that she thought it sounded delicious. "Coffee with milk, please. But it's my turn to pay." Rose whipped out her employee card.

"No way!" Jarred exclaimed, but then caught

himself and cleared his throat. He hadn't come down her to snap at her. Yikes, he was really on a hair trigger these days. "Why don't you find us a table?" he said in a calmer voice.

Rose did, in fact, sit down at the nearest table while Jarred brought coffee and plenty of chocolate to the register.

"Who's supposed to eat all that?" she grinned when he returned.

"I told you I was hungry."

"Normal people tend to eat food for lunch. Like... food with nutrients?"

"Do tell! But I thought that was one of the advantages of being an adult. I can eat what I want, when I want." He pushed a coffee cup across to her before unwrapping the first candy bar and taking a bite. "Dee-licious," he proclaimed between bites.

"Need help with that?" Rose asked innocently once she'd finished half her coffee.

"If you insist," he replied teasingly.

"I can't just sit here and let you ruin your teeth alone," she said with a wry grin.

"I appreciate the concern."

"At least you're in a better mood now," she said and then immediately froze, as though shocked she'd said it.

"Seems so." She was right. He needed to get a grip on his emotions. "You want to tell me what was wrong back there?" Worth a try, anyway. All she could do was say no.

"I don't have time right now—I have a meeting in a few minutes."

Well, that wasn't a no. Then again, was it really all that smart of him to ask? No? He still wanted to, of course. "Maybe later, then."

"Yeah, maybe."

They tossed their empty coffee cups and candy wrappers; Jarred took the last two chocolate bars with him. Once Rose had left for her meeting, he left one on her desk along with a note. In case they didn't see each other before he left for his father's house, at least he'd have gotten one more smile out of her.

ROSE

"These nightly phone calls are becoming part of my routine." Rose was lying on her bed, equal parts worn out and keyed up.

"I'm always glad to hear from you. How was your birthday? I can't wait to hit the dance floor tomorrow and celebrate properly."

"Yeah, I'm looking forward to it, too. Dancing's like vacation."

"Something like that. So! Yesterday you had Aaron-drama and Jarred-drama. How about today?"

"Should I wait while you make popcorn?"

"Don't keep me in suspense! I live in the country now, it's boring here."

"Yeah, right. That whole town is a total gossip mill. My mom told me her neighbor moved out because he met a woman half his age, and now there's always some young stud leaving his disgraced still-wife's house. That's top-shelf drama! Probably even the censored version."

"*Surely* you're not making fun of me."

"Just a little."

"Come on, don't build this up. Did Jarred confess his undying love or what?"

"What? No! We had tea. Twice. It was nice."

"Nice? Woman, you're driving me up the wall."

"And then I got a bouquet of Baccara roses. You can't even *imagine* how beautiful they were."

"What? Wow! How many? I guess there wasn't a diamond-encrusted ring attached... a birthday present?"

"Thirty! But the roses were from the wrong man."

"No! You don't mean—"

"Aaron."

"The nerve! Did he write a card? Oh, God, who cares, we want nothing to do with that idiot anyway. So did you burn the flowers or what?"

"I took them to the reception desk, because I couldn't bring myself to just throw them away. He wrote that he missed me, and that he'd realized how much I meant to him, and that we should give it another try."

"He's out of his damn mind. So he didn't buy it

that you were married, I guess? You'll just have to tell him to go to hell face-to-face."

"Hm."

"What, hm? You aren't actually considering giving him a second chance, are you? Let me be the first to remind you that we still do not know for sure if he was having an affair throughout your entire relationship?"

"That's true. We don't."

"Then how could anything have changed? He might be writing 'I miss you' cards to more than one person."

"Well, of course that crossed my mind, I'm not *that* naïve."

"Did Jarred say anything about it?"

"He left me a note on a candy bar."

"I'm... not sure I understand. But whatever. What'd it say?"

"'Good mood guaranteed.' Plus his phone number." Rose's heart was *still* hammering in her throat.

"Wait, and you're talking to me? What the hell for? Go call him already!"

"No, no way. We work together, and I'm sort of his boss, even though that's just temporary until he joins the executive board or whatever, I assume. I mean, workplace relationships are always risky. Plus I don't necessarily know why he gave me his number."

"So call him and find out! Rob and I worked at the

same company, you know," Mandy pointed out. "And don't even start with how this is soooo different. I mean, whatever, he wasn't my boss, or vice versa, but just imagine if he and I had made some hard and fast rule about not dating coworkers."

"Jarred's the son of the owner."

"Well, if you want to call him, call him. If not, don't." Mandy, pragmatic as ever.

"Maybe I will. Just to thank him for the candy bar."

"Sure, yeah, good idea. Sweet dreams!" Mandy laughed and signed off.

Rose did consider calling Jarred, but eventually decided to just relax with a glass of warm milk.

CHAPTER 12

JARRED

The taxi ride to Kensington was nearly an hour in heavy traffic. Jarred spent most of it staring out the window. Luckily, the cab driver was the quiet type, and mostly left him in peace.

Jarred hadn't been back to his childhood home in years. His mother had moved to Notting Hill after the divorce. Once he'd returned to the city after finishing his studies at Oxford, he'd visited her often. For a while, anyway. Until he'd started living in the fast lane, and every deal he closed called for a party to celebrate his success. Working hard and playing hard had left little time for anything else.

The clammy, oppressive feeling in his chest grew with every minute of a taxi ride that suddenly felt like it would end much too soon. But there was no way around this—he would just have to suffer through dinner with Dad and Marlene, demonstrate that he understood their concerns, and convince his father that he had his life back under control, that he was all done with the party scene. That had to be enough to get his credit card unblocked, right?

Jarred had even remembered to bring flowers. Blue orchids. Marlene was sure to like them. *You don't even know the woman, Jarred.* Okay, that was true. He'd only met her a few times. He'd been in the wedding party, as ordered, but he'd left as quickly as decorum would allow. Everyone thought Marlene was a gold-digger. What else would a woman her age want with a senior citizen? Dad was turning seventy this year. Surely he didn't want more children…?

The cab pulled up to the stately white home, and he paid the driver. The front yard was neatly kept, but he'd expected nothing else. Though Jarred still had his own key, he went ahead and rang the heavy, brass-fitted door. Marlene opened it almost immediately, as though she'd been waiting just on the other side. The first thing Jarred noticed was how young she looked. Marlene was only in her mid-thirties; she could have just as easily been his older sister. It would be a cold day in hell before he referred to her as "Mom."

"Come in, Jarred! Are those orchids? They're absolutely gorgeous, thank you so much!" Marlene beamed at him as though they were old friends reuniting after many years. Fortunately, she made no move to hug him or touch him in general. He gave her a polite hello as he stepped in. A little stiff, maybe, but he wasn't here to put on a show. He did manage a smile, at least, which made her blue eyes sparkle even more.

She was wearing a navy blouse and dark trousers; her blond hair was up in a simple ponytail. In her flat shoes, she barely reached his shoulder. Laughing happily, she led the way into the living room; the bouquet looked gigantic in her arms.

"Arthur, look, aren't these flowers beautiful?" she chirped as they walked in. Jarred stopped in the doorway, astonished. This room, which was easily a thousand square feet, had always been way too dark for Jarred's taste: black leather couches, dark rugs, huge, heavy-looking paintings. Now the couches were modern and beige, and the rugs were gone, allowing the wood floors to shine. The old oil paintings had been replaced with friendly landscape photography, and the fireplace mantle was now lined with family photos. He was tempted to check them out, but he forced himself to stay by the door, waiting to see what his father's first move would be.

"How kind of you to honor us with your presence. Care for a drink?" His dad was already en route to the bar to pour Jarred an aperitif. Jarred declined the offer, a response that was met with general astonishment.

"Dinner will be ready in ten minutes, Arthur." Marlene slid the flowers into a vase atop a glass-top coffee table, neither of which Jarred recognized. The table probably wasn't child-friendly, but it fit the new modern décor well. He liked it. Cozy, in a way. Had Marlene done the redecorating herself?

"Can we help?" his father asked, a warm smile playing on his lips. Jarred's jaw nearly dropped. Was that his father? Offering to help in the kitchen? Wait a minute... was *Marlene* cooking dinner? They'd had a chef for so many years—where was she?

"No, no, I've got it. You guys stay here and catch up. You don't get to see each other much." Marlene stretched up on tiptoe and gave his father a quick kiss on the lips. He watched her practically skip out of the room.

Jarred, meanwhile, was still in the door frame, doing a very bad job of looking relaxed.

"How's work?" his father asked.

"I only started back yesterday." Dad knew that; why was he even asking? Jarred took a seat on the couch and waited. His father nodded and sipped his drink. Something clear. Jarred was trying not to resort to alcohol tonight. He could always get drunk later, at his place. Right now, he needed to play the perfect son. Polysyllabic answers might help with that, but it had been so damn long since he'd sat down and talked to his dad that he didn't know where to start.

"How's it feel to be back?" his father asked out of nowhere.

Dad? Wants to talk about feelings?

"Unusual." He nearly phrased it as a question. "But good," he hastened to add.

"That's good."

He wondered if this was where his dad launched into a big explanation of how he had only the best intentions. Jarred would be twenty-nine this year, which was practically thirty, which was an age when a person was old enough to decide what was best for them. Theoretically.

"I felt guilty about your mother for a while, too. But guilt doesn't help anyone. It certainly won't bring your mother back. At some point, you've just got to let go and move on. Work obviously isn't a cure-all, but having a routine helps keep you from sinking into a deep, dark hole. And you always did like your job. If it's too much for you right now… you can always talk to me or your siblings. We're family."

"We were never a normal family, Dad. It's fine, I can take care of myself." So suddenly his father wanted to act like everything was peachy? How did he even know that Jarred had felt guilty? Had Alice blabbed to him? No, she'd never do that. Jarred discarded the absurd thought immediately.

"If you say so. Let's eat—Marlene's probably waiting." His father drained his glass, set it on the bar counter, and left the room.

Jarred followed him reluctantly. His heart was thumping in his chest. Dad was acting so… caring. It confused him.

The dining table was set for three; apparently

Sean had better things to do tonight than enjoy Jarred's company. Which suited Jarred just fine—they'd only end up going after each other again.

The dining room had been redecorated as well. It was all pastels now, bright and cheerful, and it still had personality even though all the useless little knick-knacks had been cleared out. The room opened out onto the yard, which was where Jarred had spent all his time as a kid. Nearby Holland Park had been a perfect place to let loose, he recalled. Playing ball in the house had been strictly forbidden, of course. For fear of breaking those ugly decorations.

It turned out that Marlene really had cooked the whole meal, and Jarred had to admit that the chicken with roasted vegetables was delicious. He appreciated the simplicity of the food as well—no quail eggs, no squab, no caviar, no foie gras.

Marlene and his dad chatted all through dinner; Jarred listened with half an ear, but his mind kept wandering. The two of them seemed to enjoy each other's company a lot. To love each other, even. It was an odd experience for Jarred, who almost felt like a third wheel, even though they both kept trying to draw him into their lively conversation—Marlene especially.

Jarred reached for his water glass and suddenly felt their eyes on him. Crap. Had he missed a question? "What was that?"

"I asked if you knew anyone who was selling a central, high-end condo."

"What makes you ask? There are real estate agents for that..." What was Marlene getting at?

"The people I know who are in the market have had some absolutely terrible experiences with agents. They're looking for something modern. Everything they've toured so far left a lot to be desired, quality-wise. I guess it's harder to find a good condo than I realized. Even the new buildings aren't worth the high prices."

"What's with our buildings?"

"They were very disappointed."

What? Disappointed by Campbell Investments? No way. The construction industry was corrupt, of course, and everyone cut corners wherever possible, but how could a brand-new luxury residential building right in the middle of London be in any way inferior?! Crap. He needed to look into that before word got around that their company was selling crappy, overpriced real estate.

"*I'm* looking for a buyer. How big of a place do they want?"

"You want to move out?" His father didn't look pleased.

"What am I even doing in a skyscraper? I don't like it there anymore."

"Where do you want to live instead?"

"Depends whether you want me to pay you back." Jarred wasn't even sure how much of his father's money he'd spent in the past several years, but repaying him for Atlantic City was probably the least he could do.

"Don't be ridiculous. It was never about the money."

"Do you have some concrete idea what you're looking for?" Marlene asked, patting his father's hand —she was obviously trying to keep the two of them from arguing. "I can ask around. Jill and Joe live in Hampstead, in the north, if you're interested in seeing their house. They're trying to move somewhere central. They work and travel quite a lot, so their priorities are being close to the financial district and London City airport."

Hampstead might be nice, though it was at least an hour away from Greenwich... wait, why was he even thinking about how far away from Rose he'd be living? "I'd be glad to check it out. Shall I call them myself, or do you want to set something up?"

Well, this was a nice turn of events. At least his financial problems might be solved soon.

CHAPTER 13

ROSE

Friday evening was a welcome relief: now she had not only a fun night out with Mandy to look forward to, but a visit to her parents in Watford as well. Jarred had been friendly all day; he'd valiantly fought his way through the mountain of information on their ongoing projects, but whenever she'd given him a task, he'd completed it without the slightest complaint. Now her progress report was ready for her meeting with Sean, and she'd finished her trend analysis for next quarter as well. If this kept up, she'd finally have time to tackle those luxury condos. She wondered whether she ought to voice her concerns to Jarred and get him involved.

Aaron hadn't been in touch again, thank God. She'd blocked him months ago, so he'd have to write her company email address or come to the office.

Hopefully neither. The worst option would be if he showed up at her door. Just thinking about that turned her stomach.

"Should I loan you Rob for a while?"

Mandy and Rose were at their favorite club in Soho; both were on their second or third cocktail.

"Wait, no, that would mean he was actually at home, so I'd want to enjoy him myself." Mandy made a swooning motion.

"You guys planned your weekend away yet?"

"Oh, yeah! We spent a long time talking about it today on the phone. Hopefully Ella won't get sick."

"If you tell her I'm taking her to the aquarium, I'm sure she'll be extra-careful about wearing her gloves and boots so she can stay healthy." Rose grinned. Now this was what life was all about: hanging out with your best friend, yummy drink in hand, great music in the background. Just like old times.

"Hey, maybe you should ask Jarred to play your boyfriend."

"You did not just seriously suggest I fake a relationship with Jarred. Right? I think you're throwing those cocktails back too fast."

"Yeah, probably not a good idea." Mandy sighed theatrically. "But you guys would be so great together!"

"Whatever. C'mon, let's dance." Rose dragged Mandy to the dance floor before she had a chance to protest. It was her only hope of escaping any more questions—which would eventually mean confessing that her heart raced whenever she was around Jarred. Probably good they wouldn't see each other until Monday. A whole weekend to get her head on straight again. He was completely wrong for her, and her heart was bound to understand that eventually.

They had old-school dance music on tonight, and the beat flowed straight into her blood. Euphoria flooded through her as soon as she started dancing. It was incredibly freeing—just bobbing around to the music, seemingly weightless, letting loose within the safety of the anonymous masses, until her heart was threatening to leap out of her chest...

The hairs suddenly stood up on her sweaty skin. She felt eyes on her.

She spotted him. Now her heart was racing for two reasons. His eyes were fixed on Rose; he seemed completely indifferent to the mass of dancing, writhing bodies all around him. Rose met his gaze, held it. What now? The noise around them seemed to fade; they were the only two people in the room... until some huge guy shoved his way into Rose's line of sight.

When the man finally moved aside, Jarred was gone. Maybe she'd been imagining him or something. Then Mandy danced in a circle around her, drawing her attention back to the music.

JARRED

Out of all the venues in London, he just *had* to pick the one Rose was at. He'd decided not to risk the members-only clubs in South Kensington—the drugs would be too tempting, and people would probably notice he wasn't buying everyone round after round like usual.

Now Jarred was sitting at the bar, not sure whether to trust his capacity for self-control now that Rose was here. Watching her body moving to the music had done something to him that he hadn't felt in a long, long time. He'd liked what he'd seen way too much. He wanted to touch her, to press himself against her, to run his hands over her curves, to feel her lips on his, to give himself over to this maelstrom of desire an—*okay, Jarred, shut that shit down already*. He was not having a workplace affair. The. End.

He used the last of the crumpled cash he'd found stashed in a drawer at home to buy a beer. Maybe this was a sign that it was time for a change. Time to make sure he was never dependent on anyone else again, instead of sitting around waiting for Daddy Dearest to unfreeze his credit card. Time to accept personal responsibility. Alice did it, so could he.

He'd start by selling his condo. If he negotiated well, he could get a decent price for it, even in this market. Then he'd find himself something cheaper. Maybe a bit further from central London, and not necessarily a whole hour away from Rose…

Jarred finished his beer and returned to the dance floor. Even if he couldn't have Rose, he wanted one last look at her before he went home. She was still in about the same spot. A few strands of hair had come loose from her messy up-do, and were clinging to her face. He felt like tucking them behind her ears. Her T-shirt was tight against her chest; her slim legs were encased in opaque tights beneath her short shorts. Judging by her height, her heels were maybe half as high as the ones she normally wore at work.

God, the way she moved was so hot. Just watching her dance was weirdly satisfying in itself. Her eyes were closed—but then snapped open abruptly, as though he'd touched her. There was something in the air, and he knew she felt it too. She gazed at him expectantly.

Afterward, he wasn't entirely sure whether he'd approached her or vice versa. All he knew was that suddenly they were standing so close, he'd barely had to move his hand to touch her face. Every alarm bell in his head was sounding; his mind was practically tripping over itself. He wanted to kiss her, but he couldn't. Her dark eyes reflected the desire he felt.

All at once, she stretched up on tiptoe and kissed him. The touch of her lips was like an arrow straight to his heart. She cupped his face gently with both hands. The kiss was tender, almost chaste, and yet there was something incredibly intimate about feeling her soft lips on his. When she released him, he pulled her in again and started dancing with her. It was too loud for them to say anything, but there was no need. Everything was perfect the way it was.

ROSE

She had no idea what was happening here. All she knew was that she'd *had* to kiss him. She'd had no choice. The connection she felt with him was like nothing she'd ever experienced. Nestling against him was the most natural thing in the world, as though things had never been any other way. Except, of course, that Jarred would mean her professional undoing, because if she got involved with him, everyone at the company would assume she'd slept her way to the top. This little crush she had on him could never be more than that.

Automatically, Rose pulled away from Jarred. Kissing him had been a mistake—what the hell had gotten into her? She'd come here tonight to get away from all her obsessive brooding; now everything was a hundred times more complicated. If she went home with him tonight, would that be enough to help her get over the crush, or would it only make things worse? No, no, when she saw him in the office on Monday, she'd just chalk the kiss up to all the cocktails, and then they'd go right on working like always.

Rose signaled to Mandy that she was ready to leave. But before she had a chance to decide how to leave things with Jarred, he drew her into his arms and gave her a goodbye kiss that went on and on, until Rose's cheeks were flushed, until her knees were jelly, until she was sure he'd devour her if she didn't stop him... but he tasted so good. His tongue sent little flashes of lightning through her body as it danced against hers; every teasing touch made her moan and press herself into him even more.

When Jarred finally released her, she felt empty. His passionate gaze rested on her face; his ribcage rose and fell heavily. Was he as light-headed as she was?

She had to put a lid on this, stat. She stumbled over to Mandy, who'd been waiting patiently on her. Jarred disappeared into the cloud.

If she didn't still feel his lips on hers, she'd be tempted to tell herself that she'd imagined the whole thing. She ordered an Uber with trembling hands while Mandy retrieved their coats.

Mandy held off on her Spanish Inquisition until they were in the car. "Unless my eyes were deceiving me in the diffuse light, that was... Jarred. Right?"

"Oh, my God, I kissed him. And I danced with him... like, *right* up against him. I'm so dumb, I'm so dumb." Rose buried her face in her hands with a groan.

"We've been over this. Rob and me, remember? Anyway, it was just a kiss, you weren't selling company secrets to the competition or anything."

"What? What are you talking about?"

"Chill out. I'm just saying, listen to your heart. From where I was standing, it didn't look like you took *all* the initiative there."

"He's always got women around him, though. Look at him, what woman could possibly resist him?"

"Well, me, for one. Husband, remember? Anyway, I'm not telling you to go jump in bed with Jarred tonight or anything, but you've been talking about him for literal *years*. I mean, how many sketches have you done of him?"

"I hardly talked about him at all in the past two years."

"Only because you had that dead weight who must not be named hung around your neck."

"So what do I do now?"

"Talk to him about it on Monday so that things don't get weird. Or call him tomorrow—he did give you his number."

"We'll be in Watford tomorrow," Rose reminded her.

"So? Phones work there, too, honey."

Okay, Mandy was right—it was probably best if she got this unpleasantness behind her quickly. Except why was she already looking forward to hearing his voice?

CHAPTER 14

JARRED

Despite getting little sleep, he still woke up full of energy, with a sense of big things on the horizon—something he hadn't felt in a very, very long time. His condo was so clean it practically glowed; his housekeeper had outdone herself this week. Which was good, because Marlene had called him the day after dinner to tell him that her friends wanted to see Jarred's place as soon as possible. They were coming over today at noon.

He couldn't have known he'd run into Rose at the club. She'd been all he could think about ever since: how soft her lips were, how good she'd felt in his arms. For the first time in months, he'd fallen into a completely dreamless sleep. He decided to call her as soon as he'd finished showing the condo.

And pointedly ignored the nagging worry that

this was the very definition of mixing business and pleasure.

Jarred's door buzzer sounded at noon on the dot. He'd donned a suit for the occasion, but with no tie and a dark-green shirt that he probably wouldn't wear to the office. He was going for an elegant, professional look, one he hoped would underscore how serious he was about the opportunity. Patek Philippe watch, check; Oxford signet ring, check. He planned on asking at least two million pounds for the place, and he wasn't about to do that in jeans and a tank top.

Marlene had offered to accompany Jill and Joe so that she could introduce them all, and Jarred couldn't think of any plausible reason to turn her down. She'd sounded every bit as enthusiastic over the phone as she had at dinner; maybe her energy would be the extra push needed to close the sale.

"Jarred, hi! I'm so glad you were able to see us on such short notice." Marlene greeted him with a cheek-kiss and a wink before introducing the couple behind her, who stepped into the apartment and glanced around, looking cautiously intrigued. They looked to be in their early thirties. Both were dressed in dark suits—white shirt for him, white blouse for her; Marlene's yellow Burberry dress was the only splash of color. Jarred recalled that the couple were stressed with work and business travel. As it turned out, Joe was leaving for the US in a matter of hours, which was why it had been so important for them to see the place today.

"I've got copies of all the information about the condominium for you. Have a look around for yourselves if you like. There are two parking spots included with the lease, and the building has a private movie theater, a lounge bar, and a twenty-four-hour reception desk." The reception desk, at least, was standard in luxury buildings, but Jarred felt like he ought to mention it anyway.

From what he knew about Jill and Joe, Jarred thought his apartment would be perfect for them. Modern, stylish, plenty of natural light. The dark wood of the open kitchen contrasted nicely with the white living room. His furniture was white as well, but not the harsh kind—more of a pale ivory that created a soft ambiance. The whole apartment was about thirteen hundred square feet; though not all that large for a three-bedroom, it was bound to be the biggest option available in this price range, and certainly the biggest in this central location. The two bathrooms had a mix of dark and light tile; each had a rain shower and a separate bathtub, with dark hardwood cabinetry.

Jarred hung back as Marlene strolled from room to room with Jill. Joe finished looking at everything in five minutes flat, and then promptly turned his attention to his phone. Apparently, Jill was the one who decided whether they were interested in a place.

"I'll just give you a moment alone, Jill. Take all the time you need; I'm going to talk to my stepson for a moment." The fact that Marlene had no problem calling him her stepson bewildered Jarred. She emerged from the second guest room, beaming. "I'm giving her a minute to think, but I've got her hooked," she whispered conspiratorially.

"Is she the one who gets final say?"

"Oh, they'll decide together, but they have different criteria. Joe flies to America a lot, so the location is way more important to him than the décor, although of course he does expect a certain standard. Jill mostly wants the place to be impressive-looking."

Joe finished his phone call and gazed thoughtfully out the window. Jarred excused himself from Marlene and strolled over. "Marlene mentioned that you travel a lot for work."

"Yeah, mostly to New York. Finding decent hotels is a nightmare," he grumbled.

"I know my way around New York a little. What area would you prefer?"

"Lower Manhattan."

"How about Chinatown? There's this boutique hotel I like, maybe you've heard of it." Jarred looked the place up and then handed his phone to Joe. Not knowing much about Joe or his company's price range, he resisted the urge to sell him on the place, but the photos on the hotel's home page spoke for themselves. The view from the upper floors was phenomenal, and the suites all had their own balconies. Not really compatible with Jarred's fear of heights, but Joe's expression brightened a shade.

"Would you mind sending me this link? And if you have a second alternative, please send me that as well."

"Of course, I'd be glad to."

"Joe, I've looked at everything. What do you think?" Jill returned to the living room. At first glance, it wasn't obvious what she thought of the place, but Jarred had been playing poker for so long that he was an expert at spotting tells. She was breathing a little faster, and there was a sparkle in her eyes that hadn't been there before. She was also rubbing her palms as though they were tingling in excitement. She was guaranteed to make an offer, though they weren't likely to admit that now—it would weaken their negotiating position.

"I think we're done here. Thanks very much for your time, Mr. Campbell. You'll hear from us on Monday." Joe's handshake was firm and decisive. This deal was totally in the bag.

"No, no, thank you for coming. Have a great trip, Mr. Rutherford. Nice meeting you, Mrs. Rutherford." Joe walked the couple to the door.

Marlene gave him another cheek-kiss goodbye. "Congrats." She was still smiling from ear to ear as he closed the door behind her.

So she'd noticed, too. Maybe he'd been completely misjudging her this whole time. Maybe he should have just given Marlene a chance, instead of automatically writing her off as another gold-digger.

ROSE

"Mum, Paps, we're here!" Rose called as she unlocked the door to her parents' house. Ella came running in from the living room a moment later. Rose stepped aside to let Mandy hug her first, but Ella promptly grabbed one of Mandy's legs and one of Rose's at the same time, nearly knocking all three of them over in the process.

"I'm playing chess with Grampa-Rose, and I beat him twice already!"

Just then, Rose's father appeared in the entryway with a good-natured smile on his face. "The kid's talented, what can I say?" he winked before taking Rose and Mandy's coats and drawing them both into a bear hug.

Next to her dad, Rose still felt like a little kid. He was about Jarred's height, around six-two, but Dad had at least sixty pounds on Jarred. He'd been writing short stories in his free time for years; once Rose and her brothers had flown the nest, he'd finally tried his hand at a full-length crime thriller, to great success.

Not quite enough to live on, but since he'd retired from his teaching job the year before, he had both the time and the money to enjoy his favorite hobby whenever he liked. Rose's mother was just happy to know that he was keeping busy. She worked part-time in a flower shop, and her garden was her true passion.

"Rose, Mandy, there you are!" Their mothers came into the entryway. The two of them were best friends as well. Rose would have liked to continue the tradition over a third generation, but she was already more than four years too late—she wouldn't be able to give Ella a little best friend of her own.

"Come in, come in. Rose, did you hear anything else from Aaron?" *Way to dive right in, Mom*. Rose had mentioned Aaron's return the week before; in hindsight, that was probably a bad move, because Mom actually sounded hopeful now. Like Rose, Mom had been waiting anxiously for Aaron to propose, and when they'd broken up, Mom had been more disappointed than anyone. Her dad had liked Aaron as well.

Rose hadn't said a word about Jarred being back.

"No." She had exactly zero desire to discuss Aaron, especially because that would make her memories of Jarred fade even faster, which was the opposite of what she wanted. Hm. Maybe she ought to call him today after all.

"Well, I think I'd have given him a piece of my mind," Mandy's mom exclaimed.

"Oh, no, she was at work, that would have cast her in a bad light," Rose's mom pointed out.

"True. But still. And just acting like everything was fine? I'd never have managed," Mandy's mom sniffed. She had a searing hatred of anything that smacked of opportunism or injustice.

"Sure, but Baccara roses! Thirty of them, on Rose's thirtieth birthday." Rose's mom was hell-bent on seeing the good in everyone.

"Bah! I don't care if they're a hundred roses on your hundredth birthday. If they're from the wrong man, they're worthless."

"Oh, I suppose you're right. But isn't there anyone else at your office you like, Rose? They always say you'll meet your spouse at school or at work."

"Or at classes! Why don't you sign up for a dance class? Or better, start rowing again," Mandy's mom suggested. "Plenty of men in rowing."

"I haven't rowed since university."

"What does that matter? It's probably just like riding a bike."

Both mothers nodded firmly and then left the living room to check on dinner. Rose took the opportunity to bring her bag to her old bedroom. The house wasn't particularly luxurious, but it had plenty of space: four bedrooms, all upstairs, with a master bath connected to their parents room and a second one in the hall for the three kids. Sharing a bathroom with her two brothers hadn't always been easy... especially once her brothers were older and started getting interested in girls, and often stayed in the bathroom longer than she did.

Rose's mom had converted the children's rooms into guest rooms, which meant there was plenty of space for her brothers and their wives to visit. Rose's Scorpions poster was gone from the wall… her brothers had grown up on German and Swiss rock, and Rose had developed a taste for it as well. Guano Apes, Unheilig, Krokus… but Scorpions most of all, though she doubted she was their target audience. She'd probably listened to "Wind of Change" a thousand times, and she still liked the song.

Hardly any of the old décor remained. Rose's flowered wallpaper had been replaced with white ingrain; the new lilac bedspread matched the curtains. Only Rose's old pine desk and wardrobe remained, and now they were empty.

What Rose had always loved most about her room was the view of her mother's garden and the adjoining meadow. Mom had trimmed the bushes back for the winter; their bare branches stretched toward the sky, spindly monuments to the lush spring foliage to come. There were plenty of evergreens as well, especially several varieties of heather, which her mother couldn't get enough of—even in the dead of winter, it shone in brilliant color. Mostly red, at the moment.

"Dinner's in twenty minutes, Rose," her mother called from downstairs.

"I'll be down in a bit!" Rose decided that this was

as good a time as any to call. She sat by the window and held her breath as she tapped Jarred's name on her phone. Which she'd saved, because of course she had.

He answered unexpectedly quickly. "Hey."

Hm. "Hey" gave her no information either way as to how he felt about them kissing. "Hey yourself."

He laughed softly. "How are you?"

"Fine. Just visiting my parents for the weekend... so if I hang up with no warning, don't take it personally."

"Good to know," Jarred said, sounding amused. There was a brief pause. She heard him clear his throat. "So are you calling because you regret it?"

"No, just because I wanted to hear your voice and... well, basically, now what? Do you regret it?" Rose gazed out the window as she asked. The garden calmed her down, which she very much needed, because everything about this situation was a maze of questions and potential problems. Obviously, she didn't want to stop kissing him quite yet, but that didn't change the fact that they worked together. Plus, Jarred wasn't exactly known for being the relationship type. More like the polar opposite of the relationship type. So wasn't this an automatic recipe for heartbreak? Too bad she'd felt way too good in his arms. She definitely liked him. A lot.

Business as usual, really.

"No, not at all," he replied emphatically. "When will you be back from Watford?"

"You remember where my parents lived?"

"You did just mention it a couple of days ago. I'm not quite that old, I still have some short-term memory left."

"How old are you, anyway?"

"Almost twenty-nine. You?"

"Thirty. So you kissed an older woman." Rose was expecting him to retort that it wasn't the first time, but he didn't. To her relief.

"Well... I really liked it. So when are you coming back to London?"

"Tomorrow evening. Do you want to... um, should we meet up?" Was it completely stupid and naïve of her to hope that this could turn into more than a one-night stand? She'd had a few of those, but she wasn't really a fan—they hardly ever worked out as advertised, usually because guys overpromised and underdelivered. Or were too drunk to do anything for her in bed at all. At least nobody had ever fallen asleep *on* her during sex... that had happened to Mandy once. When she'd heard that one, Rose had laughed so hard she nearly fainted.

"I think that would be advisable."

What was the question again? Oh, right, about getting together tomorrow. *Advisable*? What was that supposed to mean? "Okay, then. Meet at Bank station in London City?" she asked, trying to sound as matter-of-fact as possible.

"Sure. When you know what train you're going to take, let me know and I'll come meet you."

"Okay. Hope I manage to find you!"

"I'm sure you will. You're not getting rid of me that easily."

Wait, did that mean what she hoped it meant? *God, Rose, don't grasp at straws here.* "You mean because I'm your boss?" she quipped.

"That's definitely not why."

"Rose? You coming?" her mother called.

"I've gotta go. You have plans today?" Of course he did. He probably had ten thousand friends; why would he be sitting around at home on a Saturday night?

"I'm looking for a new apartment. I may have sold mine today, which means I'll be homeless soon, since I haven't gotten to the part where I find a new place to live."

"So you're more the spontaneous type. Respect."

"Or the idiot type. But you've got to go, so see you tomorrow."

"See you."

"I'm looking forward to it."

"Me too."

CHAPTER 15

JARRED

So he was officially breaking his own rules, and his family's. Sean and his dad would lose their minds if they knew. It was almost ironic, because he'd genuinely come here thinking he was just going to keep his head down and do his job.

Well, if and when the Rutherfords bought his apartment, he'd have some financial flexibility again, so at least that was one problem solved. Provided he got his ass in gear and found a new place, anyway. He'd browsed a few real estate sites, but hadn't seen anything that caught his eye. He wasn't especially keen to move to Hampstead, especially since he doubted there was anything nice in that area within his budget.

Maybe Greenwich? Around where Rose lived? Eesh, probably playing with fire.

On a whim, he dialed Henry's number.

"What's up? You need money?"

"Thanks, I'm well. You, too, I hope."

Henry merely grunted in reply.

"No, I think I'll be okay financially, because it appears that I may have just sold my condo. If so, I have a new problem."

"Let me guess, genius. You don't have anywhere else to go."

"Ding-ding-ding! We have a winner."

"Well, what are you calling me for? I'm not a real estate agent. You're the one who knows a million people all over town. Where do you want to move, anyway?"

"Dunno," Jarred admitted. "London?"

"Dumbass. Start with that."

"Brilliant advice."

"Anything else?"

"No." He'd been planning to tell Henry that he suspected he'd been wrong about Marlene. Stupid of him to think for a second that Henry would be interested. He missed Alice, who was still in California. As soon as she returned from vacation, he'd ask her for advice. "Sorry to bother you."

"Wait." Henry sighed. "I have to go to Texas next week. If you really need to move out that fast, you can just stay at mine. Put your furniture in storage or whatever."

"Texas? On business?"

"Of course, why else would I go to Texas? I'm not

sure when I'll be back, but it doesn't matter, my place is big enough for two."

That, it was—a palatial building in Chelsea. Work-wise, things were going great for Henry; financing start-ups apparently paid off, at least when you were blessed with Henry's natural business talent.

"Thanks."

"Anything to keep your sorry ass off the streets... oh, and I won't charge you rent, don't worry."

"How kind!"

"Somebody's got to help the runt of the litter. Try not to demolish any of my furniture if you can help it."

"Jackass."

"I love you too." Henry cackled before hanging up.

ROSE

Apparently she'd had no reason to worry about finding him at the station. He was standing just across the road from the west entrance, but as soon as he spotted her, he started waving wildly and screaming her name over and over like a lunatic. Rose laughed, blushed, and got butterflies all at the same time.

Working out which of them would go to whom turned out to be a challenge in itself; in the end, Rose practically flew down the steps to the underpass and found Jarred in the middle of the tunnel, waiting for her with a huge smile. She stopped right in front of him, anxious to find out what kind of hello this was going to be.

"Hey," he said, breaking the silence.

"Hey yourself." She felt like a teenager. Her hormones were running wild, and something forbidden hung in the air, as though her parents had just caught her kissing the coolest guy at school. And yes, she definitely wanted to kiss him. Try as she might, she couldn't get her feelings for him under control. The look in his light brown eyes held her captive. He bent to her and brushed her lips with hers, a brief touch that felt like an electric shock. God, how did it get this bad? They'd barely known each other before a week ago... what people said about sparks flying, was that actually a thing? Had Jarred felt them, too? Her lips tingled long after he broke the kiss; his warm breath on her face gave her goosebumps.

"Are you cold?"

"No, breath on my neck just tickles, that's all." That was one way of putting it. Her neck was one of her biggest erogenous zones. She cleared her throat a little, trying not to blush.

"Noted," Jarred replied with a mischievous smile. "Let's get something to eat, yeah?" After shouldering Rose's bag and pointing her to the correct exit, he led the way to the old Midlands Bank building, which now housed a five-star hotel with no fewer than eight restaurants. Jarred took her to one that served traditional English food. Rose had never even been in the building, and struggled to hide her amazement. Massive green columns lined the giant room, supporting a ceiling that was well over twelve feet high. Private dining experiences were clearly not the goal here: the whole room was packed with old, uncomfortable-looking upholstered chairs, tables, and couches. This place probably reached jet-engine decibel levels over the lunch hour, but Sunday evening didn't seem to be one of their busy times.

"If I'm being honest, I was expecting we'd meet somewhere less public."

Jarred stiffened noticeably. "We can talk about that over dinner."

They walked past the bar, and Jarred spoke briefly to a man in a black suit. Why couldn't they have just waited at the entrance until somebody came over and seated them, like normal people? Jarred was obviously incapable of following even the simplest rules. She vaguely remembered the unconventional approach he'd taken as the department head—meddling with projects he'd previously delegated to teams, for example. Sometimes he'd even obtain important information on his own and then forget to mention it to anyone else… so Rose would call the person for that same information and *then* find out that they'd already clarified everything with Jarred, which meant *she* had to field all the questions about why they were so disorganized. It had always left her feeling like a total idiot. So yes, in short, Jarred had been a total control freak. What other negative qualities of his had she forgotten over time?

They were given a table near the edge of the room, one with a tiny bit more privacy than the others. Seeming pleased, Jarred gave the host a friendly smile before helping Rose out of her coat and into her chair. Ever the gentleman.

"What would you like to drink?"

"A beer, please."

"Two, then." He nodded impatiently to the waiter, as though eager to shoo him away. The free-and-easy Jarred that had picked her up from the train station had already vanished; now he was more like Unapproachable Boss Jarred. In his white shirt and dark suit trousers, he really did look like he was at a business dinner. Was that intentional?

"Jarred, this is a really nice place, and I love British food, including pub food, but… is this a business dinner or a private one?" She could hardly believe that she had to ask the question, but his behavior was making her uneasy. *Well, it's Sunday evening, Rose, which do you think it is?*

"Private. Why do you ask?" He never even looked away from the menu.

"Can I treat you, then?"

"Certainly not," he replied, finally meeting her gaze. There was a hard look in his eyes; the small smile he put on a moment later seemed intended as a distraction from it.

"So you are a total macho-man, hm?" she retorted teasingly.

"I never claimed otherwise."

No, of course not. Had she completely misinterpreted everything?

The waiter glided silently across the patterned carpet and placed two beer glasses in front of them. Rose was suddenly in the mood for a Guinness—nice and bitter, just like her. "Have you decided?" The waiter stood there waiting, but Rose gave no response.

Jarred raised a questioning eyebrow that made her want to call him several names. "I'll have the perch on the bed of vegetables, please."

"Sir?"

"The lamb, please."

The waiter disappeared as quickly as he'd come.

The Welsh lamb had caught Rose's eye as well, but after the huge lunch at her parents' place, she was in the mood for something light. Hopefully the perch wasn't fried... but it probably would have said so in the menu. Anyway, too late to change her mind now.

Just as he and Rose crossed the room, he spotted his old friend Benjamin. Oof. Taking her here for dinner had been risky. The place was exactly halfway between his condo and his office, so he'd eaten here a lot once upon a time.

He should have explained himself to Rose rather than treating her like some kind of minion, because he knew she was right: they did need to talk about where they were going with this, and how they would act around each other in public. He'd have to urge her not to tell anyone about what was happening between them—for her own sake. When it came to his personal life, he hadn't exactly developed a sparkling reputation over the past two years.

Once he did manage to look Rose in the eye, he saw that she was scowling at him in absolute rage. Like, the ready-to-claw-Jarred's-eyes-out type of rage. "Listen—"

That was as far as he got in his efforts to address the situation with Rose.

"Jarred? Jarred Campbell? I knew it! What are you doing here? When did you get back?"

"Benjamin, what a surprise." Jarred removed the napkin from his lap and rose to shake his old friend's hand.

"Last I heard, you were living it up in the States." A look of admiration came over Benjamin's face. Now *that* was a guy who knew how to party. Then his gaze shifted to Rose, and he made no secret of appreciating what he saw.

Jarred, on the other hand, did not like Benjamin ogling her one bit. "Rose Murphy, Benjamin White."

Benjamin greeted her with an air hand-kiss,

which made Rose's cheeks flush. That was Ben's trademark move, as Jarred had seen time and time again back when he was a regular at the private clubs.

"You staying a while?" Ben asked.

"That's the plan. Provided I find a new apartment." Goddammit, why had that slipped out?

"Looking for more space?" Ben's querulous gaze shifted back and forth between Rose and Jarred.

"No, less," he admitted, though he certainly didn't want people speculating that he was having financial problems. That wasn't why he wanted a smaller place. Well, not only that.

"Got it."

Jarred very much doubted that Ben got it.

"Anyway, I just wanted to come say hi real quick. Give me a call."

"I will." Jarred most definitely would not. It would only lead to trouble. He sat down again.

Ben walked a few feet away, but then stopped and turned around. "Oh, I almost forgot. Marie and Finn are getting married. They're looking for new digs, if you hear of anything. At least three bedrooms, modern, park nearby, the usual. Get in touch with him—I'm sure he'll be really happy to hear from you."

Hm, that wasn't a bad idea. If Finn was looking for a condo, that meant his would probably be on the market soon. And Jarred couldn't be sure that Jill and Joe would end up buying, so it couldn't hurt to have a backup in the pipeline.

Jarred sighed and ran his hands through his hair

before downing half his beer in one gulp. It was only a matter of time before everyone knew he was back.

"You saw Benjamin as soon as we walked in, didn't you."

"Yup."

"Which answers my question about how we ought to behave around each other in public." Rose took a large swallow of beer, as though for liquid courage. "And in private?"

"We could take it slow." His right hand reached for the fingers of her left, but when he realized what he was doing, he froze and then withdrew his hand. "Dammit. This is going to be harder than I realized." He shook his head, chuckling softly. Somehow he'd actually believed he could keep his hands off Rose in public. "Next time you could come to my place." His voice took on a husky note.

"I thought you were going to be homeless soon? Maybe you ought to come to mine instead."

"Sounds good."

Their food arrived. His lamb was so tender, it practically dissolved in his mouth like butter. Rose liked her fish as well.

"What's the plan tomorrow at the office?" Rose asked as she set her cutlery aside.

"I'd like to start Project Spike up again."

"You want your old project back? We're not responsible for that."

"I'll talk to Sean."

"A lot has changed since you left," Rose pointed

out. "You won't be able to take on those big projects by yourself as easily anymore. According to the new company guidelines, you'll need to bring a lot more partners on board than last time."

"What the hell? I had one partner, and that was plenty." Even working with one partner had felt like having a babysitter... so, what, now he needed several babysitters at once? Good thing he was already finished eating—the thought would have spoiled his appetite otherwise.

"Hey, don't shoot the messenger. I'm just saying that times have changed."

Yeah, clearly. He didn't like it one bit.

ROSE

Jarred didn't look particularly happy, but that wasn't her problem. He'd have to work that out with his family. Rose turned down the offer of coffee or dessert, but she wasn't particularly eager to go home quite yet. She wished she could draw Jarred. He was unbelievably attractive, just her type. His angular face had a faint five-o-clock shadow today; she liked how it made him look older and a little reckless. "Where'd you get that scar?"

"Swing set! I ran right in front of my sister when she was on it."

"No magic powers, then?"

"Not related to Harry Potter, unfortunately. I hope you're not too terribly disappointed."

She loved his smile.

"Let's go." Jarred signaled to the waiter, while Rose slipped away to use the ladies' room. She decided she'd draw him as soon as she got home. Not just any old pencil sketch, either—she felt like breaking out the oil pastels and doing a proper portrait, her first in a long time.

Jarred had already paid the bill by the time she returned to the table. He helped her into her coat and then led her out of the restaurant with a hand on the small of her back—the one intimate gesture he'd made in the past hour. She wondered whether he'd kiss her goodnight.

"I'd like to walk you home," he whispered in her ear once they were outside.

"Are you sure?" Rose blurted out. "I mean, that'd be great, but it's quite a ways."

"Doesn't matter, I don't have anything else planned for the day." The street lamps weren't providing much light, so there was a shadow on his face, but she could still make out his twinkling eyes. Her heart skipped a beat. So much for taking things slow.

"You could come up for some tea, if you like," she said and batted her eyes innocently.

"Sounds perfect."

They strolled to the subway station. Rose felt like taking his hand, but she knew better. If she did get involved with Jarred, it would have to be a complete secret. No hand-holding, no spontaneous kisses, no snuggling on the subway. And she couldn't blab to her parents, either. That would probably be the hardest part—her mom had a razor-sharp sixth sense when it came to Rose's emotional life.

CHAPTER 16

ROSE

On their trek from the tube station to Rose's apartment, Jarred took in the scenery, while Rose mostly stole glances at Jarred. Greenwich was a purely residential area; the only thing halfway interesting around here was the view of Canary Wharf, and even that was mostly blocked by other apartment buildings. Only when they reached the canal that fed into the Thames did they see the faint, twinkling lights of the tallest skyscrapers.

"The observatory in Greenwich Park has the best view of the city. Have you ever been?"

"Not in forever. But we could do that together." He drew her to him, so close that his breath caressed her face, and then he kissed her.

His soft lips turned Rose to wax, even more so

when his tongue brushed her lips, asking to be let in. She was breathing hard now—she couldn't get enough of him. His beard stubble tickled her as his lips wandered to her cheek, covering it with tiny kisses.

"Is it far?" he asked against her ear in a near-growl, sending a shiver down her back.

"No, we're practically there." She pointed to a door on the opposite side of the street.

"Well, then, let's go!" he exclaimed with a laugh before grabbing her hand and practically dragging her across the road.

"There's one other tenant, on the ground floor. Maybe you noticed that the others are all row houses? Mine is the only one that's divided up, but it looks like my neighbor isn't home."

"Even better," Jarred commented.

"Oh, yeah?"

"Yeah, then he can't complain about the noise we're about to make."

"What noise? Do you drink tea so loudly that the whole building shakes?" Grinning, Rose opened the front door, which Jarred instantly shut behind him. His lips were on hers a fraction of a second later. "Wait, wait, we're in the stairwell, let's go upstairs." She pushed him gently away. If she didn't put a little distance between them, they'd end up tearing off their clothes right here and now.

Even though her neighbor didn't seem to be home, she certainly didn't want to risk him walking in on anything. She barely knew him, and she didn't want to start their acquaintance off on the compromising-position foot. As she and Jarred hurried upstairs, Rose silently prayed that her apartment wasn't in the complete state of chaos she remembered. And of course she remembered that when they were right outside the door. How fitting.

JARRED

"Welcome to my humble abode."

Jarred stepped in and glanced around with curious interest. They were in the entrance hall to the open living room, which was separated from the kitchen by a bar counter. Another narrow hallway led to two more doors, probably the bedrooms, and then he could just make out a third door at the end. Rose pointed it out and explained that it was the bathroom.

He set Rose's bag on the floor and helped her out of her coat before hanging his own as well. They deposited their muddy shoes on a metal rack, and then Jarred began wandering idly through her apartment. He hadn't expected anything this colorful. The kitchen was white, but the fridge was covered with kids' drawings. A little girl smiled out at him from several photos. Others showed what he assumed was Rose's family: parents, grandparents, a couple of adult men... brothers, maybe? One wall in the living room was painted yellow; the large throw rug was a warm blue color. The coffee table was made of the same dark wood as the flooring. The sofa was beige, with yellow and blue decorative pillows. A rocking chair sat by the large living room window, with a small bookshelf and a DVD collection nearby.

An oversized folder with loose sheets of paper caught his interest. He approached the antique writing desk.

"Wait!" Rose called. Too late, though. He'd already opened the folder, and was staring at the first sketch in astonishment. "I like to draw in my free time," she explained, walking over. "That's my dream house."

It was a pencil sketch of a two-story single-family home on a hilltop; a child's swing dangled from the old chestnut tree beside it, and part of a slide was visible in the background. The distant London skyline peeked out from behind the treetops. A curtain billowed in the breeze, and a cat crept stealthily out the door.

"That's really nice. You've got talent. Does the house actually exist?"

"No, unfortunately."

"You mind if I look at the others?" Best ask permission this time. She hesitated. "If you'd prefer I didn't, I'll respect your wishes," he added, but couldn't help sounding disappointed.

"Um, no, it's fine, but... well... the thing is... I

drew you, too." She brushed a strand of hair out of her face, looking bashful.

"You drew *me*? When?"

She shrugged as though she couldn't remember.

Intrigued, he flipped through her sketches: snapshot images of people he didn't know, a view of Greenwich Park, a few drawings of the Cutty Sark—an old sailing ship that was now home to a museum—the Promenade in London, the Tower Bridge... and then he was suddenly looking in a mirror. Several times, actually. He looked so young. These were probably older works. She'd been drawing him even back then? He didn't look particularly friendly in any of the images. More like cold and distant. When had she seen him like this? "Wait, did you draw these during meetings?" he asked, surprised and a little put off.

"Only when they were really, really boring," Rose protested. "I didn't want to stop paying attention, but it honestly didn't matter how involved I was, because Tony always got all the credit either way. The rest of us just got to play his assistants."

"Tony?"

"Anthony Johnson. Just a little taller than me, blond hair, beer belly, loud laugh, indecipherable Cockney accent. He would have been about forty-five then, and he always used this really pungent aftershave..."

"Anthony... yeah, I remember him vaguely. The

aftershave really was obnoxious. He was always talking himself up. Hone, though, isn't he?"

"Yeah, he went to the competition—couldn't develop his career fast enough at Campbell Investments, or so he claimed when he left." She wasn't the only one who hadn't exactly wept when he'd left. Rose carefully returned the drawings to the folder.

"Hang on, that's the guy from T&H Invest... why'd you draw him?" It was a simple, direct question, but Rose just stood there, seemingly unsure how to answer. "Is he the one who sent you the roses?"

"Yeah, we used to be together. It was a long time ago, and it's a long story."

ROSE

She had no intention of going into detail. It felt wrong. Plus she and Aaron had broken up nearly a year ago, though it felt like yesterday. Rose noticed Jarred watching her as she walked to the kitchen, but luckily he didn't press the issue. He turned his attention to the family photos she'd put on display.

"Those are my brothers, Trevor and Justin. Trevor's in Manchester, Justin's in Liverpool... My mom is from Switzerland originally." As she rummaged around in the kitchen cupboard, she realized that all of her mugs had goofy jokes on them. Jarred was probably used to fine china or something. "Um, so… one says, 'I am not an early bird or a night owl; I am some form of permanently exhausted pigeon'… one that says, 'Of course I talk to myself – sometimes I need expert advice' and one that says, 'Drink coffee: do stupid things faster with more energy'. And then there's a princess cup, but one of the points on the crown broke off."

Jarred burst out laughing. "I'm torn between the one about coffee and the princess cup."

"You go for princesses, hm? I'm not sure I like having that kind of competition." She tried to keep a straight face, but she could feel the corners of her mouth twitching a little.

"No princess could hold a candle to you, Rose." Jarred blew her a kiss before turning back to the photos. "Do you ski?"

"It's been a long time, but I think I could probably get down a mountain in one piece. Why?"

The kettle whistled. She filled her metal tea ball with an herbal blend, hooked it inside her Chinese jug and poured the water in. She always kept a few lemons around, so she cut one into wedges and put two on a plate along with some rock sugar.

"My family has a vacation home in Verbier. We could fly out there."

"You want to take me to Verbier? To ski?" He made flying to Switzerland sound like taking the bus to the grocery store. And Verbier! The biggest ski area in Switzerland! "You meant the Verbier with a hundred miles of slopes, off-piste runs, and heli-skiing? *That* Verbier?"

"So you're saying you enjoy skiing?" Jarred looked every bit as happy as she felt.

"Love it!"

"Good enough! We could fly there next weekend." He knew he had enough miles for two tickets to Geneva and a rental car.

"Oh, can't, I promised I'd spend the weekend with Ella," Rose realized just in time. "My goddaughter. She's four."

"Then the weekend after." He replaced the photos. "You like the classics, I see," he remarked as he perused her small library. Rose wasn't sure if he was looking at her books or her DVDs, but either way, he was right.

"I really like Audrey Hepburn. Not just as an actress and a dancer, but as a UNICEF ambassador, too. Did you know she had to give up on becoming a professional dancer because she was so malnourished during World War II that her muscles didn't develop properly? But she certainly made the best of it, and her humanitarian work was so impressive."

"Wow, you really do admire her."

"Yeah. Sorry, I always get carried away." Rose's cheeks flushed hot, but what could she say? When it came to a strong woman like Audrey Hepburn, she just couldn't hold back.

"No need to apologize. Do you have a favorite movie of hers?"

"Breakfast at Tiffany's. Not because I'm looking for a rich husband—because nobody sings Moon River as beautifully as she does. I tear up every time I hear it," Rose admitted. "What's your favorite movie?"

"A few, but they're more action films... probably the same answer you'd get from most men." Jarred shrugged apologetically.

"No judgement here. I like Bond movies a lot, even though the women are mostly just decoration. And to come back to what you were saying about skiing, Willy Bogner's shots of the Swiss Alps in *On Her Majesty's Secret Service* are amazing, aren't they?" The fact that the movie had come out long before she was born did nothing to diminish Rose's appreciation for that incredible camera work.

"Yeah, for sure... does that mean I should arrange for a helicopter?"

"Yikes, I think I'd be terrified. Those slopes are probably more than I can handle anyway. Have you ever tried heli-skiing?"

"Nah, helicopters aren't really my thing," Jarred admitted, coming over to join Rose at the counter. "Hey, you didn't offer me the boss mug!" he exclaimed in feigned outrage.

"Gotta earn that one," Rose said teasingly as she finished pouring her tea. Before she knew it, he'd rounded the counter and started tickling her until tears were streaming down her face and she was begging for mercy.

"What do I get if I stop?"

"A kiss?" she wheezed. Her ribs hurt so much from laughing that she'd have promised him almost anything.

What started as a tender kiss soon turned stormy. Jarred's body felt so damn good under her hands... she was dying to feel his skin against hers. Jarred didn't seem to mind any of this one bit, either... Should she ask him if he wanted to stay over, or was that taking things too fast? Probably, but God, it felt good...

Instead of her bed, they landed on the couch, with Rose straddling Jarred's lap; soon her moans filled the room. She couldn't remember ever going into such ecstasy just by kissing someone. Only when she was so light-headed that she had to stop for air did she pull away. She felt Jarred's heart pounding, and his lips were as swollen as hers felt.

"We don't have to rush it," he said, though he sounded like he was struggling to hold back, too. No, of course they didn't have to rush anything, and it was probably better to stop here, because soon there'd be no turning back. Now she just had to convince herself that she wanted to turn back, that she didn't want to sleep with him right then and there.

CHAPTER 17

ROSE

Jarred had stayed until late Sunday evening. On her way to the office the next morning, Rose told herself over and over again that they'd done the sensible thing, that it was better not to rush it, that they ought to get to know each other first. The thought of seeing Jarred at the office and treating him like he was just another work acquaintance was making Rose uneasy already.

When she walked in just before eight, she discovered that she was the first one in the office—Jarred hadn't arrived at some ungodly hour, like he had every day last week. She took a desk by the aisle and began looking through her messages. One of them had come yesterday, Sunday, from T&H. Aaron. She flinched a little as she opened the email, crossing her fingers that it was just a simple thank-you for the meeting, garnished with a few standard pleasantries. No such luck. He'd written to ask if she'd received the flowers, and to ask if she had time for lunch. Rose formulated a polite, but firm response declining the offer.

Her phone rang not five minutes later.

JARRED

"Hey, little brother, how's London?"

He'd been planning on trying to reach Alice in the next hour, but she'd beaten him to the punch. "You still in L.A.?"

"Yeah, but I'm leaving early tomorrow morning. Well, technically today—it's past midnight already. I'm meeting Henry in Texas."

"In Texas?" he echoed. "What's so urgent in Texas that you're all suddenly running out there?"

"I wouldn't say urgent. Henry invested in a ranch that specializes in rustic weddings."

"Henry. A wedding venue. You're fucking with me, right?"

"No! Do you remember Franco Fratelli? Anyway, his girlfriend works there, and he and Henry were always talking about going into business together somehow. Well, now they've got the perfect location."

Jarred vaguely remembered Franco, and how Henry had once wanted to open some kind of event agency. At some point, he'd assumed Henry had just filed the plan away and forgotten about it.

"Didn't Franco go back to Rome?"

"Long story. Ask Henry when he gets back."

"So why are you going to Texas now, then? Have you made your decision?"

"Yeah. My consulting days are coming to an end. I'm not totally sure where I'm going to open up the beauty salon."

"What's your target clientele? If you want to do something ritzy like Mom did, I'm sure you'd do well in Kensington or Chelsea."

"Maybe I'll do something a little hipper. Depends what I find that's affordable."

"Affordable? In London? Nowhere," Jarred laughed.

Alice laughed as well. "That's what I need Henry for!"

"I'm selling my condo," Jarred said after a moment.

"Seriously? If you're that hard up for money, I can loan you some. Plus, you're not working there for free or anything, and if you keep on being a good boy, Dad will unlock your card eventually."

"No, it's not that. I just don't feel comfortable in it, and Marlene knows a couple that want to buy it. I received their offer this morning."

"Marlene? Damn, you've been busy this week. Sold your place, made friends with Marlene... what next? You in love?"

Hm, good question. No matter what he said, Alice would jump to her own conclusions. Probably better to just keep his mouth shut.

"Jarred. That was a joke. Unless it... wasn't a joke?"

"Um, well, I may or may not have broken my own rules," he admitted, wincing.

"You slept with someone at Campbell Investments?" Alice exclaimed in horror.

"With my boss, but no, we only made out. I... it's hard to describe. I like her a lot, even though we've only known each other for a little while, and I'm perfectly aware of how stupid this is of me and how I should stay the hell away from her. I just don't know how I'm going to manage it." He knew Alice was going to tell him that he was being an ass. If worse came to worst, Rose would bear the brunt of the company's wrath, not Jarred.

"Don't toy with her emotions, Jarred. If you're not serious about her, tell her before it turns into some big drama... which it probably will anyway. Think about your darling half-brother Liam."

"Rose isn't like that! She'd never claim I got her pregnant just to weasel into my bank account."

"If you say so."

"What happened with the bartender?" he asked to change the subject. The last thing he needed right now were more reminders of Liam and his supposed true love.

"I'll tell you when I get back to London. Did you find a place to live yet?"

"No, but my old buddy Finn is looking to move as well. Maybe I can help him and then buy his current place. In the meantime, Henry said I can stay at his."

"I'm shocked that you would choose his palace over my tiny two-bedroom."

"If your tiny two-bedroom weren't on the twentieth floor, you'd have been my first choice."

"Yeah, yeah. I gotta go. Say hi to Marlene for me."

Alice was the only one who had never had anything bad to say about Marlene. Not that she and Alice knew each other all that well, but Alice never passed judgement on Dad for anything. Jarred wondered if it was time he took a page from her book…

When he stepped into the office, he saw that Rose had saved him the desk beside hers. She was wearing a dark-blue suit and a pink blouse today; her hair was pulled tightly back, as usual. She was twirling a wayward strand of hair with one hand and holding her phone with the other. Her fantastic lips were pressed into a thin line, her brow furrowed. She looked annoyed.

"I'm afraid I really do have a lot to do … No, today doesn't work … No, not tomorrow, either… Yes, I know I do have to eat sometime…" She sighed and fell silent, still twirling her hair while listening to what seemed like an extended monologue.

She didn't notice Jarred until he set his laptop on the desk and sat down. Her expression brightened instantly, and a gentle smile played on her lips before she turned her attention back to the phone call. "Fine, yeah, Wednesday. See you." She hung up and cleared her throat.

"Morning," he said in a loud voice. "Everything okay?" he added in a whisper.

"Morning!" she replied, equally loud, and then nodded imperceptibly. "I have a meeting in a minute. Do you have time to look over one of the residential projects?"

"Sure, just tell me which and I'll get to work." He'd actually been wanting to talk to Sean about his old project, but with his luck, he probably wouldn't get a slot on Sean's schedule before Friday anyway. So he'd just do whatever work Rose gave him and continue polishing his reputation. Though that didn't necessarily mean keeping his hands off Rose. He just needed to figure out where he could take her without either of them being recognized.

ROSE

Rose's hand shook a little in excitement as she paid the cab driver, and then stepped out directly opposite a pristine Chelsea home right near the Botanical Gardens and the Thames. It was already about eight, and apparently this neighborhood went to bed early —she hardly saw anyone out on the street.

She crossed the street and approached the dark wooden door at her destination. Her finger was still on the buzzer when Jarred opened the door, grinning from ear to ear.

"Where are we exactly?" Rose asked in a whisper once he'd closed and locked the door behind them. The foyer was incredibly elegant; those dark marble floors looked like they'd cost a fortune. She couldn't make heads or tails of the modern art on the walls, but she assumed each piece was worth more than she made in a month.

"My half-brother Henry lives here. He's in Texas. I'd have liked to invite you back to mine—I still will eventually, don't worry, and I know you said we could go to yours while I'm looking for a place, but I have a surprise for you, and we'll need Henry's house for that." Jarred finally stopped to take a breath.

"You're kind of cute when you're nervous," Rose remarked.

"Cute?" He closed the distance between them and began planting tiny kisses on her lips. "Or would you prefer wild?" He pulled back a few inches and regarded her, gaze clouded with lust.

Rose's heart went into overdrive. Of course she wanted more, more of everything. Instead of replying, she held him close and poured all of the emotions that had been building up inside her the whole day into the next kiss. She would have happily stood there all evening, just kissing Jarred.

"I've been wanting to do that all day," he murmured with an affectionate smile when they came up for air. Then he planted a loud, smacking kiss on the tip of her nose. "Okay, let me take your coat. Dinner's waiting in the kitchen."

Rose pulled off her boots and then followed him through the house, craning her neck to take it all in. She cast a quick glance into the living room, which was all black, gray, and white. Stylish, but oddly impersonal. The bar looked well-stocked.

"I guess your brother didn't do his own decorating."

"No, we all hired interior designers. God only knows why—hotel rooms have more personality. There'll be none of that at my new place."

"Have you found one?"

"No, not yet. Haven't the foggiest where I ought to be looking. I wasn't going to mention this until tomorrow at the office, but I think I'd like to take a look at one or two of our buildings on the east side of the city."

"Oh, yeah? To live in?"

"No, to find out what's wrong with them."

"So you noticed something was off, too, hm? I've been planning to go out there myself and see what the problem was, but I haven't had time. I'm glad something's finally going to be done about that—I'm running out of excuses for why sales would be so sluggish."

"I can follow up on that tomorrow. But tonight, I'm taking you out to the pub."

Before Rose could ask what he meant, Jarred opened the kitchen door and gestured for her to lead the way. The kitchen was state-of-the-art, but it was white with wood wainscoting, not the sea of sterile chrome she might have expected. The dark wooden table in front of the kitchen island was already set, complete with candles to set the mood. The lights were dimmed, and music floated softly through the room. An absolutely intoxicating scent hung in the air, and Rose's stomach promptly responded with a growl.

"Your brother has odd taste," she remarked, glancing at the beer signs hung on the walls.

"I stole those from his billiards room," Jarred laughed. "Sit down, I'll get you a Guinness. I think the food's just about ready."

"What's for dinner?" Rose trotted after Jarred as he went to the oven.

"Chicken pot pie."

"What? Really? I love any kind of pie. How'd you manage that so fast?" Rose marveled. How long had he been in the kitchen today?

"Um, well, that's the other reason we're eating here tonight: Henry has a chef, and she helped me. Er, more like I helped her. But the mushrooms were sliced with love."

Crazy. When did he plan all of this? He glanced at her bashfully from the side before murmuring, "Five more minutes." Then he gestured for her to make herself comfortable and went to get their drinks.

JARRED

He was more nervous tonight than he'd been in a long, long time. He wanted to make this evening perfect. If he'd had more time, he'd have liked to cook for her on his own. He'd enjoyed cooking once upon a time, and had often invited friends over for dinner.

Rose seemed to like the food, which in itself was no surprise—Henry's chef was truly talented.

"God, that was delicious!" Rose finished the last bite on her plate and patted her stomach in contentment. "What was your household like growing up? I mean, did you have a bunch of staff?"

"We always had a cook and a couple of cleaners, plus the gardener," Jarred replied. "Though we normally brought in a catering service for bigger social events. And my dad sometimes uses a chauffeur." Sean, too. Too good for the London Underground, apparently.

"But you don't?"

"I have a cleaning lady. The rest I do myself. Grocery shopping and everything!" he added with a wry grin. "I like my privacy." He took her hand, which was resting on the table, and began stroking her fingers. "When you're finished, I'll show you the surprise. We'll just have to grab our coats and shoes."

"There's more?" Rose blinked.

"I hope you like it."

Rose followed Jarred back to the foyer, gathered her things, and then followed him up the stairs.

"The house has two floors for bedrooms, each with connected baths, and then there's an office on the ground floor. But the best part's all the way at the top."

He waited for Rose to catch up before continuing to the top floor, which was all one room—a kind of loft with a billiards table, a big-screen TV, and a pair of cozy-looking sofas. The view stretched out over the park on the south side of the Thames.

"The real highlight is the roof terrace."

Rose slipped into her coat and boots before following Jarred outside.

"Wow, gorgeous!" The lights of the skyscrapers danced in the distance above the treetops. She couldn't make out which was which from this far away for her, but it was still a spectacular sight. Almost like in Rose's dream-home sketch.

He pulled her close to warm her. He'd have happily spent the rest of the evening out here, but it was too damn cold for that. There was one thing he still wanted to do before they went in, though: "May I have this dance?"

"What, here?"

"Just one song, and then you'll get your tea. Promise."

"Well, I can hardly say no to that."

He returned to the loft and switched the stereo on. He'd already deposited the speakers by the terrace door, so all he had to do was move them outside.

He pressed the button on the remote before returning to Rose, and swept her into his arms just as Audrey Hepburn began to sing "Moon River." They danced close, entangled in one another until the song finished and started over again. He felt like the happiest man in London.

CHAPTER 18

ROSE

"Oh my God, Rose, that's so romantic. You're making me tear up over here." Mandy blew her nose noisily.

"I was blinking them back myself," Rose admitted. She'd been too excited to wait until after work to call Mandy and tell her all about her amazing evening. Now, of course, acting totally neutral around Jarred in the office was going to be even harder.

"So are you guys officially together now or what?"

"We haven't talked about that."

"And you didn't go any further than kissing?"

"No—and I think that was what made it so romantic! I realized just how much I underappreciated kissing."

"You've got it bad, girl." Mandy sounded a little

worried. "I hope Jarred's not just playing you... So you're still meeting Aaron for lunch anyway? Even after that?"

"If I don't, he'll keep calling and calling until I agree to see him, so I might as well just get it over with."

"If you say so. Are you going to tell Jarred?"

"Probably not. Don't want him reading too much into it."

"Hm. I hope you know what you're doing."

Rose hoped so, too. She wouldn't be seeing Jarred until this afternoon; she couldn't wait to hear about his little field trip to the condo complex.

JARRED

He'd decided today was a red Ferrari kind of day. Even managed to find parking about five minutes from the house. Once again, Marlene opened the door almost as soon as his finger hit the buzzer. She beamed brightly at him as always; her perpetually sunny disposition was starting to rub off on him.

"Let me just grab my coat, and we can go." Marlene was wearing a stylish burgundy sheath dress and black knee-high boots. She threw her black coat over her shoulders, slung a gigantic handbag over one shoulder, and locked the doors behind them.

"Good Lord, what have you got in there, a tent?" Jarred blinked in amazement.

"Oh, nothing! Just a ruler, a notebook, a camera, a Dictaphone, and the usual girl stuff."

Laughing, he opened the door for Marlene. She was certainly taking this visit seriously. Then again, Campbell Investments hemorrhaging money because they were trying to sell economy condos at business-class prices was a pretty serious matter. Jarred shuddered to think what this was doing to the company's reputation.

He climbed in, started the car, and maneuvered into traffic.

"Nice toy you have here." Marlene ran an appreciative hand along the dashboard.

"It's way too fancy, totally impractical for city driving, but this seemed like the occasion."

"I hear you got an offer on your place?"

"Yeah, yesterday, but I haven't accepted it yet—a friend of mine is looking to move as well, and I was thinking I'd show it to him." He really ought to call Finn soon.

"If the Rutherfords' offer is good, I'd give them priority. Having them in your network is really worth it. Oh, and Joe said to thank you for the hotel recommendation. What neighborhoods is your friend interested in? Would Hampstead be an option for him?"

"I'll call him and find out."

"Great! Let me know, and I'll set up a showing. Are you coming to dinner tonight?"

What he really wanted to do tonight was see Rose. Not inviting her to spend the night with him yesterday had taken every ounce of self-control he could muster. But yes, he knew he probably ought to stop by his dad's again. Maybe he could go to Rose's place afterward?

"I think so."

They drove into the visitors' parking lot shortly before ten. Phase two of construction appeared to be well underway, and just as the report had said, the Phase One apartments—the units on the lower floors—were mostly rented. Jarred was surprised to see soccer balls, tricycles, and even hula hoops on many of the balconies.

"I didn't think families were necessarily your target demographic here?"

"Neither did I."

The front desk was manned until 8 pm every night; the receptionist welcomed them warmly and handed over the keys to the upper-level units. The empty lobby was extraordinarily elegant, with plush accent rugs covering the stone floors and radiantly white walls. Everything down here seemed spotless; the seating area near the front desk looked like something out of an interior design magazine.

"Well, this area looks just like the brochures,

anyway," Marlene remarked. "Shall we start with the penthouse?"

"How about you check out the penthouse, and I'll start on the sixth floor?"

"Sure. Just text me when you're done, or if I get done faster, I'll text you."

Jarred highly doubted that Marlene would be faster, lugging around all that gear. But he could also take the opportunity to call Finn. Actually, he probably ought to do that first thing.

He dialed Finn's number when he stepped out on the sixth floor.

"So the rumors *are* true! Consider me shocked. When'd you get back, man?"

"A week ago. Hey, speaking of rumors, I hear you're finally settling down, hm? Congrats!"

"Yeah, thanks, man. I was shittin' myself worrying that Marie would shoot me down. We've been together so long, and… I dunno, hasn't always been roses and sunshine, has it?"

Hadn't it? Jarred couldn't really remember.

"So, you got time for lunch today or what?"

He knew Marlene was meeting a friend for lunch after this, and there was no way he'd be able to keep his hands to himself around Rose, so lunch with her was definitely out. Just thinking about her lips… "Um, sure, yeah. I'm out and about at the moment, be free by noon."

"Perfect! I'll book us a table. Indian or Thai?"

"Thai."

"Right, let's do that place by Tower Gate. Brand-new, not on the fortieth floor or whatever. Really nice food, classy place. We can meet outside Campbell at one if you like—you're still working for your dad, aren't you?"

Jarred agreed and hung up. Okay, one thing ticked off the list. Now for the real reason he was here. He glanced around in the hallway, which was already a whole lot shabbier than the lobby. There were four units on this floor: two two-bedrooms, two three-bedrooms. He walked up to the nearest door and unlocked it.

ROSE

She caught herself humming Moon River while she worked. She never would have guessed Jarred was such a romantic, but after last night... she was falling for him harder than ever. She tried her damnedest to focus on the report in front of her, but her mind kept wandering. Just like when she'd first gotten together with Aaron. Ugh. Aaron. She had no desire to eat lunch with him tomorrow... maybe she ought to just get it over with already.

She texted him to say that something had come up for tomorrow, but that she had a little time today. He replied promptly, suggesting one of their old favorite places. There were way too many of those in

London City, unfortunately—they'd met for lunch all the time—so she went along with the suggestion.

Her phone rang a few minutes later, and seeing Jarred's number on the display brightened her mood immediately.

"Hi, Rose. Can you set up a meeting with Sean?"

"Hi, Jarred. Sure, I'll call his assistant now. I take it our suspicions were confirmed?"

"Honestly? I'm stunned. Every single apartment I looked at needs a full renovation. The caulking in the bathtubs looks like it was done by children. The parquet's loose in places, the doors don't close all the way, and the carpets have this weird patchwork thing going on... The kitchens look okay at first, but then you realize that the fridges don't work right."

Rose's eyes widened slowly as she absorbed the information. "Even in the penthouse?"

"Even in the penthouse."

"Which means that the rented units are in a similarly desolate state."

"Right. Marlene got it all on camera."

"Good, I'm sure Sean will want those as proof. I'll see about getting a meeting with him this afternoon."

"Thanks." She heard Jarred take a deep breath. "See you later?" he asked in a low voice.

"Gladly." She had a hundred other things she wanted to say to him—how much she'd enjoyed last night, how much she missed him, how she couldn't wait to spend time with him again—but she forced herself to hang up and focus on scheduling the meeting.

She was busy explaining to Sean's assistant that no, this really couldn't wait until next week, when a text arrived from Jarred. Just one emoji: two little pink hearts, spinning around each other.

CHAPTER 19

ROSE

It had taken a lot of convincing, but Rose had finally managed to score a spot on Sean's schedule late that afternoon. She wasn't sure how he'd react. Campbell Investments had already burned through a lot of money on this project, and there was always a chance Sean would be furious when he realized Rose had kept her suspicions to herself for so long.

Probably best not to drive herself any more insane than necessary. She was so preoccupied that she was almost late for her lunch... thing.

She found Aaron waiting outside the Indian restaurant, which was on a side street about fifteen minutes from her office. He was certainly looking dapper in his anthracite-colored coat and blue suit—the one that had always been her favorite, because it brought out his turquoise eyes. His dark-blond hair was mussed from the wind. Rose had always liked his hair better when it wasn't perfectly combed. A smile flitted across Aaron's face when he saw her approaching.

"Hi, Aaron. You didn't have to wait out here in the cold." Back when they were together, he'd always waited for her outside, even in the pouring rain, so that she wouldn't have to look for him. God, he even remembered that little quirk of hers...

"Hi, Rose. I wanted to." He bent down to greet her with a kiss on the cheek, and she caught a whiff of his aftershave. Scents were evil, they triggered so many emotions. Probably better if she kept her distance—after all, she was here to make sure Aaron understood that he could save his breath trying to win her back.

"Thanks. Shall we?"

Aaron opened the door to the restaurant and gestured for Rose to lead the way; as soon as they stepped inside, an energetic waiter bustled over to seat them. Though it had been a long time since she'd last come here, she didn't remember it being quite this cramped—the whole place was so packed with tables that she could barely squeeze through.

After they'd checked their coats, the waiter led them to a two-person table; though no less cramped, it had the advantage of being by a window fairly near the entrance. Anyway, it was apparently the very last available table in the entire restaurant, so it wasn't like she had a choice.

"You look really pretty, Rose."

Aaron had never been shy about compliments; once upon a time, Rose would have been flattered. "Thanks." Ugh. *Deep breath, Rose. Well, not too deep. He's wearing your favorite aftershave.*

"What'll you have? The usual?" Such a familiar question, coming from Aaron. No doubt he'd get the tandoori chicken. Nice and spicy, just the way he liked it.

"Prawn curry, I think." She normally always got chicken. Actually, she preferred chicken. Aaron looked her expectantly. "Or maybe just the chicken, I guess." Rose shut the menu with a sigh. He knew her too well. Hell, they'd been involved for two years, it wasn't exactly shocking.

Aaron ordered for them both, plus mineral water for Rose and beer for himself.

"Thanks for the flowers, you really didn't have to go to that trouble." Just being in his presence triggered some very confusing responses within her, but Rose kept her voice firm and forced herself to look directly at him.

Aaron toyed with his fork. His expression radiated confidence, but warmth and affection as well. Rose suddenly felt like a mouse facing down a snake. "I saw them and thought of you immediately. Did you have a good birthday?"

Rose nodded, though it hadn't been anything

special—just working like always. She and Aaron had had a million plans for how they'd spend their thirtieth birthdays. Rose had hoped to spend hers somewhere in the Southern Hemisphere, while Aaron had wanted to spend the whole night partying in New York. Presumably he'd done just that, except without her.

"Do you still draw?"

"Yeah, here and there."

"Constantly, in other words. That's good, you always enjoyed it."

"Listen—" Rose began, but the waiter interrupted with papadum and chutneys. Once he'd left, she began again: "Listen, I don't think we should see each other."

"Why not?" Aaron broke off a piece of papadum, dabbed it with spicy chutney and popped it into his mouth.

"Because we broke up?" Rose hissed, irritated.

"We could still be friends."

"Yeah, right," Rose muttered before sipping her water.

"Who says we can't? Does your *husband* have a problem with it?"

"It's a friendship ring," Rose explained. She'd never been a good liar. Then again, Aaron had probably already figured her out.

"I know. Does Mandy have the same one? It's pretty. I might have guessed you'd pick something from Tiffany's."

So he'd made a point of tracking it down. It was an eye-catching design, though. Probably not hard to find. "You actually Googled my ring? It was really that important to you?"

"I was trying to gauge my chances."

"Think 'snowball in hell.'"

"And yet here you are."

"Let's just eat and go our separate ways." Her stomach was already growling, but she'd be damned if she was going to reach for that papadum and give him a chance to "accidentally" touch her hand. Back in the day, she and Aaron would always fed each other bits of papadum and usually left the restaurant with globs of yogurt sauce on their shirts. Like you do when you're in love.

Their food was served soon after, thank God. Rose ate her curry in silence. Aaron didn't seem to mind keeping up the conversation on his own, though. She learned that he lived in Whitechapel, just twenty minutes from his office, but hoped to buy a cottage near the sea depending on how business went this year. She learned that he'd enjoyed New York a lot, but had returned to London for personal reasons. And she learned that his sister had gotten married and was expecting her first child.

Rose liked Aaron's sister, and had regretted losing touch with her. She wondered if the "personal reasons" for his return involved his sister, but refused to do him the favor of asking. The cottage by the sea was a very obvious reference to plans they'd made back when they were together. She tried to shake off the wave of melancholy washing over her, to quit asking herself whether she'd been too hasty in leaving Aaron. She'd probably never know for sure. But the way he was looking at her now... so open, so honest... had she made a huge mistake?

Or was he manipulating her?

"I'd better get to my next meeting." She and Aaron had finished eating, and there was no sense hanging around. She could get her tea in the canteen. They split the bill at Rose's insistence—she refused to be in Aaron's debt for any reason whatsoever.

The moment they stepped outside, Rose reached out for a goodbye handshake.

"We can walk back together, I'm headed the same direction."

"Um, no, sorry, I'm headed that way, something else I have to take care of." Mostly she needed a break to clear her head. He still had an effect on her. Maybe he always would, no matter how often she told herself that she didn't care about him one way or the other.

"In that case, thanks for lunch." He gave her another kiss on the cheek, brushing her ear with his lips in passing; the tickle of his warm breath on her neck sent a shiver down her spine.

JARRED

Finn was already waiting outside, at the bottom of the escalator leading up to the Campbell building. He'd hardly changed at all. "Is that a beer gut coming on?"

"Nobody around to make me go to the gym." Finn's horn-rimmed glasses slipped down his nose as he laughed. Same old Finn.

They hugged enthusiastically, and Jarred found himself wondering how he hadn't missed the warm feeling that came over him. Probably because he was too busy wallowing in self-pity and abusing every substance he could get his hands on. "We'll have to fix that, then," he replied impulsively as they started toward the restaurant. Finn looked genuinely delighted at the thought. "Where'd you propose to Marie?"

"We were at that Christmas market in Leicester Square, you know? I'd been carrying that ring around for weeks, thought up a million different ways to do it, but pretty much every one of them put me in a panic. So then I decided to just do it right there. Cheesiest place in London, but a bit away from all the commotion, at least." Finn looked sheepish. He'd always been on the shy side, and Jarred admired the fact that he'd worked up the courage to propose in public.

"How do you two like Hampstead? Is that an area you'd be interested in?"

"Marie's looking for somewhere a bit greener. And public transit doesn't matter too much, so... yeah, why not? You know someone there with a place?"

"Yeah, the people who are interested in buying mine. I can set up a showing for you."

"How come you're selling your place, anyway?" Finn asked.

Is that Rose? There was a glare off the windows of the small restaurant, but he thought he saw Rose sitting inside. But... no, probably not. Actually, he didn't even know what she'd worn to work today, since she'd already left for lunch by the time he arrived. The woman had turned away again; all he saw was her dark pants suit and her red shoes. He couldn't see who was with her.

"Jarred?"

"Yeah? Oh, sorry, I thought I saw someone I knew."

"Some*one*, as in singular? I'm amazed we haven't stopped ten times so you could take a call or tell someone hello."

"I've got my phone on silent." *Which is how I should have always done it*, he added in his mind. But gosh, it had been so wonderful, hadn't it? Knowing that he was so popular, that everyone wanted to talk to him all the time. God, he'd had such an ego back then.

"That's good." Finn glanced at him, obviously bewildered.

What would he say if he knew why Jarred was

back in London? Actually, the real question was whether he could tell Finn without half of London finding out. Or, worse, without someone selling the story to the press.

No, he could trust Finn. He was pretty sure.

ROSE

Rose didn't notice that she'd missed a call from Jarred until she was on her way back to the office. She texted him to tell him about her 4:30 appointment with Sean, and asked him to let her know if he was free—ideally a few minutes before, so that they could prepare.

She returned from an afternoon meeting, stressed already, to find Jarred sitting at his computer, typing a blue streak. Rose went straight to his desk. God, he looked good enough to eat. Her heart did a happy somersault when he looked up and smiled at her.

"If I'd known you could type that fast," she remarked, "I'd have given you a few extra reports."

"You look tired. Let me guess: process optimization?"

"Quality assurance. Double signatures and all that. I assume process optimization is next."

"Tea?"

"No time, we're supposed to see Sean in half an hour."

"I've already got our documentation ready." Jarred stood up and gestured to his chair. "Why don't you read that over while I get you some tea?"

Could he *be* any more perfect? Rose gave him a grateful smile before sitting down to read.

Jarred brought the tea along with a chocolate bar. *You look incredible*, the back of the wrapper read.

"Thanks. Your report is really good. I suggest I start by talking about our analyses and the conclusions we drew independently, and then you can go into your observations from this morning. Your stepmother certainly did provide plenty of photographic evidence."

"Yeah, she did. But are you sure you don't want to go meet Sean on your own?"

"No, why do you ask?"

He gave her a meaningful look but didn't explain further. Was it about the two of them, was that why he couldn't say it out loud? Was he afraid Sean might notice?

"We'll both go," she said in a firm voice. It wasn't like she was going to sit there making puppy-dog eyes at him, and Jarred had the best poker face of anyone she knew. Easy breezy.

Going to Sean together seemed risky, but Rose seemed so confident that Jarred knew there was no point trying to argue.

When they stepped into Sean's office, he stood up, walked over to Rose, and shook her hand. The look he gave her was a lot friendlier than the one Jarred got. Didn't offer Jarred a handshake, either. Jarred followed them to the couches and poured himself and Rose each a glass of water; Sean waved the offer away.

Jarred had already noticed that Rose liked to speak her mind, and this time was no different. To keep himself from staring at her lips in fascination, Jarred sipped his water and watched Sean's face to see how he reacted.

"You were there today?" Sean eyed him coolly.

"I was. Marlene went with me." If he'd gone alone, Sean would have had an excuse to doubt his observations, and would likely have wanted to go see for himself—whenever his schedule permitted, of course. Meanwhile, Campbell Investments would keep losing money. "You know we'll need to investigate this." Jarred gave him a challenging look. What was going through Sean's mind right now? He hated scandals, as he was oh-so-fond of reminding Jarred. Would Dad sweep this under the rug, or would Sean have the guts to publicly admit that mistakes had been made?

"Rose, when do you think you can get a report to me?" Sean asked, ignoring Jarred.

"By the end of the week."

Sean nodded and stood up in a way that was probably supposed to signal that the conversation was over... but as long as Jarred was here, he figured he could bring something else up as well.

"Can I talk to you real quick?"

The brothers waited until the door closed behind Rose.

"What is it?" Sean muttered. "You here to moralize?"

"Of course not," Jarred said in a sugary-sweet voice. "Nothing could be further from my mind. You're the boss."

"Then what do you want?"

"Spike!"

"Dream on." Sean turned to face his computer, pointedly ignoring Jarred, who stayed right where he was.

"Why not? I would have completed Spike. So now I'll do it two years later." Two could play the stubborn game. "You think I'm a risk to the company and might run off again at any time?" *Spit it out already, Sean.*

"That's part of it."

Ouch.

"The project is also just too big—it's cost far too many people ungodly amounts of money. How would I explain that to our shareholders? It would mean committing another huge chunk of our budget to a project that's already obsolete. My desk drawer is overflowing with modern, innovative proposals. Nobody's interested in Spike anymore."

"I thought we'd switched to an electronic filing system," Jarred remarked, just to provoke his brother.

"Snide remarks won't get you far," Sean retorted. "Anyway, just finding partners would take you months."

"Partners, plural? Since when do I need more than one?"

"You've been gone a long time. Things have changed."

Not the first time he'd heard that.

"If the residential buildings aren't exciting enough for you, we have several commercial projects in the pipeline in Manchester. Pick your favorite."

Manchester?

"I've got an appointment in a minute here, but I'll see you at dinner—you can tell me what you've decided then."

Sean wanted him to decide in the next two hours whether he was moving to Manchester? He couldn't be serious!

CHAPTER 20

JARRED

He was still seething as he drove to dinner. Manchester! He'd be commuting at best! Such bullshit. He had no desire to leave London. Rose was in London. They both knew that this clandestine office romance couldn't last, but every cell in Jarred's body still objected to the thought of telling her that they'd only be seeing each other on weekends.

The exact same parking spot he'd used that morning was free again tonight. Marlene welcomed him with a hug he was only too happy to return.

"Was Sean satisfied with our work?"

"Think so. He'll take care of everything."

Marlene furrowed her brow, as if surprised by Jarred's lack of enthusiasm.

"And I've decided to take the Rutherford's offer

on the condo." He'd just decided at that very moment, in fact. Marlene had made such an effort, and he liked the thought of making her happy.

Marlene cheered and threw her arms around him again. He laughed and caught her before she could drag them both to the floor. "We'll have to drink to that! What did your friend say? Should I ask about scheduling a showing?"

"Yeah, but during the week will be difficult—do you think we could set something up for Saturday morning?"

"I'd imagine so. Saturday morning was when Jill and Joe wanted to look at your place. I'll call Jill tomorrow—right after you tell Joe you're accepting their offer."

"I can have a purchase agreement drawn up by the weekend."

"How much did they offer?"

"Two million, one hundred seventy-five thousand."

"Are you coming away with a profit?"

"About twenty percent."

"Not bad! Bet big, win big. Especially since the buyer pays the fees, right? Well, they did manage without an agent, so that saves them a ton of money. Anyway, as long as the Rutherfords are happy."

Jarred had been expecting them to go straight into the living room, but Marlene pointed him toward the kitchen—where he found his father mincing herbs, and wondered if he was hallucinating.

No way, not in a thousand years. Marlene had obviously thrown Dad out and brought some guy home that happened to look like his father.

"What are your thoughts on cilantro?"

Amazing. This man wearing a bright red apron over his button-down shirt and suit trousers even had the same voice as his father, though Jarred was reasonably sure that his real father had never said that combination of words in his entire life.

"Jarred sold his condo! Isn't that great? And you should have seen him at the showing—Joe was very impressed with how professional he was."

The hell? Marlene was giving him the credit? She'd done a lot to make the sale a success. "Don't sell yourself short there, Marlene," he hurried to reply. "I wanted to thank you for all your help." He'd never stolen anyone else's thunder before, and he wasn't about to start now.

"Oh, that's what family's for. I think we're a pretty good team!" Smiling, she moved to the stove and stirred something in a large cast-iron pot. Whatever it was, it smelled delicious. "Are you done there, Artie?"

Artie? His father hated nicknames. Which was why all of their names were short enough that they'd sound stupid shortened any further. Although, now that he thought about it, Henry and his best friend Franco had called each other "H" and "F." Which was pretty hip, actually. Maybe he should start going by "J."

"I am. Where's Sean?"

"Just getting out of the taxi. Should be here in twenty seconds."

Then Jarred noticed the tiny monitor beside the phone on the kitchen island. So that was how Marlene always knew he was coming.

"I'll get the door, then," Jarred said, wanting to do something more helpful than stand there and watch his father and stepmother cook. "Hey, what ever happened to our old cook?"

"Sarah? She retired ten years ago. We've got a new one, but she's only part-time, no point having another full-timer when it's just the two of us," his father said in a perfectly dry tone, as though explaining how the stock market had developed over the previous quarter.

Aha.

"Jarred, did you want to go let Sean in?"

Oh, right. He'd rung the doorbell three times already. Grinning, Marlene accepted the minced cilantro from Jarred's father, who then embraced her from behind as she stirred the herbs into the pot. It was such a familiar scene, Jarred could hardly tear his eyes away—but Sean would probably start trying to break the door down if Jarred didn't open it already.

"Did you fall asleep on your way to the door or something?" Sean grunted.

"Sorry, I got distracted."

"By what, for God's sake?"

"Dad and Marlene in the kitchen."

"She cooks, so what?" Sean apparently found that less impressive than Jarred did. Once he'd hung his coat, Sean went straight to the living room to pour himself a drink. "You want one?"

"No, I drove."

"You got your Ferrari out of the garage? How the hell are you going to pay for the gas?" Sean tossed back his first whiskey in one gulp and immediately served himself a second.

"I sold my condo."

"So, what, you're just going to cut and run again already? Why, because I wouldn't give you the Spike project back?" Sean gave him a troubled look, which was in itself an unusual sight—Sean normally had his feelings tightly under control.

"What are you talking about, Sean?" Neither of them had heard their father come in. Arthur's eyes shifted back and forth between his sons.

"Jarred wants to build his skyscraper. I told him no. For good reasons, mind you."

"I'd have to disagree there," Jarred responded, "but you're the boss. And no, I'm not leaving town."

"Have you found a new place, then?" Arthur asked.

"You're welcome to live here, if you like," Marlene piped up as she stepped into the living room. "And dinner's ready."

"Thanks, but no need. I'm staying at Henry's while he's in Texas." Jarred stepped back, allowing Marlene to lead the way. His stomach was growling, and he was looking forward to seeing what was on the menu.

Ten minutes later, he thought he'd died and gone to heaven—Marlene's chili had his tastebuds in ecstasy. Even Sean seemed impressed. When it came down to it, they all had fairly simple taste; none of them needed extravagant meals.

"Have you thought about whether you're going to take one of the projects in Manchester?" Sean asked.

Jarred had only had time to skim through them. The Manchester skyline was transforming rapidly, and these upcoming construction projects would create whole new neighborhoods. The tallest structure would be fifty-one stories—a hundred and fifty-two meters tall. He'd been assuming Sean wanted to pawn some second-class job off on him, but honestly, Manchester was enough to make any investor's heart skip a beat. No comparison to the London real estate prices, of course, but heaven wasn't free in Manchester either. Tens of thousands of apartments would be going up there in the coming years.

"What, after two hours? I think I'll go have a look at them myself first. With your Highness's permission, of course."

"Knock yourself out."

They dueled with razor-sharp glances until Marlene broke in to ask about what type of property Finn was looking for. Jarred rattled off what details he knew: three bedrooms, sunny, with a yard or near a park.

Marlene nodded, looking pleased. She seemed to genuinely enjoy playing real-estate agent.

Jarred took his leave at around nine. He'd played dutiful son long enough for one evening, and he'd certainly had his fill of Sean's company. Especially since he was planning on spending the rest of the night with someone infinitely more charming.

ROSE

She'd whipped out her easel and had been happily painting away for hours. Jarred's face was crystal-clear in her mind, but her concentration skills were leaving a lot to be desired. When his text message arrived, she took it as a sign from the universe that it was time to hang it up for the night. She rinsed her brushes and aired out her little studio, the space that would normally have been the guest bedroom. She left the unfinished painting on the easel—she'd show it to Jarred once it was finished.

Rose took a quick shower and changed into a pink T-shirt and a comfortable pair of black pants. She left her hair down; disheveled, maybe, but just the thought of combing it back made her scalp hurt. Then just a dab of lip balm and—yikes, doorbell already? Had Jarred come by helicopter or something?

Rose flew downstairs to open the door. Jarred

smiled at her. Her heart went into a frenzy as he stepped inside and pushed the door shut behind him before kissing her until she could barely think straight.

"I missed you," he murmured.

"Missed you too."

"Not touching you in the office is torture."

"C'mon, let's go upstairs." She took his hand and climbed the stairs with him. Now that she finally had him here, she'd be damned if she was going to let him go... Well, okay, he had to take his coat off first. She sighed and released his hand with a sigh, sneaking glances at him as he slipped off his shoes.

"What?"

"Oh, just thinking maybe you don't need to stop at the shoes," she replied with a provocative flick of her eyebrows. What the hell were they waiting for, anyway?

He hesitated for exactly one second before grabbing her hand and making for the two closed doors on the other side of the apartment.

"Left."

As soon as they reached the bedroom, he pressed her against the wall and kissed her like a drowning man until they were both gasping for air. His lips drifted first to her earlobe, then down the side of her neck. "You smell so good," he growled, inhaling deeply. "And you're wearing far too many clothes."

"Hang on, the window." Rose ducked underneath the arm he was using to prop himself against the wall, and reached out to pull the curtains shut. Then she dimmed the lights, bathing her bedroom in a romantic glow, before crawling onto the bed and fixing him with a challenging stare. "I'm waiting."

Jarred began a slow, deliberate striptease, tossing his jacket onto a chair by the window before undoing his shirt buttons one by one. "You could follow my lead instead of just sitting there staring at me."

"Oh, but I very much enjoy staring at you, Mr. Campbell."

"I'm aware of that, Ms. Murphy. But perhaps it's escaped your notice that the sentiment is mutual." Slowly, he slipped off the shirt, revealing his muscular torso. Real-life Jarred was every bit as breathtakingly perfect as the beach-photo Jarred she'd recently had the pleasure of ogling. She wasn't sure where to look first. A bolt of heat shot through her as he undid his pants and let them drop to the floor along with his underwear; he casually tugged off his socks and laid them neatly on the chair, giving Rose a glorious view of his backside. Oh, yes, her nickname for Jarred was more than applicable. Another wave of heat coursed through her as he turned back and rolled on the condom.

"You look like you're trying to memorize my body," Jarred remarked, jolting Rose out of her trance.

"Can't help it," she murmured bashfully. *That and imagining all the things I want to do to you*, she added in her head. She started removing her own shirt, but he put up a hand to stop her.

"Let me." He sat down on the bed, slid the hem of her T-shirt out of her waistband, and began pushing it up slowly, leaving tender kisses on every inch of skin he revealed in the process: her navel, her ribs, her cleavage. After tugging the shirt over her head, he undid her bra clasp with a practiced motion. He stopped to gaze at her in silence for a moment before running his fingertips over her breasts in reverence. "Beautiful."

The desire in Jarred's eyes turned Rose on even more. She wanted to touch him, to kiss him, to surrender completely to her lust. The electricity in the air made her skin tingle. Their lips met in a passionate kiss, and Rose frantically freed herself from the rest of her clothes. She was every bit as impatient as Jarred, could hardly wait to melt into him—any remaining doubts she had about whether this was a good idea evaporated. Whatever difficulties they would have to face suddenly struck her as trivial. Right here, right now, it was only him and Rose and the connection she sensed with every fiber of her being, a connection she never wanted to be without again.

Her hands wandered down his back and continued to his butt as though of their own free will. God, she was wet. She wanted him inside her, *now...* but he was pressed so tightly against her that she could only grind against him, which made her even hotter. They kissed feverishly, gasping, moaning… and all at once, he lifted her hips and sank into her with one long, smooth thrust.

"Fuck, you're so tight," Jarred gasped, "so perfect." As soon as he settled into a steady rhythm, Rose felt an orgasm building inside her. *Jesus, speaking of perfect,* she thought.

She felt his hot breath against her ear, felt him kissing and nibbling her earlobe, making her even wetter than she already was. His right hand drifted down to play with her nipples before diving lower to stroke her clit, and Rose immediately went over the edge, screaming his name as she came, writhing beneath him. Jarred went right on stimulating her. It was too much; her senses could barely process it all. Now she felt his lips on her nipple, his tongue teasing her, and she came again—sweeping him along with her, as she heard from his animalistic cry.

She couldn't tell which way was up anymore; they were one giant tangle of arms and legs. Rose's body felt feather-light yet wonderfully heavy, so much so that she dozed off almost immediately.

CHAPTER 21

JARRED

He hadn't planned on staying the night—morning-rush traffic was no joke—but having Rose in his arms felt so damn good that he couldn't bring himself to leave. Not after that phenomenal sex, not now that he was finally starting to understand just how much she actually meant to him. He fell asleep eventually; when his alarm went off at five the next morning, he realized that they'd slept cuddled together. Before tonight, the only person he'd ever done that with had been his ex Vicky, and that was years ago; everyone else, he'd discreetly shooed out of the hotel room as soon as the fun part was over.

Damn shame they both had to work today; he'd have much preferred to spend the day with Rose. In bed, ideally. He began tracing tiny circles on her stomach. Her incredibly soft skin smelled like roses. And like Rose.

"Awake already?" she mumbled, half-asleep.

"I should get going."

"Why? What time is it?" Rose jolted upright and clicked on the bedside lamp. The sight of her naked body was enough to make his mouth go dry. He was more than willing to pick up where they'd left off a few hours before.

"It's only five, but I need to stop home to shower and change." *Cold shower. Very, very cold.*

"Five? Oh, thank God, I thought we'd overslept." She sank back against the pillows and snuggled against him. "Are you absolutely sure you want to leave?" she whispered, nibbling his earlobe.

"Of course I don't. But do you think my boss will buy it if I call in sick?"

"Hm, I hear she's a clever one, she'll probably see right through your lies." Rose giggled against his neck, and her long hair tickled his chest. He'd never felt so comfortable with a woman... it made him a little nervous. He took a deep breath in and out, trying to calm his racing heart.

She propped herself up on her elbows and gazed at him dreamily. "Why don't you shower here, and I'll make us breakfast before you go?" Now it was her fingers tracing languid patterns on his chest.

"I'll smell like roses the whole day."

"I have men's stuff, too—they practically throw

free samples at you in the department stores. I've got the one you use."

"You're scary, Rose."

"You mean it's scary how amazing I am."

"That, too. I guess I'd better hurry—traffic's only going to get worse." He jumped out of bed, ignoring Rose's pointed sigh, and headed into the bathroom. A moment later, she followed him in, bearing fresh towels. She'd put on a long T-shirt, and she looked so goddamn hot in it that he promptly pulled her into the shower with him.

Still in a bathrobe, with her wet hair under a turban, Rose insisted on whipping up scrambled eggs, toast, and coffee.

"Wow, thanks. Proper breakfast. Do I get the boss mug today?"

"Hm, I'm not sure."

"I could bribe you." He kissed her long and deeply, and then gave her a questioning look.

"Fine. Just this once."

They sat down and began to eat. He couldn't remember the last time he'd actually eaten breakfast in a sitting position.

"I asked Sean about the Spike project yesterday." The subject he'd been dwelling on ever since.

"Let me guess: he shot you down."

"You got it," Jarred replied with a bitter smile. He

toyed with his mug for a moment before continuing. "He offered me Manchester."

Rose stared at him in silence. "Did you say yes?"

"I want to go check it out first. And I wanted to talk it over with you."

"The projects out there are very promising. With all the skyscrapers they're planning? You could really live it up."

"I'm not so sure I want to live it up so far away from you. Actually, scratch that, I'm sure that I *don't* want to." He pulled her onto his lap and held her tightly.

"You and I both know that you won't stay my assistant for long," Rose murmured. "I don't want you missing opportunities on my account."

If only they weren't right at the beginning of a relationship. Jarred wasn't even sure whether Rose saw him as anything more than a fling. But if he started spending the whole week in Manchester, they'd never have a chance to get to know each other.

Maybe Sean suspected something was up, and that was why he wanted to send Jarred away. Or was he upset that they'd told him about the problems they'd noticed? Either way, Jarred highly doubted Sean would reveal his motives, whatever they were.

"I'd better get going if I don't want to be late. See you later?" Jarred undid Rose's turban before planting a kiss on her damp hair.

"Of course. You do still work for me, after all." Smiling, Rose leaned in for a goodbye kiss. "And before you quit, you'd better find and train the new guy."

"New girl, if anything!" he retorted.

ROSE

"You think Jarred will decide to go to Manchester?" Mandy looked worried.

"Career-wise, he'd be a fool not to. From a purely selfish standpoint, I wish he'd turn it down."

It was lunchtime, and Rose was on her way to the Thames again. The wind was gusty today; passing clouds reflected in the glass facades of the skyscrapers. In moments like these, Rose loved London just a little bit more.

She took a deep breath, feeling the tension drain from her body for the first time since breakfast. After Jarred had brought up the job opportunity, things had been a little weird between them all morning. He'd been as helpful as ever, but she could tell that he was preoccupied with Manchester.

"Do you think getting involved with Jarred was a mistake?"

"No, no way. Besides that one little hiccup when he first started, he's never given you any reason to doubt him and his loyalty. Not that I'm expecting either of you to swear your undying love after dating for a week, but he did want your blessing on

Manchester, which says a lot about how he feels. Maybe you should see this as an opportunity. You won't be hanging around together, so you won't have to hide how you feel. And I'm sure having a few quality projects will make Jarred happier career-wise... and you guys can always see each other on weekends. Or just drive up to visit him in Manchester. It's a great town, and you won't have to worry as much about somebody at the company spotting you."

"You always make everything sound so positive."

"You could even go visit your brother while you're there."

"Less positive now," Rose laughed.

"So tell me, if you got an opportunity like that, would you turn it down for Jarred?"

"An opportunity to go to Manchester?"

"Yeah. Or let's think even bigger, say New York or Boston or something. I dunno where all you guys have projects happening."

"So whether I'd put my career ahead of my relationship? I dunno. Wouldn't the relationship be more or less doomed to fail? I'd certainly discuss it with my partner, but I can't really see myself doing it."

"I'm telling you, men are just wired differently. You remember our neighbors, the Jacksons? They were in Sweden for two years, and then in Switzerland for three years. Beverly had just written me from Geneva to say how happy they all were, how the kids were doing great in school... and then a month later, her husband gets offered another promotion, so they all have to pack up and move to America. How self-centered is that? He's got a family!"

"I've gotta admit, I'd even have given everything up for Aaron. I'd have moved to America with him without hesitating for a second. I don't remember thinking that way when I was younger... maybe it's a hormone thing?" Rose made a frustrated noise.

"I wouldn't know, I'm the same age as you. For me, it's the pressure to have a second child, even though I was only twenty-five when I had Ella... Sometimes I feel like Rob and I were way too young to be parents. Maybe that's why nowadays he acts like missing a single party would be the end of the world, and he throws himself into his work like he's somehow trying to catch up. Anyway, it's your life and your decision—don't let anyone tell you what to do. Just don't get your heart broken, Rose. No man is worth being miserable over."

JARRED

He'd gone to Manchester the next morning, and even spent the night so that he could really get a feel for the city. Overall, he'd been pleasantly surprised. Perhaps he'd misjudged Sean after all. The one bitter pill left to swallow would be that, if he took the assignment, he'd only see Rose on video chat during the week.

Cross that bridge when they came to it, though. Tonight, he'd invited her over for dinner, and he had another surprise up his sleeve.

The doorbell rang at six-thirty. He'd left Rose's name with the doorman so that she could come straight up.

"Hey, come in."

"Thanks." Rose's gaze swept around the room before coming to rest on Jarred. "I brought dessert," she added, nodding to the completely unmissable pastry box in her hands. She was obviously just as nervous as he was.

"Yeah, I'll bring that to the kitchen for you... can I take your coat?" He placed the pastry box on a side table before accepting the coat and hanging it up.

Unlike Jarred, Rose waited patiently rather than just wandering about the place, opening random artist portfolios and thumbing through photo albums. Then again, his apartment didn't feature either of those things. He'd already packed most of his stuff, so that he could bring it to Henry's in the morning.

"I'm glad you came." He stepped in and kissed her. It felt even better than he'd remembered.

"So am I," Rose said with a small sigh. "I missed you."

"Likewise," he replied before reluctantly releasing her. "I didn't have time to cook, but the

Indian place around the corner's great. I hope you like Indian?"

"I love Indian food. I went out for Indian just the other day."

"Oh, maybe I should have picked something else, then."

"No, no, I could live on curry. Well, maybe not *just* curry, but… anyway, let's see what you've got!" Rose followed Jarred into the open-plan kitchen, where a giant stack of foil-wrapped packages awaited them. "Are ten of your friends stopping by as well?"

"I wasn't sure what you like."

"So you got one of everything," she said with a teasing smile. "Ooh, garlic naan, yum."

"As long as we both have some." Jarred watched in amusement as she opened one container after the next, and soon a mélange of enticing aromas lingered in the air. He retrieved several china serving bowls from the cupboard and began transferring the contents of the containers.

He'd decked out the dining room table: underplates, candles, the works. Even created a centerpiece of snowdrops, wild roses, buttercups, and tulips.

"Where'd you find the snowdrops? Are they blooming already?"

"A few. You like those?"

"Oh, for sure. My mom loves gardening—she'd always take us kids around to different gardens as soon as the snowdrops were properly in bloom. But I didn't discover the biggest, most beautiful gardens until I started at Cambridge: there's an old estate about ten kilometers to the west of there. Belongs to the National Trust. The park there has something like three hundred different varieties of snowdrops."

Rose's eyes sparkled as she spoke. Jarred pictured her standing in what was no doubt an enormous park, giddy with excitement. The mental image made him happy. He didn't have any comparable memories of his own. "We could go out there sometime if you like," he suggested.

ROSE

"Your apartment's really nice," Rose remarked as they sat down to eat. Fingers crossed that she wouldn't spill anything—curry stains were tough to get out, and dunking the naan into the sauces was a surprisingly effective way of getting sauce all over things. Hm, maybe she ought to be polite and eat with a knife and fork. She wasn't trying to get orange stains on the chairs or the carpet.

"And really bare. I want my new place to be completely different."

"Yeah? Different, how?"

"More colorful, for sure. I think I'll buy some paintings, too. I know this one really talented artist, I might ask her if she'll sell me a few of her works."

Smiling, Jarred tucked a wayward strand of hair behind Rose's ear.

"I bet she'd be happy to give you a few."

"Would you become a full-time artist if you could make enough to live on?"

"That'd be a dream come true." This, she realized, would probably be the moment to tell him about her side job.

"Well, never say never. But let's eat before it gets cold." Jarred loaded Rose's plate with a small portion of everything: chicken tikka masala, lamb vindaloo, fish masala, prawn curry, baingan bharta, saag paneer, mushroom kofta, aloo gobi, and rice.

"How long have you lived here?" She accepted the plate with a nod of thanks; just looking at this incredible spread was making her mouth water. A perfect evening already.

"About four years, but I was practically never here for the last two. It doesn't feel like home."

"That's a real shame."

"There's still a box of my things stashed away somewhere in my dad's house. Stuff from my childhood. I should really go pick it up—I can't even remember what's in there anymore. We all got sent away to boarding school at age eleven, and then Mom moved to Notting Hill after she and Dad divorced, so my sister Alice and I went to live with her. Mom liked it a lot better there than in Kensington, especially that big crazy outdoor market on Portobello Road. I liked it, too... Anyway, mom had all the old photos of me and Alice, and Alice took them after my mom died. My dad handled the... you know, the estate and everything, because I... I wasn't doing so great, like, she was only fifty-four, it was so sudden and I, just... you know..." Jarred broke off and took a deep breath before continuing. "I couldn't bring myself to sit there going through her stuff, figuring out what to keep."

God, how sad is that? "I'm sorry," Rose said, taking Jarred's hand. It sounded like he'd had a pretty lonely childhood—her heart grew heavy just thinking about it. She couldn't even imagine. And then losing his mom, from one day to the next? And so young, too. She suddenly wished she could take him to Watford to meet her own family, but that was out of the question. For now.

"It's ok, it was a long time ago," Jarred murmured, but Rose could tell it still weighed on him—he'd suddenly gone from eating his food to poking at it.

"So, you've got... how many siblings?"

"Alice is my only full sibling, and then we have three half-brothers—each with a different mom. Dad had a real revolving door of wives and girlfriends going on."

"Do you and your siblings all get along? My two brothers and I, we absolutely tortured each other as kids, but I suppose that's normal." Rose rolled her eyes and grinned. "My friend Mandy helped me fight back—every prank they pulled on me, we'd think up two to play on them. Nothing too bad, of course.

Once we tied the laces on all of their sneakers together... the meanest thing we ever did was probably washing my middle brother Trevor's favorite shirt on hot. He actually cried!"

"So what terrible thing did he do to deserve that cruel fate?"

"He painted the hair on every single one of my dolls. Green, red, blue, black. Waterproof paint, too. Absolutely unforgivable."

Jarred grinned. "And what prompted him to do that?"

"Oh, well, I may or may not have spread it around school that he had a crush on the prettiest girl in his class."

"Sassy little thing, weren't you?"

"Sometimes," Rose winked.

"Did your mom name you Rose because roses are her favorite flower?"

"Pretty obvious, right? Eh, there are worse names."

"I read somewhere that Jarred means Rose in Hebrew. Well, that's one of the translations, anyway. I hope it's actually true."

"Yeah, me too!"

"So what are *your* favorite flowers?"

"Sunflowers. Especially the bicolored ones. They're unconventional, I like them."

"Is that why you rowed in college? Because it was unconventional? I hardly know any female rowers."

"I guess that was part of it, but mostly it was just a

hell of a lot of fun. I guess my bucket list has a few 'unconventional' things on it. I want to do a road trip across America in a truck, for example."

"Like a pick-up truck? Interesting. What else?"

"Hm... I always wanted to live in California. Don't ask me why, I mean, I'm already thirty and I've never even visited. It just sounds so fantastic. Warm all the time, beach right outside your door."

"Not to be a dream-killer, but August in San Francisco feels almost like winter. Sixty degrees and foggy. Not great."

"Where else have you visited?"

"I was in the South Pacific a few weeks ago. It was incredible. You can't even imagine how blue the water is there."

"I'll bet... sounds nice! So where would you want to live if not England?"

"Australia. Ideally the West Coast. I like the people there. They're a lot more relaxed than we are. I suppose it could get on my nerves after a while, but I think I'd enjoy it for a while."

"West Coast, hm? Got any photos?"

"Millions. I'll show you next time. Got something else planned for today. Are you finished eating?" They'd managed a little over half of the food.

"Yeah, thanks. It was great." Rose wiped her mouth with the starched white napkin, pleased with herself for having made it through the meal without globbing sauce anywhere it wasn't supposed to go. "What exactly have you got planned, then?" Not likely to be any roof terraces in their future—not with Jarred's fear of heights, anyway.

"I'll show you in a minute. I hope you like it." He grinned from ear to ear, seemingly sure that she would.

CHAPTER 22

ROSE

"Wait, there's an actual movie theater *in his apartment building?*" Mandy gaped. It was just after ten in the morning, and Mandy and Rob had just arrived to drop off Ella.

"Yeah, I guess the tenants can just reserve it whenever they like."

"How romantic. Did you guys spend the whole movie making out?" Mandy grinned impishly.

"Most of it," Rose admitted. She'd also spent the night at Jarred's, though she'd made an early exit since he had things to do that morning. "But I have *Breakfast at Tiffany's* memorized backwards and forwards, so it didn't matter that I didn't catch much of it this time."

"You must be sad that he's going to Manchester soon."

"I don't want to bitch and moan or anything, but it's really not going to be easy. I'm not good at long-distance."

"Well. You've also never done it."

"True. And it's way too soon to call it a relationship, anyway. I just… like spending time with Jarred, that's all."

"You think you're in love?"

"I dunno? I had a crush on him for years even though I barely knew him, so now I'm just working on swapping out fantasy-man for actual-man in my head. I want to get to know the real Jarred and give him a chance. Not just my idealized version of him, know what I mean?"

"Sure, of course. But you're also really observant; you notice things about people that other don't. So I bet your 'fantasy' Jarred isn't all that far from reality. And if he's not always super open with you, well, Rob doesn't always tell me every little thing, and he's not even in the public eye—just imagine what it must be like to grow up in a billionaire family! You probably don't ever know who your real friends are… anyway, to me it sounds like things are going great with you and him."

"Ever the optimist," Rose added, and then blurted out: "So I went to lunch with Aaron the other day."

Mandy looked horrified. "What? Why?"

"He just wouldn't take no for an answer," Rose sighed.

"Did you at least make it crystal clear to him that it's over?"

Rose shook her head.

"Maybe you should start by figuring out how you feel about Aaron. Otherwise, you and Jarred are never going to get anywhere, right? Anyway, we'd better get going. Call us if anything comes up!"

As if on cue, Ella came scurrying over and launched herself into Rose's arms. "Aunt Rose! Aunt Rose! Did you see how fast I can run? Daddy only caught me one time!"

"How about we say bye to Mommy and Daddy now, and you and I go to the aquarium? Does that sound good?"

"Yeah! Let's go!"

"We'll send you photos," Rose said, hugging Mandy tightly. "Don't worry about us—enjoy your time together!" If she said it often enough, maybe Mandy would actually take the advice to heart. Mandy was even worse at relaxing than Rose.

Rob sidled over to give Rose a quick hug; only then did Rose notice how tired he looked. Not unhappily so, but this vacation was probably a welcome break for him as well. "Drive carefully," Rose told him. "And let me know if the hotel lives up to the reviews."

"It's by the beach—that alone is worth the trip. Even in January."

Ella gave her father one more impassioned hug, and Rose grinned a little—she'd been expecting the goodbye to take a while. Then she and Ella stood by the curb and waved until Mandy and Rob's car disappeared from view.

"Okay, let's go! Which fish are you most excited to see?"

"The sharks and the jellyfish. And Nemo and Dorie, they're sooo cute!"

Ella talked a blue streak the whole way to the transit station; in the cable car, she gaped in astonishment at the city below, giving Rose her first great photo opportunity.

JARRED

Hampstead was only a 30-minute tube ride from his apartment; the Rutherfords' four-story house was just off Hampstead Heath. Marlene was already outside, and Finn and Marie arrived right on time as well. Jarred introduced them all.

"I'm glad you're back. We missed you!" Marie gave him a hug and a kiss on the cheek. Green-eyed and dark-haired, Marie was a real firecracker who could hold her own in any situation. It was no secret that Marie, a banker, brought home the bigger paycheck; Finn would never be able to afford this place on his software-analyst salary.

"I missed you too."

"Well, then, try not to flee the country again, yeah? Your friends are here for you when you're going through a rough time. Got it?" She punctuated the last question with a smack on the arm.

Jarred laughed and nodded before turning his attention to the property. "So this is it, hm?"

"I'll lead the way!" Marlene turned to Jarred. "Did you remember the contract?"

"Of course, you didn't think I would?"

"What I think is that you seem a bit distracted. So what do you think? Pretty nice, right? Just don't get in a fistfight over it or anything," she laughed.

The brick exterior seemed like it was in good condition, and the small front yard looked well-kept.

"There's parking spots, too," she went on. "But let's go inside, it's a little chilly today."

Jarred considered mentioning how underdressed Marlene was for January—knee-length skirt, thin silk stockings, strappy heels—but then he realized he'd never seen Marlene in anything *but* skirts and heels.

Too bad he couldn't have brought Rose along. She'd probably have enjoyed this.

Joe answered the door. Though impeccably dressed in a gray suit, he looked far more relaxed than he had the previous time. Once Marlene had finished making the introductions, Jill started showing Marie and Finn around. "The ground floor here has a nice open kitchen," she said, "and then there's the living room, the dining room, and a guest bathroom. The five bedrooms are on the three upper floors; two have en-suite baths, and then there's a bathroom in the third-floor hall as well."

Jarred explored the ground floor while the others went upstairs. The décor was modern and elegant, with light-colored wood floors that gave the place a warm, cozy feel. The purple dining room chairs weren't really Jarred's style, but he also didn't have to sit on them. No backyard—just a small stone courtyard—but it probably didn't matter too much, with the park so close. Incredibly, Joe and Jill were asking around four hundred thousand pounds less than they offered for Jarred's condo, even though this house was exponentially bigger. Apparently location mattered more than he'd realized.

"Shall we get the business part out of the way?" Joe seemed glad to have an excuse to let Jill handle the tour.

"Sure... I've got the contract here; take all the time you need looking it over. I've signed it already, so if everything looks good to you, just sign this copy and mail it back to me."

"Will do. So will I be seeing you at the Sheraton next week?"

"No, my father's usually the one attending those." Him and Sean. The annual charity fundraiser at the Sheraton was reserved for business-world bigwigs, and Sean was clearly standing between him and anything too high on the career ladder. Back in the day, it would have bothered Jarred that he wasn't going; these days, he saw the event in a different light.

"Oh, well, your father's sent his regrets, so I'd be glad to see you there instead. I know Campbell Investments sponsors more than one table, but my wife and I would love to have you at ours... By the way, that hotel you recommended in New York was an excellent find! I've never shown up to an important meeting so relaxed."

Jarred knew that being invited to the fundraiser was an honor, and Marlene had mentioned more than once that Joe was kind of a big deal. Probably best not to risk offending him. Jarred forced a smile and accepted the invitation with a firm handshake. He'd have to go solo, since he couldn't exactly take Rose, but that was probably just as well—there was no topping those charity events for sheer decadent excess. So far, every one he'd ever attended had rubbed him the wrong way. He wasn't jaded enough to put the sick, suffering people supposedly benefiting from those charity events out of his mind while he stuffed his face with pricey food and fancy champagne. The jarring contrast between the two sent cold chills down his spine.

"There you are, Jarred." Marlene strode in gracefully. "Everything all right?"

"Everything's great," Joe replied. "Jarred's going to join us at the Sheraton on Tuesday."

"Wonderful! Arthur has pressing obligations he can't reschedule, such a pity."

"I'm sure Sean and Jarred will do a fine job of representing him." Joe's phone rang; he glanced down at it and then excused himself.

"You don't have to go if you don't want to," Marlene whispered as soon as Joe was out of earshot.

"It's a once-in-a-lifetime opportunity," Jarred said half-heartedly, trying to convince himself.

"There's always more than one opportunity. That whole... social scene makes me sick. I mean, how many more foundations does Arthur have to found before they'll finally leave him in peace? He's nearly seventy, for God's sake."

"So there are no pressing obligations he can't reschedule?"

"Tickets to *Mamma Mia* in the West End! The tickets were thirty pounds each, and we're going out for Italian beforehand, and afterward we'll go to bed with perfectly clear consciences. I can't stand decadence, and neither can Arthur."

Jarred also preferred donating directly rather than through charity events. He abruptly realized he hadn't been to a single casino since Vegas, which was over a month ago. He hadn't missed poker in the slightest. Oh, maybe he ought to just suck it up and drop by the event... Rose wasn't available today, and the nursing home they were fundraising for could obviously use the money.

"If you do decide to go, you should probably talk to your father first," Marlene remarked. "He can give you tips on who's worth talking to and who's just an opportunist. Come on, let's go look at the house—you're here to help your friends make a decision, right?"

Crazy—Marlene sometimes actually sounded like a mom. The fact that Jarred was only a few years younger didn't seem to bother her at all.

ROSE

She couldn't believe they'd spent almost three hours at the aquarium, and Ella hadn't complained about being tired once. Good thing they'd eaten lunch beforehand.

"Nemo was so pretty! When I'm big, I'm gonna swim to Nemo. Hopefully he'll wait for me."

"I loved the coral reef, too. The colors were magical!" She'd never seen a manmade coral reef before. Then again, it wasn't like she'd traveled anywhere with coral reefs, manmade or otherwise.

"Will you draw me a picture? But everything has to look exactly like Nemo. Can you do that, Aunt Rose? Aunt Rose? Aunt Rose, can you do that?"

"Sure, of course." Rose was only half-listening, because she'd just spotted Aaron jogging in their direction. He was wearing sunglasses and staring at his watch, probably checking whether he was making his planned run times. Aaron had always been ambitious in everything, and athletic achievement was no exception. He did the London Marathon every year, so he was likely training for it now... and since today was Saturday, he was probably doing twelve miles. And of course he didn't look up until he was practically nose-to-nose with Rose.

Ella tugged her coat impatiently, trying to get her attention.

"Okay, honey, okay. We'll draw some pretty pictures later, what do you think of that?"

"Rose?" Aaron stopped, pulled out his ear buds, and stopped his watch.

"Hi, Aaron."

"Rose, what a coincidence!" he exclaimed.

"Yep, sure is," she replied unenthusiastically. "Sorry, we need to get going—don't want to interrupt your training."

"Oh, that doesn't really matter."

Since when? Rose had never met anyone as obsessive about training goals as Aaron, though it was probably appropriate considering what insane fitness goals he set for himself.

"Heyy, who's that hiding behind you?" Aaron said in a higher, babyish voice. He'd probably seen the little hands clutching Rose's coat.

"That's Ella. Mandy's daughter?"

"Ella! Of course!" He knelt down. "Wow, you've grown so much! Do you remember your Uncle Aaron?"

"Mommy said you went to America and made Aunt Rose cry." Ella narrowed her eyes at him.

"Did she? Well, I'm sorry. I'll try to make it better. How's Mr. Fox?"

"Good, but she's a girl, not a boy. She had babies," Ella added solemnly. "I'll show you next time."

Aaron put on his most charming smile.

Yeah, Ella had liked him, too. Not only had he given her a stuffed animal, but he'd also enjoyed playing with her. At the time, Rose had considered it a plus.

"Ella, honey, we need to go."

Aaron straightened up and checked his watch, brows knitted. His strict training plan didn't allow for such long breaks. "Ella, it was very nice seeing you. Rose, I'll be in touch." But he only got a few feet before stopping and jogging back to them. "Oh, by the way, Rose, will you be at the Sheraton ball this Tuesday?"

Was that a serious question? Not that the whole industry hadn't been talking about it obsessively or anything, but everyone also knew that you had to be more than a piddly middle manager to get an invite. "No, Arthur and Sean Campbell will be in attendance."

"Rumor has it that the old man won't be there. Maybe he's in the mood for something else."

Why did that sound so dirty coming out of Aaron's mouth?

"I'd be delighted if you'd come with me."

What the hell? Jesus, what would people say?

"It's quite common for invitees to bring a guest," he went on.

Joining the Campbell Investments top brass was probably not in her future—not that she wanted to remind Aaron of that or anything—but the offer was still tempting. It'd be a fantastic networking opportunity, if nothing else... and she'd be old and gray before Sean would ever get around to inviting her. Well, she did have a few gray hairs already, and... no, dammit, don't go on a tangent, let's not forget about the main problem here. Aaron. He was her ticket in, which would mean she'd have to be nice to him, and she'd be in his debt. Or would it make them even, because he cheated on her? And vehemently denied it... whatever, forget it, been over this a million times already.

"Let me know on Monday, then." His lips brushed her cheek, which felt *way* too good. Again. As she stood there watching Aaron jog away, she suddenly swore she could hear Mandy's voice, asking her what a guy would do in her shoes. Which came first, her career or her injured pride? It wasn't like accepting the invite automatically meant she had to sleep with Aaron. And Sean was the one who'd put her in charge of the T&H Invest meeting, so he had no reason to object.

"Aunt Rose, I'm hungry." Ella tugged on Rose's coat. Eesh, no, no whining, whining was what she'd been trying to avoid.

"There's a café over there. Do you know what you want for teatime?"

"Chocolate cake! That's my favorite," Ella added, looking serious. Rose knew that, of course. "I want to be the flower girl, I've never been the flower girl before."

"Um, what do you mean?" She'd obviously missed something here.

"Aunt Rose, can we please, please go on the Ferris wheel? Pleeease?"

"Honey, the line is way too long. It would be dark outside before we got our turn."

"Oh, yeeah, I want to go on the Ferris wheel when it's dark! Please, please, please?"

"Let's go to the café first, and then we'll see. Okay?"

Ella stared at the Ferris wheel for a moment, but then nodded, to Rose's immense relief. "And I want a pink dress with a ribbon right here, okay?" Ella pointed to around chest height. "And the skirt down to here—" Ella tapped her leg just below the knee. "—so that I can wear pretty socks. And I want my hair in big, fat curls. Okay?"

"Ella, honey, whose flower girl do you want to be?"

Ella stopped in her tracks, brow furrowed.

Hm. Let's try that again. "Who's getting married?"

"You and Uncle Aaron. He's not in America now, so you don't have to cry anymore. Now you can have your wedding, and I'll be the flower girl. Mm, I can't wait for cake!"

Oh, Lord. "Ella, honey, Aaron and I aren't getting married. But if I ever do get married, you'll definitely be the flower girl. Promise."

"When?"

"I don't know, sorry."

Ella stuck out her lower lip.

Though Rose felt weirdly guilty at having squashed her goddaughter's flower-girl dreams, she also didn't want to lie to her. "Wanna go to a café?"

Ella nodded.

Rose sighed in relief. Hopefully the café had chocolate cake—otherwise she'd have another crisis on her hands, and she wasn't sure whether she'd be able to avert that one as easily.

"I can't wait to ride the Ferris wheel."

CHAPTER 23

JARRED

Marie and Finn liked the house in Hampstead Heath, but they wanted to sleep on it before making an offer. The most obvious question was whether they even needed five bedrooms—Jarred had never heard them talk about wanting kids. Well, when would he have heard it? Right, okay, yes, he'd been gone for two years, he couldn't exactly claim to know much about them. Anyway, he did know they planned on getting married, so there was a certain degree of likelihood that they also planned on starting a family.

Jarred assumed those were the kinds of things people normally began thinking about when they were pushing thirty. Which meant Rose was probably thinking about them, too. Kids. God, what a huge responsibility. The very idea nearly gave Jarred a panic attack.

He paced around his living room, but after twenty minutes of completely failing to relax, he grabbed his coat again and practically ran out of his apartment. Tonight was definitely a casino night. He felt at home in casinos. As soon as he had those cards in hand, he'd be cool as a cucumber.

The London City streets were desolate on weekends. His feet carried him toward the Thames as though on autopilot; before long, he'd lost all sense of time. His phone vibrated, and he took the call without even looking at the display. "Hello?"

"Jarred? Benjamin. I got your new number from Finn. Hey, I'd love it if you came down to the club tonight. I'm having a belated birthday party, got a fucking awesome DJ coming. Bring your girlfriend, too."

"What girlfriend?" God, who were they claiming he was dating now? He hadn't seen any tabloid headlines lately but... ugh, when his dad got wind of this, he'd have to go around doing damage control yet again. You don't need his credit card anymore. Huh. That was true... weird, how had he forgotten? He was really out of it today. The one thing he did know was that he had zero desire to go to the club.

"That girl you were with when I saw you. Rose, right? Wasn't she your girlfriend? If not, even better, *definitely* bring her."

What the hell...?! "I'll see if I can make it." Standard non-answer.

"I'd love to see you. Great to have you back, man, we missed you. Later!"

The brief call left Jarred with a guilty conscience. His gaze drifted to the Ferris wheel on the opposite side of the Thames. It would be dark soon... maybe a change of perspective would help clear his head? His fear of heights was a lot easier to manage when it was dark out. Luckily, he'd brought his wallet, and his emergency cash would be enough for one ticket. Not having a credit card meant he couldn't buy the ticket in advance and skip the line, but he wasn't about to let that deter him.

Twenty minutes later, Jarred was at the foot of one of the world's largest Ferris wheels. He'd been ten when it was first built, and he'd have killed to ride on it at the time. Well, better late than never.

The people around him didn't seem to mind the wait; they chatted happily and took selfies. Lovers cuddled, older kids played on their phones. Only the littlest children looked impatient. He sympathized with them—patience was not currently his strong suit. One little girl was crying loudly enough that people were turning around to look. The girl's mother knelt in front of her, trying to placate her.

Then she turned around, and Jarred realized to his surprise that it was Rose.

"Honey, the line is way too long. What do you say we go on the Ferris wheel next time? Ella, please, let's go, honey."

The kid was having none of it. In fact, she looked like she was about to throw herself on the ground in a full-blown tantrum.

"Rose! Rose!" She probably couldn't hear him, not with the kid screaming at glass-shattering frequencies. Even this far away, he winced a little.

"Do you want us to save your spot?"

Jarred blinked. The young couple standing behind him gave him sympathetic smiles. Maybe they thought he was the girl's father. Well, he definitely needed to help Rose—she looked as overwhelmed as he felt. "Um, thank you, that would be great." He hurried over to Rose. "Hey, there you are! I've been waiting for you guys this whole time."

Rose glanced up, and then her eyes widened in astonishment when she realized that Jarred had joined them.

He put on his brightest smile, so as not to frighten the little girl. Well, he'd achieved one thing, anyway: the kid had abruptly stopped crying, and was now staring at him, looking equally astonished. "It's almost our turn, come on! By the way, I'm Jarred, and you must be Ella." By some miracle, he'd remembered Ella's name. It drew a smile and a nod from the girl.

ROSE

Jarred had obviously been sent by Heaven. Rose had been at a complete loss for what to do with Ella—once she'd gotten the Ferris wheel into her head, there'd been no talking her out of it. Rose wasn't even sure what moms normally did in such cases. Just drag the kid away? What if Ella refused to walk? She couldn't exactly carry her all the way home... and even if she could, Ella might kick and scream, or break free and run away or something. But giving in just to shut her up didn't seem like the right move, either. They'd already been to the aquarium, eaten lunch at a restaurant, and gone out for a big piece of cake. Even Rose would consider that a gold star day. So why was Ella fighting her now? Just tired, maybe?

"Come on, we have to hurry." Jarred helped Rose up and took Ella's hand; the little girl put up no resistance. "So what did you do today, Ella?"

Ella launched into a long, rambling recap, mixing up many of the details along the way. She was an absolute angel now; her tears were forgotten, and she was delighted at all the attention Jarred was showing her. This probably went against every parenting guidebook in the world, but Rose was just grateful for the chance to catch her breath. And she'd only had Ella for six hours. How the hell did single parents do it? *Respect.*

"Did you know that the London Eye is the biggest Ferris wheel in Europe? It's more than four hundred feet tall, and it has twenty-eight cars. The ride lasts more than half an hour, and it never stops, it just keeps going and going. So as soon as the door opens, we have to get in really fast. Think you can do that?"

"Of course. But I want to sit by the window."

The entire car was glass except for the floor, so Rose didn't see that being a problem. Mostly, she was just wondering what Jarred was doing here—and how he was going to manage the London Eye when he was afraid of heights. But she couldn't very well ask him in front of Ella.

"Aunt Rose," Ella said, turning toward her. "Are you guys getting married?" Oh, no. Every time she averted one crisis, another developed. How was she supposed to explain who Jarred was? They were acting too friendly to claim they were just coworkers, but if she told Ella that Jarred was her boyfriend, then her mother, Mandy's mother, and everyone else in Watford would hear it by tomorrow.

"We work together. Jarred's new in town, and when I told him that you were spending the weekend with us, we were trying to think of fun things you might want to do." She cast an uncertain glance at Jarred. It was just a little fib, right? Not technically a lie—she *had* wondered aloud to Jarred whether Ella would enjoy the aquarium or the zoo more.

"And I've never been on the London Eye before, but I always wanted to when I was a kid, so we thought maybe we'd all do it together. But we wanted it to be a surprise." Jarred played along so convincingly that even Rose bought the story. He spoke in a warm, affectionate tone that made her sigh a little. Her, and probably every other woman within earshot.

Jarred also insisted on paying, of course. Rose didn't like it one bit—Ella's ticket alone was over twenty pounds. She'd make it up to him, somehow, someday.

Once they were in the car, among the other passengers, Jarred took Rose's hand—a tiny gesture that send tingles through her. She wished she could nestle against him. And kiss him. And forget the world around them. When she closed her eyes, she could feel his warm skin on hers... taste him on her tongue... as his hands explored every inch of her skin...

"Aunt Rose! Look how small the buildings are."

Jarred let go of her hand with lightning speed, as though it were made of hot coals. Rose suppressed the slight pang in her heart as she joined Ella at the window. "The people look like ants," she said. "Look how tiny the boats are."

Ella stretched out her little hand as if to touch the sky. "I want to be a bird so I can fly up whenever I want and look down at everybody. Will you draw me a picture? Where I'm a bird, and you're in the Ferris wheel, watching me? Can you draw, too?" she asked, abruptly turning toward Jarred.

"Nope, 'fraid not."

"That's okay. I'll tell my mommy to put you in my

book. Normally I don't like boys, but you're nice. We can go on adventures."

"What kind of book?"

"My mommy wrote a book about me, but I have a different name in it. I'm Maisie. I got to help her pick my book name, and Aunt Rose draws the adventures I go on. Cool, huh?"

Crap. There's that cat out of the bag.

"I'd like to see the book sometime." Jarred glanced at Rose.

She couldn't tell if he was displeased or merely curious. Either way, her days of hiding her side hustle were apparently numbered. Hopefully she wouldn't get in trouble at work.

"Oh, you can buy it at the bookstore," Ella explained in a businesslike tone before turning her attention back to the view, humming happily.

JARRED

Rose was avoiding his eyes, and Jarred was dying to know why. Was she embarrassed that Ella had told him about her illustration work? It didn't seem to affect her productivity at Campbell Investments, at least not that he'd noticed. Hell, she was usually the first one to arrive and the last to leave. She had a sharp mind and an open ear... if anything, she expected too much of herself. He'd just have to bring the book up sometime when they were alone.

Ella was a sweet kid, and she and Rose seemed very close. He enjoyed just watching the two of them together. He kept to the middle of the car, well away from the windows, but even from here, the view was phenomenal. His problems genuinely seemed smaller up here. As long as he kept ignoring the queasy feeling in the pit of his stomach. Or trying to.

"Aw, too bad, we're back down again," Ella announced, jolting him out of his reverie.

"We really do need to get going, Ella. This time we can take the tube, and change trains in Canary Wharf… would you like that?"

"Oh, yeah! Okay, let's go. Bye, Jarred!"

"Bye, Ella, nice to meet you."

Ella was already dragging Rose away by the hand; Rose could only shrug apologetically and wave goodbye. He decided to call her tomorrow—maybe they could at least spend Sunday night together.

He was still going back and forth on whether to stop by Benji's birthday party. But he still had a few hours left to make up his mind, since there was no point showing up at the club before eleven.

Next stop: bookstore. He was curious about Maisie's adventures.

Late that evening, Jarred's cab pulled up outside an imposing Victorian townhouse in South Kensington.

Nothing about the exterior suggested that one of London's most exclusive gentlemen's clubs lay on the other side of that brass-fitted maroon door—except, perhaps, the two men in dark frock coats out front, who murmured a polite greeting in chorus as Jarred approached and knocked. The woman who opened the door was in period costume as well: a long, high-necked dress with a massive hoop skirt. To his right was a tiny reception desk, where a second woman in the same outfit gave him a brief nod in greeting. Discretion was everything here—photography was strictly forbidden, for example—so although the woman obviously recognized him on sight, she did him the favor of skipping the small talk that normally followed as soon as anyone realized who he was. Once upon a time, Jarred had gotten a kick out of being a Campbell; he'd thought of himself as a big deal, as though he'd somehow done something to deserve all that privilege. These days, it made him uncomfortable that people knew him just because of his last name.

The club hadn't changed a bit. The deep blue carpet in the foyer looked like it had just been put in yesterday. Up ahead was a winter garden full of tropical plants, the only room in the club where smoking was allowed. A burst of laughter rang out briefly as someone opened the door.

The building itself was a maze of narrow hallways and stairwells, but every room was a paragon of elegance, with fine art lining the walls. Jarred never knew who he'd bump into around the next corner:

CEOs, politicians, media personalities, world-class athletes... he'd even spotted the occasional royal.

Jarred assumed that Benjamin had rented the downstairs area, which featured a state-of-the-art dance club.

"Jarred? What are you doing here?" His ex-girlfriend Victoria moved into his field of view and immediately hugged him in delight. "When did you get back, and why didn't you call?" She pinched his side in playful outrage.

"Well, I'm here now," Jarred replied, extricating himself from her embrace. Victoria was the touchy-feely type; it didn't normally bother him, but tonight it felt weird and somehow wrong. They'd known each other forever. Victoria was an only child, a banker's daughter, so the tabloids had all dubbed them "London's next power couple" for the year they were together. Marrying her would have made Campbell Investments more influential than ever. Hm, oh well. They'd gone back to just being friends a few years ago, though the gossip hounds somehow refused to believe it—there were always random articles claiming they'd rekindled their romance. Probably slow news weeks or something.

With her long, dark hair and symmetrical features, Vicky looked like a model; she hardly needed what little makeup she wore. Her blood-red, lace-trimmed bodycon midi dress flattered her curves perfectly, though there weren't many of those to flatter—she barely had an ounce of fat on her.

Probably still working with that personal trainer. Her high-heeled strappy sandals displayed her pedicured feet.

Jarred had since developed a taste for more natural women, the kind with wild hair and a penchant for lemon muffins, the ones who rolled over when the alarm went off and weren't above wearing ugly boots to keep their feet dry on the way to the office and... yikes, Rose really was taking up *all* the space in his head.

"You're not very chatty tonight. It's okay, though, let's just have lunch sometime. Party's getting started downstairs; are you coming now or would you rather look around up here first?"

"No, I'll come down with you." He was only here to tell Benji happy birthday and treat himself to one beer.

The dance floor was full of familiar faces. Jarred couldn't even begin to guess how many nights they'd all spent down here, partying until they dropped. His life had been one long, loud, intoxicated rush; whenever he'd come down, he'd do another shot, another line, whatever, anything to keep it going. He'd usually wake up in some random place with no memory of the past several hours. Stupid, stupid. Could have ended in so many different kinds of disaster. Not that he'd have given a shit either way.

"Jarred, there you are. I wasn't sure if you'd make it." Benji's eyes were already glazed; his grin looked like more of a grimace.

"Happy birthday. What are you having?"

"Thanks. Anything and everything, as long as it's high-proof. This is my last birthday before the big three-oh, which I guess is when I finally have to grow up." Benji laughed almost hysterically, swaying a little. Knowing Benji, he'd be too drunk to talk in about half an hour. Jarred wondered if maybe he ought to stick around and make sure he got home in one piece.

"Dance with me!" Vicky's breath tickled his ear. She snuggled against him from behind, encircling his chest with her arms. Jarred felt the heat radiating from her body.

The DJ started blasting "Without You," by Avicii. Brief, fragmented memories of a woman in a plain T-shirt and shorts flashed through his mind, but the loud, jubilant singing on the dance floor wiped them away again—hell, who wouldn't let themselves get swept up in this excitement?

Maybe just once more for old times' sake.

CHAPTER 24

ROSE

Jarred hadn't been in touch all weekend, and eventually Rose decided to not-respond in kind. She wasn't trying to chase him or anything. Of course, it was possible that Jarred hadn't called because he didn't want to bother her while Ella was there, and Rose was just being childish.... Well, whatever. A little distance was probably a good thing. Space to sort out her own feelings.

After Mandy and Rob picked Ella up late Sunday afternoon, Rose set out for Greenwich Park to enjoy the sunshine. Bundled up in a scarf, a warm hat, and woolen gloves, she tromped to her favorite spot in the neighborhood: the planetarium, which had the world's best view of London City. On the way, her thoughts revolved around Mandy and Rob. The weekend away had obviously done them good; they'd been absolutely beaming when they came for Ella.

The streets were mostly empty, and when Rose reached the planetarium, she realized to her surprise that she was completely alone. She took a deep breath and then turned around.

The view gave her goosebumps every time. She and Aaron had come here often; he'd stand with his arms around her, giving her affectionate little kisses from time to time. So romantic. Sigh. She was supposed to let him know by tomorrow whether she'd come to the charity ball. The thought of accepting the invitation felt super weird. Jarred probably wouldn't be pleased. Rose figured she ought to at least tell Jarred that she was considering taking Aaron up on the offer. Just out of common courtesy.

Her phone vibrated. Text from Mandy.

Mandy: Ella's so keyed up! You didn't mention that Jarred joined you on the Ferris wheel... you think that was a good idea?
Rose: No, but it also wasn't planned. Guess I'd better avoid my mom for a while ;-)
Mandy: Better clear some things up with Jarred first. Check this out.
It was a link to a tabloid article. Rose grimaced.
Rose: Do I have to?
Mandy: You don't HAVE to do anything. But you might want to call him.

Great, now there was no way she couldn't click on the link, even though whatever it said was obviously going to make her unhappy. The headline wasn't too worrisome—Jarred's back, blah blah blah —but then the article talked about Victoria Thompson. Rose had heard of her, of course. Jarred's old girlfriend. The article was a bunch of speculation on whether they were back together, as evidenced by a photo of Jarred leaving a private club, and Victoria departing a short time later.

Wait, that was it? Rose could only scratch her head. So two people leaving the same building meant they were having an affair? The rest of the article was mostly theories on where the two of them went next.

On a whim, Rose decided to give Jarred a call, but it went straight to voicemail. Hm. Now what?

"Hey, it's me. Ella went home. She's still so excited —I think the Ferris wheel impressed her even more than the aquarium. I just wanted to say thanks. Call me back if you have time; otherwise, I'll see you tomorrow. Miss you." She hung up.

Jarred didn't call back.

JARRED

Monday morning. He was in the office, staring blankly at his computer screen. What a bizarre weekend. He'd partied all night on Saturday and then crashed hard until late on Sunday, which had completely screwed up his sleep schedule; after spending most of Sunday night pacing around his condo, he'd finally given up at about four that morning and gone for a jog along the Thames. He'd certainly have gone over to Rose's if he'd gotten her message sooner. He felt at peace when he was around her, like he'd arrived at his destination. In retrospect, going to the club had been completely stupid. He didn't belong there anymore, it wasn't his world. Being there didn't do anything for him anymore, apart from leave him feeling drained. Was this what a quarter-life crisis felt like?

Setting his jaw, he reached for his phone and called Alice.

"Jarred? What the hell are you calling me in the middle of the night for?"

"I can't hear you, are you talking into the pillow?"

"Dumbass. What's up, kid?"

"Where are you?"

"London," she said with a loud yawn. "Jet lag is killing me."

"Eight hours' time difference, so you'll be back to your old self in eight days."

"What did I do to deserve your babble this early in the morning?"

"I have a problem."

"What happened? You and Vicky forget to use a condom?"

"What? No! Jesus, where'd you get that?"

"Just joking, kid. I'd love to hear about your problem. Your place or mine? Tonight?"

"I'll be at Dad and Marlene's this evening. Want to come?"

"Sure, should be fun."

"She's a good cook."

"That's a plus, of course."

"See you there."

When he spotted Rose at the entrance, he felt like jumping up and kissing her, but he remained motionless as she gave him a brief nod before picking a desk at the other end of the room. Maybe they could grab a cup of tea together later.

Before he had a chance to ask, he got a message from Sean, commanding Jarred to report to the executive floor immediately. Sean had sent it through the Intranet messaging system, which showed Jarred's status as present, so he couldn't just claim he hadn't arrived yet. Better to just grab the bull by the horns. He already knew what Sean wanted.

As usual, his half-brother was seated at his gigantic desk, surveying his royal domain.

"You wanted to see me?"

"When were you planning to inform me that you were coming to the charity ball instead of Dad?"

"Today."

"Huh. See, Marlene has known since Saturday. How strange."

This conversation was already draining what little energy he had. Sean really did remind Jarred of a raging bull; Jarred was half expecting him to flare his nostrils and stomp his hoof... er, foot.

"What's going on with you and Vicky?" Sean continued.

"Nothing."

"You do know that she'll be there tomorrow as well, yes?"

"What do you want me to say, Sean? You insisted that I come back to England, and now I'm here, and you can't stand it."

"Just... don't cause any trouble."

Jarred snorted in frustration. "I'm not a child."

"No, that you aren't," Sean agreed, which only confused him even more. "How was your trip to Manchester?"

"Good. I'll let you know when I've made up my mind." Obviously, he and Jarred were never going to stand there clapping each other on the shoulder in appreciative delight, eyes sparkling as they bounced new ideas off one another. But Jesus, they were brothers. Where was the warmth and affection that other families had? Surely they were more to each other than just... coworkers?

"See you this evening, then." Sean turned back to his computer, seemingly dismissing Jarred from the conversation.

Fresh air. I need some fresh air. Now.

ROSE

Jarred disappeared without even acknowledging her existence. Rose had been hoping to talk to him before everyone else arrived. Guess not. Well, whatever, she had better things to do than wait around for him. Sure would have been nice if she at least knew whether he'd made a decision about Manchester. Did he still work for her or not?

She started swiping through her messages in frustration. Hopefully Jarred would be back soon and they could talk. An hour later, he still hadn't returned, and Rose's patience finally ran out. Impulsively, she texted Aaron to accept the invite. She wanted to go back to focusing on her career; men were nothing but a distraction, and this game of hide-and-seek with Jarred was the icing on the cake. She wasn't going to tolerate this kind of crap anymore.

So why are you just now asking yourself whether it's wrong of you to go to the event with Aaron?

Oh, shut up, stupid conscience.

She'd have to go shopping for a new dress tonight... and maybe stop by the hairdresser's as well? Before she could talk herself out of it, Rose booked a hair appointment and then threw herself into her work. Work was always the best medicine for broken hearts. *Broken hearts?!* She sighed and shook her head, exasperated at herself.

. . .

"Rose, you're killing me. Seriously, keep this up and I'll be able to throw our TV out. Your relationship chaos is more interesting than any soap opera I've ever seen."

"Surely you're not making fun of me."

"Maybe just a little," Mandy said with a smile. "What ever happened to good old-fashioned face-to-face conversation?"

"Are you saying you have something against notes on candy bars?" Rose asked innocently.

"Is that kind of like foreplay for you guys or what?"

"I'm starting to think you don't get out enough. We can't sit there texting each other back and forth all day—that would be way too obvious."

"Didn't you literally just decide today that you were sick of playing hide-and-seek?"

"You're using everything I say against me," Rose whined.

"Oh, it's not like you're not going to do whatever you want anyway, no matter how irrational it is. C'mon, show me the clothes you're trying on. That's why you called, isn't it?"

"Of course, that was the only reason." Rose laughed.

The first dress was black and, as required by the event organizers, floor-length. It was sleeveless, with crystals adorning the Vs in the front and back.

"That one's amazing!" Mandy exclaimed in delight.

"Amazingly expensive, too."

"Put it on, I want to see it on you."

"I just hope it doesn't make my butt look too big... or my stomach. What do you think, are my boobs too small to fill this out?"

"Are you always this difficult? Put the damn thing on already."

Rose set her phone down in the changing room before stripping to her underwear and slipping into the dress. She managed to get the zipper up without help, but one look in the mirror made it abundantly clear that there was no way she could wear a bra under this one. Once she'd peeled it off, the dress fit like a glove. Her stomach looked flat—probably thanks to the material—and the top kept her cleavage perfectly in place. This dress was worth every penny.

She picked up her phone. "Mandy, it's perfect."

"Let's see! ...Wow, the cut is awesome. I'm not sure about the color, though. Black makes you look really pale. Why don't you find something dark red or green?"

"Anything else?"

"Don't forget the lace panties. But only if they won't show through in the back."

"Okay, off I go." Once she'd peeled herself out of the dress and put her own clothes back on, she began rifling through the racks with Mandy's help. One dress seemed like it was designed for a pregnant woman, another looked like a curtain, a third was too short, and a deep-blue dress with feather-light fabric was so long that Rose nearly tripped on the hem.

"Wait! Stop!" Mandy exclaimed. "What's that?"

"A princess dress," Rose whispered. She'd just spotted it as well. "Same price as the black one," she added in disappointment.

"Put it on, put it on!"

The bodice of the burgundy-red dress was embroidered down to the hips, with a plunging V in the back; the tuille skirt would be the perfect length once she had heels on.

"Girl, you'll knock 'em dead in that."

"It's not what I'd call modest."

"You don't need modest. You need 'Here I am, and I'm fucking spectacular at my job.'"

"Are you sure you want to keep writing children's' books? You'd make a hell of a life coach."

"Nah, I'm content with just telling you what to do all the time," Mandy giggled. "Plus Ella would be disappointed if Maisie didn't get to have any more adventures."

"Speaking of Maisie... I forgot to tell you that Ella told Jarred about Maisie."

"What? When? Oh, on the London Eye." Mandy looked horrified. "Are you in trouble?"

"Not yet."

"Thank God. I have a couple of new book ideas, and I don't want to have to look for a new illustrator. We're a team!"

"The best team! So let's hear them."

"What do you say we send Maisie around London and have her tell the history of the city as she goes? In a playful way, of course."

"Like how Jarred explained the Ferris wheel to her?"

"It's just an idea."

"We could connect it to different jobs," Rose suggested. She was thinking about how fascinating they'd always found skyscrapers, and pictured Maisie climbing up the scaffolding of a construction site. Not that kids were allowed on construction sites, but there was no rule against drawing them there.

"You've got that twinkle in your eye again. Show me the sketches later. Anyway, back to the dress. Buy it. What are you doing with your hair?"

"Crap, I'm going to be late to my stylist appointment. What do you think, should I have it straightened? Or just get an up-do?"

"Up-do," Mandy said. "But not too tight, it makes you look old."

"Thanks very much."

"Anytime, sweetheart. Big hugs, have fun!"

"Thanks, Mandy."

She'd just ask her stylist's advice—he'd known her hair for a while now, so he could probably come up with something simple enough for her to replicate at home.

. . .

The Oxford Street salon was open seven days a week. There was an area for normal humans and then a section for VIPs, with its own dedicated entrance. Two, actually: if the celebrity wanted to let the paparazzi snap a few photos, they went through the big glass door; if not, they'd use the back door, which was even protected by a separate gate that allowed private cars to drive up to the door unnoticed.

Rose used the normal-person entrance, which had a large window front flanked by planters. She squeezed herself and her massive shopping bag through the narrow lobby. Barely made it on time! What the hell had she been thinking, shopping at Harrod's? Traveling back and forth across the city during the evening rush, what a brilliant plan.

The lobby was empty, which was often the case here. It felt like the staff turnover here was a lot higher than most places. She didn't recognize any of the other stylists. The owner was nowhere to be seen. Probably in there drinking champagne with the VIPs. With kind of attitude, she marveled that he even managed to keep the place afloat.

Everyone seemed busy; nobody paid any attention to Rose. She saw Olivier, the shop owner, standing in the back with a slim woman. She looked like she was trying to talk him into something, but he kept shrugging apathetically. Rose couldn't make out what they were saying over the noise of the hairdryers and the chatting stylists. Suddenly, the woman turned and began walking in Rose's direction. Hm. Had they met? Her face looked awfully familiar.

"Rose, darling, so glad you're here." Olivier swanned over enthusiastically, practically shoving the woman aside in the process, and gave Rose a hello-kiss on the cheek. God, did he reek of alcohol. Rose tried to block it out by breathing through her mouth. Well, great. Hopefully the stylist would be sober, at least. "I'll do your hair myself today, what do you say? *C'est une bonne idée, n'est pas?*"

Oh, dear God, no. How was she going to talk her way out of this?

The woman beside him made a throat-clearing sound.

"Are you still here, Alice?"

"Yes, Olivier, I still need a few things... unless you only display your products for decoration?"

"Sassy little minx, aren't you? Just because you're a Campbell, it gives you absolutely no right to—"

"Right, right, I heard you the other times. Here, I made a list. I'll be happy to wait," she added in a sugary-sweet voice.

"Rose, *ma chère*, won't you be a dear and take a seat? I'll be right over."

Seriously?! No way. Was that Jarred's sister?

"What's wrong?" Alice raised an eyebrow at Rose.

"Um, nothing." Maybe she should just go. This was a disaster waiting to happen. She'd spent way too much money today already, and what good would a nice dress do her if she walked out of here with ruined hair? Olivier had disappeared into his office, which seemed like a good opportunity to flee the scene. Probably the cowardly option, but so what? "I just... realized that I have to go do something. If Olivier asks. And if not..." Rose shook her head and hurried out, never looking back until she reached the next corner, where she breathed a sigh of relief.

Okay, now what?

She felt like hailing a cab, but that would be way too expensive. Maybe she could snag an Uber? The thought of wedging herself into another underground car was not exactly filling her with joy.

"You want to tell me why you ran out like you'd been bitten by a tarantula?"

Rose nearly jumped out of her skin when she heard the voice right beside her. She spun around to discover Alice, holding a heavy-looking box and grinning from ear to ear. They were about the same height, but Alice was so thin that she looked almost fragile. Rose doubted she'd be able to haul that box around for too long.

"I've been invited to a charity fundraiser tomorrow, and I'm not about to let a drunk stylist wreck my hair."

"Trust me, you don't want Olivier wrecking your hair even when he's sober. Maybe he used to be brilliant, but his best years are well and truly behind him. Now he's all showmanship and air kisses... So, a charity fundraiser, you say?"

"Yeah. I should get going. Nice to meet you."

"We haven't met yet. I think your name was... Rose?"

"Um, yeah?"

"Which charity fundraiser?"

Was Alice always this curious? Or had Jarred mentioned Rose to his sister? Nah, doubtful. Then again... he *had* mentioned being close to Alice. But that would mean Rose meant more to Jarred than he'd cared to let on. Unless he'd told Alice that she was naïve and an easy lay...? *Oh, come on, Rose, what the hell is wrong with you?*

"Tough question, I guess?" Alice winked.

"No, no, of course not. It's at the Sheraton."

"Oh, wow, cool. Not easy to get an invite to that one. Respect! Well, I don't have my own salon yet, but what do you say I do your hair? Is that your dress for tomorrow in the bag? Because if you have it on, it'll be easier to figure out what style will look the best with it."

"Excuse me?"

"Not to toot my own horn, but I'm good."

"I'm not sure... although..."

"Although what?"

"I... um, I'm friends with Jarred and I just wanted to mention that, except now that obviously sounds like I'm trying to get some friends-and-family discount, and no, of course I would pay you, it's not like that. But if I did book you..."

Alice burst out laughing. "You're a lot different from his other friends. How did you two meet?"

"Um, well, I'm his boss," Rose whispered.

Alice stared at her in wide-eyed silence, and then a Cheshire Cat-like grin spread across her face. "C'mon, let's go! Way too cold to be standing around out here, and this box is getting heavy. Can you hail us a taxi?"

"A taxi? Yeah, of course. Where to?"

"Canary Wharf," Alice replied. "Where do you live?"

"Greenwich."

"Perfect! That's practically at your front door."

When the taxi pulled up in front of them a moment later, Rose decided to ride with Alice. She could always transfer to the cable car in Canary Wharf and ride home from there.

CHAPTER 25

JARRED

The mood at the dinner table was ice-cold. Alice had cancelled at the last minute, and Sean was pissed that their dad didn't feel like attending the upcoming charity ball. Meanwhile, Dad was pissed at Jarred for any number of reasons, but the most recent batch of tabloid headlines was obviously at the top of the list.

"Oh, come on, all of you, this is unbearable. I can't fathom why you're getting so worked up, Sean. If the thought of representing Campbell Investments alone really upsets you that much, well, you had plenty of time to ask Jarred if he'd join you. Now he's sitting at Joe Rutherford's table, which I think is a great networking move and shows what impressive connections you all have." Marlene refused to let anything spoil her good mood. Jarred was amazed that she was able to find positive sides to everything, even his family's most hopelessly ingrained behavior patterns. But eventually she'd probably run out of patience and throw in the towel, and then the next young wife would take her place.

"Victoria will be there tomorrow as well, as I'm sure you know. Who are you bringing?" Jarred's father regarded him coolly.

"Nobody, I'm going alone." Why the hell would he even ask that? Like Jarred would be that stupid. Whoever Jarred took would immediately end up on the cover of some gossip rag. "Do you actually think I'm *trying* to wind up in the tabloids over and over?" He turned to Sean. "How come they leave you alone, anyway?"

"With you, they get the sense that you might go completely off the rails at any moment, which sells more papers." Sean smiled contemptuously.

"How delightful for your future bride," Marlene murmured.

"What?" Jarred blinked in bewilderment.

"Nothing. Have you thought about where you might want to live?"

"I'm going to buy Mom's house," Jarred said, surprising even himself. He probably ought to have given something like that more than zero thought... the words had just come out somehow.

"That dump?" Sean scoffed. "Good luck with that. But you're used to throwing money out the window, so..."

"That's enough, Sean."

"Well, I think it's a wonderful idea. Let me know if you need any help." Marlene was beaming brightly again. Jarred was getting to like her more and more. He'd probably even take her up on that offer at some point.

But he'd had enough of this for one night. "I think I'll head out. Thanks for dinner." Better to make a break for it before they wound up trying to kill each other.

"Wait, let me pack you some food for Alice," Marlene said. "You're stopping by her place, aren't you?"

He hadn't actually planned on it, but it sounded like a good idea. Alice ought to know that he wanted to buy their mother's old house.

ROSE

"Come in!" Alice exclaimed, holding her apartment door open for Rose. "It's not very big, but the view is amazing."

Rose, glancing around with curious interest, dropped her massive shopping bag in the tiny hallway before pulling off her coat and boots. "Wow, I can probably see my apartment from here!" She traipsed through the living-and-dining area on her way to the narrow balcony.

"Here." Alice approached from the open kitchen area, which was directly beside the balcony door, and handed Rose a pair of binoculars.

"Do I even want to know what you normally use these for?" Rose's imagination was already running away with her.

"See that building across the way? There's a guy over there who's always walking around his apartment naked," Alice explained in a perfectly matter-of-fact tone.

Rose snorted with laughter. Alice was definitely a quirky one.

"What, you don't believe me? Wait another hour, that's when he usually gets home. Today's Monday, right? Yeah, an hour then. Right when he gets inside, he'll start stripping down. First he'll take about a ten-minute shower, and when he gets out, he'll dry off on his way to the kitchen. Then he'll get himself a beer and stand there drinking it in the middle of his living room, in all his bare-assed glory."

"Dare I ask how you found this out?"

"Random chance. I'm a tax advisor. We work murderous hours, so even when I'm sick, I'm usually still on the job, just working from home. I spotted him on one of those evenings, maybe six months ago."

"Well, it *was* a long, hot summer," Rose pointed out.

"But he's still doing it now, at the end of January."

"Doesn't your boyfriend get jealous?"

"My boyfriend? That's a long, complicated story. You want something to drink?"

"Sure, as long as I don't have to drink it naked in the living room," Rose giggled.

"Why don't you put on your new dress? You can use that room on the left, it's the guest room... and the office, and the storage room. Pull the curtains shut if you like, but nobody can see you from that side." Alice winked before turning away, chuckling.

"Gotcha. Be right back." Rose passed a tidy bathroom with a bathtub on her way down the hall. The wooden floors gave way to beige carpet in the small guest room, which had a separate balcony; the double bed had a white bedspread and plenty of emerald-green pillows. Rose wedged herself between it and the dark wooden desk to change, and then checked her reflection in the oval mirror propped against the whitewashed wooden closet door. The dress really was unbelievably pretty, she thought as she ran a reverent hand along the embroidery.

She closed her eyes and started humming "Moon River" under her breath, imagining herself dancing to it. Preferably with Jarred, nestled against him, inhaling his scent.

Then she heard a voice in the living room and froze. Was she hallucinating already? Curious, she padded into the adjacent room. Sure enough, Jarred was at the kitchen counter, holding a delicious-smelling package that hadn't been there before.

"Jarred?" Rose asked, interrupting the siblings' conversation.

"Rose? What the hell are you doing here?" Jarred gave her a look of confusion. His eyes widened as he gave her a once-over, but then his expression hardened into an icy glare. "What's going on?" He turned to Alice, who was placidly eating an apple in the kitchen.

"Nothing's going on. We just met today, at Olivier's. You remember Olivier, that horrible little toad that took over Mom's salon? Well, he categorically refuses to sell, at least for the price I'm offering. Anyway, Rose happened to be there also. I swear to God, that guy must have been drinking since breakfast. So gross."

"Random coincidence, huh? And you decided to bring a random stranger home with you?" At that, he turned to Rose. "Unless she wasn't a stranger," he added, eyeing Rose coolly.

"What planet are you on, kid? Rose had no idea I'd be there. I had to tie her up and drag her with me." Alice discarded her apple core and rinsed her hands quickly before walking over to Rose, who was rooted to the spot ten feet from Jarred. "That dress is amazing. Turn around? Wow. How much do they pay you at Campbell Investments that you could afford this? Or are you eating ramen noodles for the rest of the month now? Well, no worries, Jarred's brought us dinner tonight." Then she looked at her brother. "What's your *deal*, anyway? Your girlfriend comes out looking like a million bucks and you just stand there like an idiot without even kissing her hello."

"Why did you buy that dress?" Jarred asked Rose.

She absolutely hated that cutting tone of his. Like she was a bad little kid who needed to be punished. And what the hell was that about, anyway? She'd accepted Aaron's invitation for purely business reasons. You sure about that? Jarred had no right to tell her what to do!

"I've been invited to the Sheraton tomorrow," she replied as casually as possible.

"By who?" The question came out like a pistol shot.

Alice flinched involuntarily. "Oh, I thought you two were going together. My bad."

"By who?" Jarred repeated icily.

"How is that any of your business?! Who are you going with? Victoria?" Rose scowled and folded her arms.

She saw Jarred sneak a glance at her cleavage and swallow hard, but unfortunately, he composed himself again a moment later. "Alone."

Oh. Well. That was... surprising.

"Did Aaron invite you?"

"Alice, I'd better go," Rose said, looking at her hostess.

"Bullshit," Alice shot back. "Jarred, sit down. You know where the remote control is." Then she looked at Rose. "Take your hair down so I can figure out what to do with it. That tight bun can't be healthy for your scalp. Sit *down*, Jarred," she insisted again. "You're next. Got to have you looking at least as good as Sean in a tux, right?" she added with a wink.

Jarred ran a hand through his thick hair, seemingly conflicted on whether to stay or go. Finally, he snatched up the remote control and plopped down in front of the TV.

Alice dragged Rose into her bedroom, and then onward into the connected bathroom, where she gestured for Rose to sit on the stool. "Communication is important in a relationship, don't you think?"

"Why tell me that?" Rose scoffed. "I didn't realize Jarred and I were in a relationship, and *I'm* not the one in the newspaper with Victoria."

"And who's this Aaron?" Alice pulled the hairpins out of Rose's bun one by one, making her scalp tingle pleasantly. Her hands felt wonderful.

"My ex. Another long story." Rose was suddenly tired. Was it from Alice's head massage? She closed her eyes in bliss.

"My brother's never been good at showing his feelings—like, his real feelings. That whole thing with Victoria… I really doubt there's any truth to it. I'm sure they had their fun, but they were never a good fit. The story probably just sells well. Jarred's a real stickler for his own rules; the fact that he broke them and started seeing you, even though you work together, tells me that you mean a lot to him."

"He has a funny way of showing it," Rose muttered. "He's like a completely different person when we're alone, or when nobody's watching... but the secrecy thing isn't my style."

"It's important, though. Do you really want to have to listen to that bullshit? The rumors that you're trying to sleep your way to the top?"

"No, of course not."

"See? Okay, I think what we should do is sort of like oversized curls, and then pull a big section back on each side into a half-topknot. That way your hair is down without being in your face."

"Sounds good, but the curls will never last the night."

"Why, you have plans tonight?" Alice asked, batting her eyelashes innocently.

"No, no, I just mean my hair will do its own thing overnight." Rose didn't have to look in the mirror to know that she'd turned tomato-red.

Alice cackled. "Well, then, how about I meet you at Campbell Investments tomorrow before you go? I assume you're changing at the office, so I'll do your hair there, okay?"

"Why are you going so far out of your way for me?"

"Because I like you. Okay, send my baby bro in. We'll eat afterward. Jarred brought us chicken and couscous—our stepmom is a really good cook."

CHAPTER 26

JARRED

Jarred couldn't believe Rose was going to the charity fundraiser with her ex. And looking like an absolute goddess in that dress, too. That slimeball Aaron probably claimed it was just business. Right. This event was shaping up to be one hell of a gauntlet. He'd want to keep an eye on Rose, but he'd also be busy fending off Victoria… and everyone in the room would have him under a microscope the whole time. Sean wasn't the only one just waiting for Jarred to make a fool of himself again, even though there'd been years when the only reason he'd made headlines were his business successes. He wondered if anyone out there still remembered that.

"Hey, Alice is ready for you."

Jarred startled back to the present, and found

Rose looking at him expectantly. "I didn't know you liked casting shows," she grinned, glancing at the TV.

"What?" He hadn't even noticed what he'd put on. "Oh... uh, yeah, I love girl bands." He grinned back and held out the remote. A wave of warmth spread through him when their fingers touched; Rose closed her eyes for a moment and ran her tongue over her lips, which made his mouth go bone-dry. Well, hell, what was actually stopping him from kissing her?

He rose to his feet and pulled Rose close, caressing her cheek. She was so beautiful. Her eyes sparkled, her mouth was slightly open. She closed the remaining distance between them, touching her lips gently to his. They were incredibly soft and tasted like Rose. The kiss started slow and tender, but turned passionate almost immediately.

"I *hate* to interrupt," Alice remarked dryly.

Rose's eyes remained closed as Jarred broke the kiss and brushed his lips against hers one last time. When she opened them, her gaze reflected the same whirlwind of emotions that he felt himself. "Be right back," he whispered into her ear before following Alice into the bathroom. He'd been expecting his sister to give him the third degree, but she remained silent, focused intently on trimming his hair.

"I like her," Alice remarked as she admired her finished masterpiece in the mirror.

"You don't even know her," Jarred retorted.

"She's not like your previous girls, which is already a huge plus."

"As in, not an obvious gold-digger?" Jarred asked sarcastically.

"Exactly! Let's not keep your sweetheart waiting any longer."

They returned to the living room, where Jarred was disappointed to discover that Rose had already changed into her regular clothes, and was playing with her phone on the couch.

"Rose, let's eat, my stomach's growling. You want some of this, Jarred? Marlene sent, like, three or four days' worth of food."

He shook his head.

"Beer, then?"

"No, thanks."

"Did you drive here?"

"Yeah. Could have done without the evening traffic."

"When are you going to Silverstone?"

"Not sure. February, maybe." Probably better to figure out his financial situation before he and the Ferrari jaunted off to the racetrack.

"What's in Silverstone? Are you watching Formula One or something?" Rose furrowed her brow. "I thought that was in summer."

"There are a bunch of races there, not just Formula One," Alice explained. "I went to a vintage car race there once. It was great—some of those old roadsters can really get up and go. And they have one weekend a month where regular Joes can run the track in their own vehicles."

"You're taking the Ferrari? Isn't that... dangerous?" Rose looked uneasy.

Alice merely shrugged. "The family adrenaline junkie is actually Henry, though Jarred and Liam are close seconds."

"It's not dangerous," Jarred assured Rose and shot his sister a warning look, which she pointedly ignored as she went back to heating up dinner. Rose fixed her gaze on Jarred for so long that he grew uncomfortable and had to avert his eyes.

"That smells amazing. So your stepmom really likes to cook, hm?" Though Rose was politely changing the subject, Jarred was fairly sure that she'd bring the racing up again once they were alone.

"Oh, yeah," Alice replied. "She's an amazing cook. And she redecorated the house, too."

"Hey, what did Marlene used to work as?" Jarred suddenly realized he'd never thought to ask. She seemed to be a woman of many talents.

"She was an architect. Why? You want to get her help on Mom's house?"

"She already offered," Jarred admitted.

"Our mom lived in Notting Hill," Alice explained for Rose's benefit. "The house was pretty rundown when she died, and her beauty salon was nearly bankrupt. At the time, neither of us wanted anything to do with either; Jarred and I grabbed a few things from the house, but our dad took care of everything else. He's the one who sold the salon to Olivier."

"Who'd he sell the house to?"

"We don't know," Jarred replied. "Sean was mad when I brought it up, and Dad didn't say anything about it."

It was weird sitting here with Rose and Alice, but in a good way—almost like they'd known each other forever. His sister could be harsh when she didn't like someone, but Rose seemed to have passed the Alice test with flying colors. Almost like she'd decided Rose was her new BFF.

The rest of the evening was pretty relaxed. Rose talked about her love of flowers, and described the children's books she illustrated for her friend.

"How did such a gentle, artistic soul end up stuck at Campbell Investments?" Alice shook her head in theatrical horror.

"Same way you ended up stuck doing taxes," Jarred pointed out with a teasing grin.

"So what's your secret talent?" Rose asked him.

He was tempted to say 'nothing,' but then he changed his mind, though Alice was making subtle *shut up* signals in his direction with her eyes. "Poker." Well, yeah, Rose probably wasn't going to just swoon with incredulous delight at that particular revelation.

"Oh, cool! Do you do tournaments? I'd love to come watch you play sometime."

"Um." Her enthusiasm surprised Jarred. "No, I don't really have time for the tournament circuit. I just play for fun."

Alice's sarcastic snort was fortunately masked by Rose's cell phone. She glanced briefly at the display, furrowed her brow, and then put her phone on silent. "Oh, it's already after ten. I should get going." She began collecting the dishes, but Alice waved her off. "Now I missed your neighbor."

"You'll just have to come by some other time," Alice said with a wink.

"I'll bring you home." Jarred walked straight to the front hallway without waiting for Rose's response.

Rose gave Alice a goodbye hug and exchanged numbers with her before putting on her boots, and then slid into the coat Jarred was patiently holding for her. Once Rose was ready to go, Jarred gave Alice a quick hug and murmured a "Thanks" before striding through the door.

The elevator arrived promptly. He and Rose stepped in, and his lips were back on hers as soon as the door closed. Tragically, it was only a ten-second ride. "Not nearly enough," he whispered in Rose's ear before picking up her shopping bag with one hand and taking Rose's hand with the other as they walked to his car.

The temperature was right around freezing, and gusty winds whipped Rose's hair around.

"This is why I never wear it down," she groaned, trying to gather her hair with her free hand.

"I like it down."

"Even when I look like a scarecrow?"

"Even then," he grinned. "Nearly there now."

His Ferrari was around the next corner. Jarred opened the door for Rose gallantly before rounding the car, dropping her bag in the back seat, and getting in himself. Though Rose's apartment was practically within sight, the drive still took almost twenty minutes, since they hadn't yet built a Ferrari that could swim across the river separating Canary Wharf from Greenwich.

It was definitely a shame to use a car like this in regular city traffic. Jarred was dying to take it for a proper spin, to push the needle past two hundred. Not that he'd ever actually managed that—even on the racetrack, he was a shade too timid to *really* floor it. He had a healthy respect for all seven hundred of the horses under the hood.

"Why wasn't your fear of heights a problem at Alice's place?" Rose blurted out.

"Because it was dark out. As long as I don't have to go on the balcony, it's not a problem."

"So that's why you were okay on the London Eye," Rose realized.

"Yeah. Plus the cars are closed. Thank God. Just imagine how awkward it'd be if it kicked in while I was in a gondola... Other people freak out when the gondolas sway too much, but that part doesn't bother me." He glanced over at Rose as he changed lanes. "Are you still available for Verbier next weekend?"

Rose blinked. "Don't you have to go to Manchester?"

"I haven't decided, but I'd be back on time either way. I'm not planning on moving to Manchester. And... I'm sorry I wasn't very supportive earlier."

"What was wrong? You were so standoffish."

"I just want to protect you," Jarred sighed. "Treating you that way isn't easy for me."

"I'm not big on this cloak-and-dagger stuff," Rose murmured.

"Honestly? Me either. But it's better this way, can you just trust me on that?" He cast a quick glance at Rose, but she was gazing pensively out the window. "Well, if it works for you, we'd fly out of London City airport early on Friday afternoon, and we'd return on Monday morning."

"Okay, sounds good."

"I agree. A whole weekend to ourselves? Sounds perfect, actually."

CHAPTER 27

ROSE

They found parking a few minutes' walk from her apartment. After turning off the car, Jarred got out to help Rose out of the car. She'd been expecting to say their goodbyes there, but he apparently had other ideas—he walked beside her as though that had been the plan all along. Rose unlocked the front door before turning to face Jarred. His eyes seemed to bore through her, with a mixture of desire and pleading that she couldn't ignore.

Instead of inviting him up, she took his hand and led him inside. Once they were upstairs and inside the apartment, she finally kissed him softly. If only everything could be as easy as kissing Jarred. As soon as she felt his lips against hers, all of her problems seemed to evaporate.

"Are you staying?" she whispered. The apartment was still dark; the streetlamp outside the large living room window provided the only light.

"Only if we can ride to work together tomorrow."

Wait, what? Seriously? Rose fumbled for the light switch so that she could see his expression. They both flinched briefly at the sudden brightness. "Say that again."

Jarred sighed and kissed her. "I said, I want to spend the night here and then ride to the office with you in the morning. Once I've dropped you off, I'll drive home to shower and change and pack my tux, and then I'll meet you in the cafeteria for coffee. And if your schedule allows, I'd like to have lunch with you, and after the fundraiser tomorrow, I'd like to take you back to my place, so you should probably bring an extra outfit with you tomorrow."

"Why the sudden change of heart? I thought we were supposed to avoid drawing attention, that it was better for me that way."

"Maybe I'm sick of hiding."

"Why?" Was he going to tell her how he felt about her? If so, was he actually serious, or was he just playing with her? Why was she so insecure when it came to Jarred?

"Would you mind if we didn't discuss it in the entryway?" Smiling a little bashfully, Jarred removed his coat and shoes before helping Rose, who could only watch in confusion.

"Um, yeah, okay. You want something to drink?"

Rose turned and started for the kitchen. Her heart was getting its hopes up dangerously.

"No, Rose." He held her back, pulled her close to kiss her again. "I've never felt like this before, and it scares me a little, but I don't want to lose it. By which I mean... I think I'm falling in love with you."

Rose gave him an incredulous stare. He cupped her face in his hands, searching it with his eyes for a response. Never in a million years would she have dreamed that Jarred Campbell would say those words to her.

"Why aren't you saying anything?" A note of uncertainty had crept into his voice.

"I'm just... overwhelmed. I'm falling in love with you, too. I just... never expected..." If she didn't watch out, she'd start tearing up in a minute.

"Then let's go to bed, it's been a long day." He winked at her before steering her into the bedroom, kissing her the whole way. They somehow managed to get each other's clothes off without breaking the kiss for more than a second or two. Rose didn't think she'd ever get tired of ogling Jarred's amazing body. And she could definitely get used to that adoring look on his face.

JARRED

How could anyone be this beautiful? Rose felt perfect in his hands—there was no other word for it. He'd never surrendered himself so completely before when making love. It felt like their hearts were beating in unison, like they'd melted into a single person, like they understood each other without words.

Alice had always said that having sex just to get off paled in comparison to sleeping with someone you genuinely loved, but Jarred had mostly taken her word for it. Now he understood what she'd meant. Jarred's eyes never left Rose's, and their fingers remained interlaced even as the overwhelming sensations drove them each to orgasm in quick succession. It was breathtaking, a moment he wanted to freeze for all eternity.

In that moment, Jarred was certain that telling Rose how he felt had been the right move. Hell, he wanted to shout it from the rooftops. The only worry clouding his euphoria was that it might affect her professional reputation. It was hard enough being the woman in Jarred's life, let alone the *Campbell Investments employee* in Jarred's life. He'd have to find a way to fix that situation; hurting Rose was the last thing he ever wanted to do.

ROSE

"He actually used the words falling in love?" Mandy sounded a lot more skeptical and a lot less enthusiastic than Rose had been hoping.

"I was in such total disbelief that I didn't even know what to say at first," Rose admitted.

"Did you... respond in kind?"

"Yeah. I kind of had my doubts, but I think that's mostly because of how we act around each other in public."

"Is that going to change?" Mandy asked, surprised.

"We'd like to, but Jarred's afraid it would create drama at work, especially for me. But I feel like everyone in the world will be able to tell I'm in love with him just from the look on my face! God, it was such an amazing night, Mandy..."

"What about tonight?" Mandy broke in. "How are you guys gonna do that? Is Jarred the jealous type? Will he sock Aaron in the face when he sees Aaron pawing you on the dance floor like he used to? And you're not going to make it any easier on the poor guy, wearing that dress. Rose, the vamp! Maybe I really ought to be writing books for adults instead."

"You do have a hell of an imagination... And yeah, I know it's a pretty weird situation, but I dunno, it's just a business event. I'll tell Aaron to keep his grubby mitts to himself. Anything else would cast me in a very bad light."

"Sure, do that, put him in his place, that'll *totally* show him," Mandy snorted.

"What, you don't think I have the guts to spell it out that I'm not interested?"

"I mean, it worked *so well* last time."

Okay. Point taken.

As promised, Alice dropped by the office to do Rose's hair. Rose could hardly believe how well her locks were suddenly behaving—every strand was perfectly in place. Alice even seemed confident they'd *stay* in place as Rose was walking to the taxi, which would be a *real* first.

Rose stepped out into the Campbell Investments lobby and found Aaron already waiting. Her coat didn't cover much of her dress, and Aaron grinned from ear to her when he saw her. He looked pretty dashing as well in that deep-green coat, and Rose knew the tuxedo beneath it would be a sight to behold. She'd beheld that sight often enough back in the day. His hair was neatly trimmed; his blue eyes twinkled as brightly as always. Aaron could be a real charmer when he felt like it, and apparently, he really, really felt like it tonight.

"Taxi's outside." Aaron held the door for Rose and never left her side as they made their way to the cab. Rose sat close to the window, grateful that her voluminous skirt kept Aaron from plopping down right next to her. "You look really nice." Aaron's eyes took on a lustful look for a fraction of a second before shifting back to admiration—Rose wasn't even entirely sure she hadn't imagined it. She did her best to hide how nervous she was. All of the industry bigshots would be at tonight's event, and that was more than enough to send her blood pressure skyrocketing. And Aaron was technically a competitor, even though they were theoretically considering a business partnership. Plus, it was *Aaron*... yikes, this was going to be a stressful evening. She had to watch what she said tonight, from both a business standpoint and a personal one. It was no secret that they'd dated, and for nearly two years at that. She assumed she'd be meeting a few of Aaron's workmates tonight, since T&H had apparently invited their middle management as well—otherwise Aaron wouldn't be on the list. Unless he'd gotten a promotion?

"How many of you guys from T&H will be there tonight?" Rose asked, smoothly ignoring Aaron's compliment.

"About twenty. Ten of the top brass are invited every year, and we middle managers can apply for the other ten tickets." Aaron looked proud. "What about Campbell? The old man's pretty stingy with the invitations, I guess," he added with a sneer.

That was true—her own company kept its guest list small and exclusive. Besides Sean and Arthur, the heads of the Risk and Financial Divisions were the only people with standing invitations, though they'd occasionally bring along a departmental manager who'd really gone above and beyond the previous year. Rose had felt obliged to notify Sean she'd been invited. He'd sent some generic one-line reply, not offering an opinion either way.

The fundraiser started at eight PM. The Sheraton overlooked one side of Green Park, Buckingham Palace the other. The ride over was nearly forty-five minutes in evening traffic; Aaron spent most of it telling her about his time in America. From the sound of it, he'd really enjoyed living and working there—he'd only returned because there were better prospects for promotion over here.

So Rose had guessed right: Aaron was attending the ball in hopes of advancing his career even faster. He'd always been laser-focused on "making it;" he had the largest professional network of anyone she'd ever met, and he still kept in frequent contact with everyone, including his old university buddies—though half of them weren't even remotely involved in the financial industry. To Aaron, any contact was a valuable contact.

Rose supposed she could learn a thing or two from him about networking. She'd fallen out of touch with most of her old classmates; by this point, she'd probably forgotten half their names. But hell, she'd graduated eight years ago! Just remembering her current clients' names was hard enough.

"I highly recommend it," Aaron told her.

"Recommend what?" Whoops. He really did love the sound of his own voice, though, didn't he? The rhetorical questions had always annoyed Rose the most, but luckily, he hadn't resorted to those yet tonight.

"Time abroad," he said. "I wouldn't trade that experience for the world. So many doors are open to you afterward." He sure did seem pleased with himself.

"Oh! We're here," Rose exclaimed, trying not to sound too obviously relieved, and discreetly wiped her clammy palms on her dark coat. It wasn't like her to get this nervous. *Just don't let them intimidate you, Rose.* Mandy was always telling her to picture everyone naked, which worked on everyone except men of the particularly well-built variety. *Okay, Rose, shoulders back, stomach in, and the rest will work itself out.*

She'd never even set foot in the Sheraton before. The exterior alone was enough to make her jaw drop.

"The hotel's almost a century old," Aaron remarked. "Limestone façade. See that mansard roof? Gives the building a really nice flair, wouldn't you say?"

Rose looked up. Wow, a person could probably see all the way to Buckingham from there. The art deco style was truly breathtaking. The front entrance was two stories tall—so, what, twenty-five-foot ceilings? Thirty?—and flanked by columns easily thirty feet in diameter. It was a historically protected building, obviously. She hadn't seen many five-star hotels from the inside—just the odd business dinner here and there, never as a guest or anything—so it was all she could do not to gape in amazement as they strode through the elegantly lit lobby. The walls looked like they were covered in gold dust, and massive mirrors on either side made the room look even bigger than it was. The thick beige carpet muting their footfalls had the same pattern as the ceiling. Rose had never seen painted stucco before. Odd, but somehow it matched perfectly.

Aaron took her coat to deposit at the cloakroom before offering her his arm. A familiar gesture, but Rose wasn't sure how to respond at first—wouldn't they look like a couple? Just then, fortunately, a T&H acquaintance of Aaron's spotted him and came over to strike up a conversation. Rose might have thought he was a nice guy if he hadn't been undressing her with his eyes the whole time.

A staircase led to a mezzanine with a bar, where waiters were diligently handing out champagne. Rose had been expecting most of the other guests to be men, but there were a number of women in here, all primped and preened to perfection. Most of them had followed the dress code: floor-length gown, modest neckline. She glanced around the room, curious whether any of the faces in here had smirked out at her from the covers of any recent business magazines, and did her best to ignore the men's approving once-overs and the women's scrutinizing side-eyes. She knew the dress was eye-catching, but she didn't want it to distract from her as a person.

Aaron kept her close at all times, introducing her to everyone he spoke to; soon Rose's head was spinning with all the new names and faces.

She swept her gaze around the room from time to time, searching for Sean and/or Jarred, but she didn't see either. A few other Campbell Investments higher-ups were in attendance, but she didn't know them well enough to just jaunt over and strike up a conversation. A loud confusion of voices suddenly swelled from the lobby, but Rose couldn't see the entrance from the mezzanine, so she would just have to wait and see whose arrival had prompted such commotion.

It turned out to be a tall woman in a tight black gown that made her seem completely naked somehow without technically revealing anything. Her hair was in an elaborate up-do, and if the jewelry she had on was real—it did look real, anyway—it must have cost a fortune. The pendant on her diamond-studded necklace vanished teasingly within her cleavage. An exceptionally handsome older man in a tailored tuxedo held her arm; his salt-and-pepper hair was full, his fine features faintly tanned. Judging by his stature, he was obviously very physically fit. Rose almost felt like she was watching a pair of movie stars sashay down the red carpet before the Oscars.

"Victoria and her dad always have to make a big entrance," Aaron murmured contemptuously. Oh, of course, that was Victoria. Somehow she looked different from how Rose remembered. But God only knew how old the tabloid photos were.

"Did she have her nose done?" someone whispered behind Rose.

"Her tits, if anything," someone else whispered back. "Not that I'd complain."

"Like she'd let you within ten feet of her," the first guy snickered quietly. "Dream on, dude."

Now that the big spectacle was over, the people around Rose resumed their conversations. The doors to the ballroom were opened as well, and Rose discovered that they were on a balustrade. The ballroom was even more opulent than the rest of the hotel, or at least what she'd seen so far. Around thirty eight-person tables draped in white linen were scattered around the room, which was bathed in both indirect light and chandelier-light, promptly banishing any romantic atmosphere that the setting might otherwise have created.

Rose took Aaron's arm with a grateful nod as they walked downstairs to the ballroom and he led her to their table. Fine porcelain tableware, silver cutlery, lilies in the centerpieces. Thank God Victoria and her dad were on the opposite end of the room—Rose would have probably spent the whole night staring at them. She found her place card and discovered that she'd be sitting with her back to the stage, where a band would be performing later.

There was a second stage across from the ballroom entrance. A painting of the Pegasus hung on the gold-ornamented wall above the oversized fireplace; the equally oversized mirror beside them allowed Rose to keep an eye on the entrance without having to turn around, which meant she got to watch Sean and Jarred's entrance. They both looked spectacular. Sean radiated the power of his position; Rose could hardly believe he wasn't married yet. Wasn't he thirty-eight now? And so handsome, too... but most of her attention was on Jarred. Though they were only half-brothers, Jarred looked like a younger version of Sean. Jarred was a few inches taller, with a slightly slimmer build, but they were nearly equal in terms of sex appeal. Rose's pulse surely wasn't the only one racing now.

Immediately upon arrival, Sean stepped to the side and headed straight for Victoria and her father. Jarred remained in the doorway for a moment, sweeping his gaze through the ballroom until he caught Rose's eye in the mirror, though he didn't react in the slightest when he spotted her. A couple walked in behind Jarred and exchanged a few words with him before making their way to the middle of the room; Jarred followed. The woman was extremely thin, with her jaw set in grim determination; she had a clutch in one hand and a cell phone in the other. Her husband looked equally tense. Jarred was the only one of the three that wasn't making it obvious that he'd rather be someplace else.

"So Arthur really didn't feel like coming," Aaron remarked. "This is going to be an interesting night."

Rose suspected he was referring to the combination of Victoria, Sean, and Jarred in the same room. Was Sean interested in Victoria or something? Then again... as long as *she* ended up going home with Jarred, she didn't really care about anything else.

CHAPTER 28

JARRED

The Rutherfords were here in body more than spirit. They nibbled at their food and made a little small talk, but spent most of their time staring at their phones. Jarred didn't mind in the slightest; there were plenty of people around to chat with. The other women at the table flirted with him non-stop. Jarred responded politely, but his gaze kept wandering—discreetly, he hoped—in Rose's direction. Aaron really didn't know how to keep his hands to himself, did he? Rose scooted away from Aaron every now and again, but she smiled at him way too often for Jarred's taste. Despite knowing next to nothing about Aaron and Rose's relationship, Jarred already couldn't stand Aaron. And even a blind man could see that Aaron was interested in Rose. Well, who wouldn't be interested in her, especially in that dress?

Though as far as Jarred was concerned, Rose would be equally beautiful in sweatpants and a bathrobe.

Sean appeared to be having a blast. Loud laughter rang out from his table at frequent intervals. Once the official part of the program ended, Jarred would probably have to go say hello to Victoria and her father. Maybe he could skip the auction, at least? That was the part he dreaded the most. Like most of those in attendance tonight, Campbell Investments had donated a generous sum of money in advance, but Jarred really, really didn't want to sit there listening to the beneficiaries' tales of woe. Not that he didn't care where his donations went, but it wasn't like he actually went and visited the sick children and single mothers and old people he was supporting.

"Come on, Jarred, this is as good a time as any to finish our business, don't you think?" The main course plates were being cleared away, and Joe got up to leave the ballroom. Relieved, Jarred followed him to the mezzanine. Dozens of other guests were filtering out as well, presumably taking the opportunity for a smoke break. "You want a whiskey, too?" Joe asked as he headed straight for the bar to place an order. He really didn't ever waste a second of his apparently very precious time. Jarred would hate to be that hardnosed about everything... although he did seem to recall having been referred to as a slave driver on occasion. What could he say? When he was really excited about a project, he wasn't going to let a little thing like normal working hours stand in his way.

"Sure," Jarred replied as he approached.

Joe slipped the folded contract out of his inside jacket pocket and handed Jarred a copy. "Pleasure doing business with you," he said. "Cheers." He touched his glass to Jarred's and then finished the drink in one gulp. "How soon can you have the place cleared out?"

"Next week, I think." He'd have to find a moving company in the morning, so that he could move straight into Henry's when he got back from Verbier. Hopefully by then he'd know who had purchased his mother's home, and how much it would cost him to buy it back.

"Your friends put in an offer on our house."

Oh? Finn and Marie? They hadn't mentioned it.

"Are you sure you don't want it for yourself, Jarred?"

Jarred blinked. "What makes you ask that?"

"My wife said you seemed quite taken with the place when you came by for the showing."

Well, true, but so were Finn and Marie. Jarred decided not to mention his mom's house to Joe. "It's a beautiful property, but probably a little big for just one guy."

"I wouldn't think you were exactly lacking for female admirers." Joe nodded toward the ballroom as though it were obvious that Jarred's future wife were in there somewhere. "I'm sure Victoria's just waiting for you to ask her to dance."

AKA just waiting for Jarred to seduce her. Yeah, well. They'd had fun and all, but Jarred had never felt anywhere near as strongly about Victoria as he did about Rose. The realization surprised him a little—enough that he barely noticed at first when someone sidled in next to him and brushed a kiss on his cheek. Even without looking, he could guess who it was. Not many women as tall as Victoria wore five-inch stilettos.

"Jarred, don't you want to introduce me?" With a fake smile plastered on her face, Victoria took his arm and waited for him to heed her command. Yikes, had she bathed in perfume? Seemed a bit drunk as well—she wouldn't normally be this touchy-feely in public.

"Victoria, this is Joe Rutherford. Joe, Victoria Thompson."

"Pleasure to meet you," Vicky simpered, extending a hand.

"Pleasure's all mine," Joe replied automatically and air-kissed Vicky's knuckles.

"So how do you guys know each other?" she asked, still glued to Jarred's side.

"Real estate," Jarred replied before draining his glass.

"Work friends, hm," Vicky sniffed.

"Joe bought my condominium." Why was he bothering to explain himself? What he felt like doing was putting Vicky back at arm's length. She could be so damn… overbearing.

"You're moving? Where to?"

"Haven't decided yet." *Sorry, ma'am, that information is on a need-to-know basis.*

"You can stay with me," she promptly offered.

"Nice to meet you, Ms. Thompson." Joe excused himself with a nod.

Jarred found himself wishing he could follow Joe's lead. He wasn't exactly desperate to talk to Vicky. "I'm staying at Henry's, but thanks."

"At Henry's? Why? You and I could have a lot more fun." A moment later, her lips were on his; she cupped the back of his neck with one hand to pull him closer, while her other hand drifted below his belt.

His body responded before he had a chance to push her away.

ROSE

They'd been on their way outside for some fresh air, so they had front-row seats for the entire show.

"Apparently some people aren't familiar with the concept of public behavior," Aaron sniffed, pulling Rose away.

As they passed, Rose heard Jarred hiss something at Victoria angrily, but she didn't quite catch what it was. Her heart was hammering in her throat. Women like Victoria were probably used to getting everything they wanted. And Aaron getting all huffy about it was pretty ridiculous—he'd never been particularly shy about public displays of affection.

Rose took several deep gulps of cold air as they stepped out. A few smokers were clustered to one side; traffic on the damp street was light. Out here in the golden light, against the backdrop of the spectacular hotel, it was almost romantic; the only thing missing was a starry sky, and those were few and far between in cities of London's size.

Aaron wrapped her coat around her tenderly. She felt his warm breath on the back of her neck, and then his lips brushed the sensitive skin beneath her ear. The goosebumps that spread like lightning across her body were not from the chilly air.

"What are you doing, Aaron?" Rose whispered, dazed.

"You're the most beautiful woman here tonight." He pulled away with a quiet sigh.

Rose stepped to one side, putting some distance between them. Out of the corner of her eye, she noticed a dark figure near the entrance.

Jarred scowled at them, gritting his teeth. The shadow of the streetlamp made him look even grimmer.

"Campbell. That was quick." Aaron's derisive laugh was like a slap in the face. "Can't close the deal on anything anymore, can you? But what else would I expect from a player..."

Rose held her breath.

"Mind your own business." Jarred's tone could cut glass, and his hands were clenched into fists.

"I'm going back in, I'll meet you at the table," Rose said. She wasn't about to stand there watching them brawl on the front steps. She strode quickly through the glass doors, re-checked her coat, and hurried down the stairs—but then realized halfway down that the restrooms were one floor up. Ugh, but if she went back the way she'd come, she might run into Aaron, or Jarred, or Victoria. She glanced around for a moment and then spotted a small sign marking another set of restrooms.

The ladies' room was empty—she doubted too many people wandered in here. Rose peered at her own reflection. Her hair was still perfect, and her makeup only required a few touch-ups here and there. When she stepped out into the hallway again, she wasn't even all that surprised to find Jarred waiting for her. There was nothing tender in his gaze.

"What are you doing here?" Oh, Lord, was he going to make a scene?

"Making sure you know who you belong to." He closed the distance between them to press her against the wall and kissed her with a tenderness she never would have thought possible. She'd expected something rough, possessive—she couldn't have asked for a clearer sign of how he felt about her.

"What about you?" Rose whispered when they came up for air.

"What do you mean?"

"What do you think? I saw you and Victoria." She shoved his chest angrily, but he didn't move an inch.

"She's always been the extroverted type," he replied in a matter-of-fact tone.

"Are you making fun of me?"

"No, I'd like to go home." To Rose's immense disappointment, Jarred released her abruptly; his amused smile suggested that he noticed her reaction, which annoyed her even more. What the hell was going on today? Maybe she ought to just go home alone. She had no patience for games.

"Here. Your key." Jarred handed her a key card, the type she'd only ever seen in hotels. "See you later."

And just like that, he was gone.

Two hours later, Rose was in a taxi, trying to decide whether to head home. After the clash between Jarred and Aaron, everything about the event had managed to grate on her last nerve. Aaron's hand had kept wandering to Rose's knee underneath the table, and the more he drank, the higher it drifted. None of the other guests at their table had paid any attention to them; everyone seemed to be having a grand time, though as the night wore on, it felt more like some kind of ultra-decadent frat party.

Once the band finally started playing, the guests really let loose. A CEO Rose had once seen on the cover of *Forbes* had invited her to join him in a polonaise; he'd whooped and hollered as they jaunted around the room. Next, she'd danced with Aaron, who'd taken the opportunity to kiss her in front of everyone before whirling her around and then pulling her shamelessly close, almost like he wanted to grind against her or something.

That was her signal that she probably needed to exit stage left sooner rather than later. She'd managed to do a little networking, but she couldn't be sure that anyone she'd talked to would actually remember her name in the morning.

The next time Aaron spun her around, she'd spotted Jarred against the far wall, sipping a drink and watching her grimly. Victoria was right nearby, practically wrapped around him as she jabbered into his ear—which, granted, was the only way anyone could make themselves heard over all this racket. But having Victoria so close didn't seem to bother Jarred that much anyway.

Rose managed to make herself stay another thirty minutes, by which point there was no sign of Jarred anywhere. She forced herself not to wonder if he and Victoria had retreated to a dark corner somewhere.

The silence of the cab was glorious. If she could take her shoes off, it'd be absolutely perfect. Rose gazed out at the slumbering city through the window. Home or Jarred's?

She gave Jarred's address. If he wasn't there, she'd go home.

She wondered whether Sean had noticed something was up between her and Jarred. She'd felt Jarred's eyes on her so often that other people had to have noticed...

The taxi pulled up at Barbican Centre. Rose paid, gathered her purse and scarf, and strolled to the entrance. The doorman let her in without a word, and Jarred's key card worked on the elevator.

Rose unlocked the door to Jarred's apartment and... froze in astonishment. The lights were dimmed; a line of candles marked a path from the entrance to the living room. She sighed in relief as she removed her shoes, hung up her coat, and then gathered the hem of her skirt so she wouldn't accidentally set herself on fire. Soft music drifted from the living room—Adele, "Make You Feel My Love." The candle trail ended at the living room table, which held a bucket of champagne and two glasses. The red rose petals scattered across it released an intoxicating perfume. Unless that was a scented candle?

Jarred was standing at the window. He'd removed his tuxedo jacket and bow tie; the top two buttons of his shirt were undone, and his sleeves were rolled up to the elbows. He regarded Rose in silence until the song finished and restarted.

"Dance with me." He held out a hand as he approached. Rose immediately wished she'd kept the shoes on—she wasn't used to being eight inches shorter than him. He didn't seem to notice, though. They danced slowly, wrapped up in one another. It was incredibly romantic. When the song ended, Jarred kissed her passionately.

"What's up with that Aaron guy?" he asked immediately afterward.

Rose felt like he'd poured a bucket of ice water over her. She stepped back. The storm brewing in his eyes belied his calm tone. "He's my ex, you know that," Rose replied cautiously.

Disappointment flickered on his face, and he averted his eyes briefly before forcing himself to look at her again.

"We were going to get married, but…" *Don't you dare cry!* Rose took a deep breath. "I wasn't his only girlfriend. I only found out by random chance." She turned away to wipe her eyes discreetly. Even after all this time, it still killed her that she didn't know for sure whether Aaron had been cheating on her that whole time.

"What do you mean you weren't his only girlfriend? He cheated on you?"

"I never did find out for sure. Aaron knows everyone and their mother, so we didn't see each other very often—he was always getting invited somewhere for something. Business, personal, whatever. He took me with him once in a while, and I started picking up on things. I never caught him in the act, but... I dunno, it just started seeming like he had something on the back burner. Before we met, he'd had three or four affairs going at any given time, you know. And then one night I met a woman at a party who knew more about Aaron than any 'friend' ought to... at first I thought she was just jealous, but no, she knew all kinds of intimate details about him. He'd taken her on vacation to the same places, given her the same gifts... it was creepy."

"Did you call him out?"

"Of course, what do you think? He denied everything, swore up and down that he'd never cheat on me. I broke up with him on the spot anyway, though. I just didn't feel like I could trust him anymore. Not long after that, he moved to the US on business."

"And now?"

"Now he's back," Rose replied lamely.

"Do you still have feelings for him?"

"Do you still have feelings for Victoria?" Rose countered.

"We've known each other for a long time. She's my ex. That's all. I probably never did love her."

The tiny hairs on Rose's bare arms stood up immediately as Jarred traced his fingertips down them. They were a great match physically, no doubt about that. She felt Jarred unzip her dress, kissing every inch of skin he exposed in the process. He took his time about it, turning Rose on more and more. Hell, she didn't even need foreplay; she just wanted to feel him deep inside her, to look into his eyes and reassure herself that he wanted her and her alone.

She slipped out of the dress, took his hand, and led him to the bedroom. Jarred didn't need to be asked twice—he started unbuttoning his shirt while Rose fumbled with his belt and zipper. Her hand closed around his impressive erection immediately; she gazed into his eyes deeply as she began massaging it, and didn't even bother hiding the smile that automatically spread across her face when she realized how much she was testing his self-control. Once he'd finished removing the rest of his clothes, she pushed him onto the bed. After stripping off her lingerie, she rolled a condom onto him and straddled him. She didn't expect him to let her stay in control for long, but she was still surprised when he flipped her over in a matter of moments. He glided in and out of her much too slowly—probably his revenge for earlier—but it didn't even matter, because his eyes held her captive. The look on his face held all the answers she'd been searching for, the certainty that his heart belonged to her as well.

CHAPTER 29

ROSE

The following day, Rose was half-expecting Sean to call her to his office. Surely he had to have noticed that Jarred's eyes were on her all night, and that she kept stealing glances at him as well. Hell, maybe Aaron's incredibly pushy advances had actually saved her? That'd be hilarious…

Rose decided to keep a low profile for the next several days. It wasn't easy, but Jarred wasn't in the office and there was plenty of work to do… plus Rose was taking Friday afternoon off. A whole weekend alone with Jarred! She could hardly believe it.

Verbier welcomed them with radiant blue skies and perfectly snowy slopes.

"Wow!" Rose had her face pressed against the rental-car window; she could hardly believe her eyes. It was Paradise. Just looking at this place seemed to erase all the stress of the previous week. The sun was setting in an hour, so they wouldn't have time to ski tonight, but she was determined to be the first one on the lift in the morning.

"Should we grab equipment now?"

"Someone's eager." Jarred was grinning no less brightly. "There's a bunch of equipment in the chalet already. I'm sure something in there will fit you."

So the staff had already organized everything for them? Strange. They could have just stopped at a sports equipment store or something.

"We can check out Les Ruinettes tomorrow. It's at twenty-two hundred meters—there are a couple of blue runs."

"Why not go up to one of the peaks?" The reverence Rose felt as she gazed up at them, glittering in the late-afternoon sun, was probably nothing compared to how she'd feel once she was up there. She remembered exactly what it was like to stand at the top, with the other massive peaks towering around her like a wreath. It was a mixture of intimidation and exhilaration, of feeling tiny and insignificant and euphoric all at once, in a giant rush of adrenalin that whipped her down the slope. The wind in her face, the sound of crunching snow, her body on autopilot, her brain blissfully silent at last.

"Pretty steep. You think you're up for that?"

"What's your favorite place to ski?"

"I like to freeride," Jarred replied promptly.

Hm. Rose was too rusty to freeride. Best to start with something easier. "Red should be fine." Red slopes were tougher than blue, but not as challenging as black.

"If you say so."

They went on driving in silence, until finally Jarred stopped outside a gigantic chalet, an imposing four-story structure complete with towers and balconies. It reminded Rose of a castle.

Jarred drove around to the back and pulled up outside a garage door with a post in front. After rolling down the window, he pressed his thumb to the post, and the door opened a moment later. They drove into a garage easily large enough for twenty vehicles. There was a dark Porsche Cayenne in one corner, and an older Volvo near the entrance. Jarred parked their Jeep in the middle. "Let's go inside first."

Inside? Wait, what about their stuff? Rose followed Jarred to an elevator that took them to the fourth floor. When the doors opened, they stepped out into a rustic living room with a steeply pitched ceiling and two doors leading off on either side. Apparently every room in the house was set up to provide an incredible view of the village and the mountains. The sun was already starting to set behind the peaks.

"Are you hungry? I can have something brought up."

"Hey, uh, does the whole house belong to you guys?"

"Yeah... who else would it belong to?" Jarred grinned. "I can show you part of it later. There are fifteen rooms in all, but each of us has our own private area, to use however we like. This is my area. The pool, the sauna, and the fitness center are downstairs, and then the common living room and kitchen are in the middle of the house."

Rose's head was spinning already. Sometimes she forgot just how unbelievably wealthy Jarred's family was—he always acted so down-to-earth around her. "Maybe we should try the ski equipment on first."

She followed Jarred back to the elevator; this time, they got out on the ground floor. He walked down a narrow hallway and opened a door at the far end, revealing a dedicated room for ski equipment. Several pairs of skis and ski boots stood at the ready. One pair had obviously been used recently—it was dripping snow onto the floor.

"Liam must be here," Jarred said. "But we won't run into him, don't worry."

Rose was highly tempted to ask why not. Liam, the scandal-Campbell. Rose only vaguely remembered him. She was still new at the company when the whole paternity court thing was happening. She didn't even know how it had all turned out—only that Liam had officially left the company soon after. She hadn't heard a thing about him since then.

Rose sat down and started trying on boots. The

third pair fit perfectly, no pinching anywhere, at least not once they were all the way on—getting them on and off was another matter. *Okay, now who's going to adjust the bindings?* No sooner had she finished formulating the thought than she realized to her surprise that Jarred was doing it. He hadn't asked her which skis she wanted, but she figured she could always switch if these ended up being too fast or slow.

"Perfect, now we can hit the slopes first thing in the morning without having to stop off to rent skis. I'd been hoping one of these would fit you. Okay, so, how shall we spend the rest of the evening? Pool? Sauna? Hot tub? Or straight to bed?" He gave Rose an exaggerated wink, and she couldn't help laughing.

"Let's build a snowman!" It'd be a shame to spend their time just sitting around the house... although cuddling in front of the fireplace didn't sound half bad.

Jarred blinked at Rose in surprise. Clearly not the response he'd been expecting.

"What? Don't you know how to build snowmen?" she teased him.

"Pfff. I build the biggest and best snowmen!"

Rose couldn't remember the last time she'd had this much fun. She and Jarred played in the snow until it was completely dark outside. The brightly lit village twinkled below them between the pitch-black mountains, and the crystal-clear night sky stretched out overhead. She couldn't resist challenging Jarred to a snowball fight, which she'd then lost in spectacular and soaked fashion.

As she followed him shivering into the house, he briefly excused himself to take a call. Fortunately, she'd already learned the way from the ski room, where she deposited her wet boots beside the other dripping pairs, to his apartment. She peeled off her ski outfit as well—she was planning on drying it in the apartment, but she didn't want to track water all over the house.

Jarred followed her up shortly thereafter, and they spent the evening in. They even tried to sleep for part of the night, since they wanted to catch one of the first gondolas to the top in the morning.

Now they were at the top of what looked like one hell of a steep slope. Rose checked the sign again—maybe she'd accidentally landed on a black slope? But nope, this one was red. The black slope was another several hundred feet up, accessible only by chair lift.

"Everything okay?" Jarred turned to look at her, though she couldn't see his eyes through the mirrored goggles.

Rose wasn't sure whether to admit that she was freaking out. "I'm afraid I'm making the number-one mistake."

"Which is what?"

"Overthinking. My old ski instructor always

said to ski with your gut, not your head. So let's go." She grinned and pushed off. Her body knew exactly what to do. The goosebumps she'd had ever since she first stepped into the gondola spread all over again; soon she was breathing hard, and as soon as she rounded the first curve, that old familiar euphoria washed through her. Amazing childhood memories tumbled through her mind. She stopped at the next hill and glanced over her shoulder to see if Jarred was following.

He stopped right behind her, grinning like a kid at Christmas. "You're a damn good skier, hm?"

"I'm pretty rusty."

"And pretty hard on yourself. I should have guessed. Every Swiss person I've ever met is." He laughed.

"Oh? I'm only half-Swiss, though."

"Apparently it doesn't make a difference. How about I go on out ahead and you follow me?"

That was perfectly fine with Rose—she wasn't familiar with this ski area, and Jarred knew it like the back of his own hand.

They kept skiing until Rose's legs were threatening to give out, stopping only to grab lunch at a mountaintop restaurant, where several people noticed Jarred even though he looked like just another skier. Rose reasoned that the locals probably knew the Campbells since they owned a house nearby.

"You want to keep going? I can head back on my own," Rose offered.

"No, the slopes will be there tomorrow. Let's go dancing later, yeah?"

JARRED

He had half a mind to finish the day by riding all the way to the top. He was an incorrigible adrenaline junkie, period. Missing out on the ultimate thrill when it was so close at hand felt like some kind of punishment... but then again, there was no point in bringing Rose to Verbier—one of the few women he'd ever invited out here—and then ditching her. She was a much better skier than he'd expected; being here with her was a lot of fun.

He knew it was probably stupid to take her out dancing, since people around here knew him, but he had to burn off all of this pent-up energy somehow. Besides, the less time they spent at the chalet, the less likely they were to run into Liam. It was a big place, but there was still no guarantee that they wouldn't cross paths, and he didn't have the first clue how he would go about introducing Rose to Liam.

Rose didn't sound particularly excited at the thought of another run. He'd pushed her pretty hard today already, and she'd never once batted an eyelash. Little by little, Rose was turning out to be the woman of his dreams. He doubted he could keep their relationship a secret for much longer—nor did he want to. He already missed her every minute she wasn't around. Yeah, he had it bad.

"Why don't you go on ahead?" Rose suggested.

"Trying to get rid of me, hm?"

"No, just need a break."

If he went up again, he'd be out for a lot longer than she was—she'd probably be down the mountain in twenty minutes or less. And it was getting dark.

"I'll come with you," he said. "I can always go up there tomorrow. It's not going anywhere."

He loved the rush, but he wasn't trying to break his neck or anything. Rose's smile was confirmation enough that he'd made the right decision.

CHAPTER 30

JARRED

This past weekend had been one of the best he'd had in a long time. Mentally, he was still in Verbier with Rose, careening down the steep slopes. She was the woman of his dreams—there was no other way of putting it.

Jarred knocked on Sean's office door and waited for his gruff "Come in." This time, he found his brother standing at the window rather than enthroned behind his desk. Jarred walked to the middle of the room and stopped, waiting.

"How was your weekend?" Sean turned to look at Jarred. His expression was perfectly neutral, with no indication either way of whether he knew where Jarred had spent the past few days—or, more importantly, with whom.

"Good."

"That's good." Sean regarded Jarred intently for a moment before continuing. "I'm dissolving your department. It hasn't been economically viable in years. Go ahead and start assembling a team for Manchester. We'll be leasing a space downtown, so find yourself an apartment around there."

Wait, what? Sean wanted him to *move* to Manchester?? What the hell?! Jarred fought back a rush of anger. Sean obviously hadn't just come up with this idea today. So first he'd insisted Jarred return to London, only to refuse to give Jarred his old job back. Then he'd been mad about Jarred selling his condo so he could renovate his late mother's house. And now Sean was just dissolving Jarred's entire department here in London? And shipping him off to Manchester? Was this some kind of prank?

"How long have you been cooking this up?" Jarred sniffed. "How come I had a choice before, but not now? You *know* I'm planning to buy Mom's house and renovate it to live in, so *now* you're sending me to Manchester? What gives?"

"Restructuring has been on the table for a while now. Clever little monkey like you can probably put the rest together."

"What the hell is that supposed to mean—was bringing me back here just some kind of game? And what about Rose? Why would you bother promoting her if you were just going to eliminate the department?" He wondered if he'd be able to take her to Manchester with him.

"The promotion was only ever temporary, and she knows that. I was originally planning on waiting a bit longer, but given the circumstances, I think it's time to move forward."

"Given what circumstances?"

Sean scowled at him furiously. Several long seconds of tense silence ticked by. "Don't play stupid," he finally snarled. "I warned you, Jarred. Keep your goddamn paws to yourself. Which part of that was so hard to understand?"

So Sean *did* know about him and Rose. Dammit.

"You have exactly two options here: stay away from Rose, or get the hell out. You think I'm going to let a little shit like you bring down the whole fucking company? YOU GOT THAT?" Sean had worked himself up into a frenzy. He clenched his fists, seemingly itching to hammer his point home. Literally.

Jarred bit his tongue to keep himself from saying anything rash. Where did Sean get off, treating Jarred like this? Their dad was still the primary shareholder. Then again, Dad probably wasn't likely to contradict Sean.

Jarred wasn't necessarily worried about his own fate, but Rose didn't deserve to be out on the street. Especially not on Jarred's account. He knew there was no point wondering whether she'd come with him to Manchester. Giving her up was out of the question... but Manchester wasn't exactly the other side of the world. They could still get together on weekends.

Unless...

"You're letting her go?"

It was more of a realization than a question.

"The team in Frankfurt needs reinforcements."

Frankfurt in Germany? Rose wasn't about to move away from England. She was always talking about how much she liked it here. "She'd never agree to leave the country."

"It's that or find another job."

"Then I'll quit instead."

Sean scoffed. "Don't make a fool of yourself."

"What, you'd *still* fire her?"

"Spending time abroad looks good on a resume. Rose would be stupid not to take the offer."

Silently, Jarred turned to leave.

"I want a list of names for your team by the end of the week," Sean called when Jarred was at the door. "The new office will be move in-ready next Monday."

Rose was going to hate him. He'd raised the stakes too far, and now he'd lost everything.

ROSE

"I can't make heads or tails of it," Mandy assured her.

"Hm, yeah, it's a pretty fuzzy image," Rose agreed, trying to convince herself. She and Jarred had been photographed at the club in Verbier, and the picture had landed in some dumb British tabloid.

"Some random fool at the club probably just recognized Jarred and snapped a pic of you. Seriously, if you can get paid for photos *that* blurry, I'm gonna start taking them everywhere I go."

"Someone obviously thought it was worth it," Rose mumbled, scowling.

"What did Jarred have to say?"

"Haven't talked to him yet today—I don't even know whether he's seen them. I probably shouldn't care; my name isn't mentioned in the article."

"Yet."

"I gotta go. Sean wants to see me."

Rose rode up to the fortieth floor and knocked expectantly on Sean's door. She waited for his "Come in" before turning the knob. Sean was standing at the window, imposing as ever... but his expression was more regretful, unless Rose was just imagining things.

"Come in and sit down, Rose."

Uneasily, she obeyed.

Sean sat down across from her and got straight to the point: "I've decided to push forward with the reorganization process, which means I'm eliminating your department."

Wait, what?!

"I want to streamline the company. Part of our workforce will be transferred to new offices outside London, and I'll be leasing the space in this building made available as a result. Jarred will be heading up a team in Manchester, and I'd like you to support the team in Frankfurt."

"You want me to move to Frankfurt?" Rose looked at him in bewilderment.

"As I mentioned, the team there needs additional support. Construction is booming there, and you're one of the only people here who speaks German."

"What if I don't want to relocate to a different country?"

Sean gazed at her for a long moment before replying. "Then I'm sorry."

They'd let her go? Jesus. This conversation was getting worse and worse. "Wow, fantastic prospects there," she blurted out.

"See it as a chance to gain experience abroad."

You go ahead, I'm fine how I am, she thought, but bit her tongue.

JARRED

He'd left the office and walked down to the Thames. Sean made him so goddamn mad. He wasn't Liam. Rose wasn't Cheryl. But Sean didn't see the difference. The company's reputation took precedence; any and all potential scandals were to be nipped in the bud.

Dammit! The prospect of losing Rose made him feel like he couldn't breathe. But any way he sliced it, their brief relationship was history. Hell, it probably didn't even deserve to be called a relationship. And he'd have screwed it up eventually anyway, so it was just as well that Sean had kept any damage to the company and the family reputation to a minimum.

If he kept repeating this bullshit, he might actually believe it eventually. Jarred snorted in frustration, and then made a spontaneous decision to call Alice. He gave her a brief rundown of what had just happened. Maybe she could help him?

"Sean really painted you into a corner, hm?" she remarked when he was finished.

"He completely overreacted, is what he did."

"You actually offered him your job in exchange for Rose's? She must mean a lot to you."

"More than anyone ever has."

"But I can also see Sean's point of view."

"So we have no right to be happy, or what?!"

"Don't shout. You know perfectly well that Sean has to consider what's best for the company. What if you'd cast Rose into the public eye, and the press had torn her to pieces? You *know* what it would look like. They'd write her off as a gold-digger. You have no way of guaranteeing her that they wouldn't."

"Just because the public somehow can't get enough of contrived scandals."

"Oh, Jarred… what does Rose think of all this?"

"I haven't spoken to her yet."

"Why not?"

"Too mad. Too disappointed."

"If she cares even half as much about you as you do about her, she's feeling the same way."

"I guess I'd better get back to work before they send out a search party. I'll talk to you later."

The walk back to the office felt like an awful lot like a march to the gallows.

ROSE

Jarred suddenly appeared at her desk, as though she'd conjured him with her thoughts. He looked more or less the way she felt. Even before he opened his mouth, she could tell that he was going to break up with her. She followed him to the elevators with a heavy heart. "Where are we going?"

"Somewhere we can talk in private."

They headed to the auditorium on the ground floor. The room held five hundred people, but it was hardly ever used—nobody would bother them here. Jarred shut the door, took a deep breath, and… said nothing. He looked like a thousand different thoughts were flying through his head, but somehow he didn't have the words to express any of them.

"You're sending me away, aren't you," Rose murmured quietly. She'd never known him to be this out of sorts.

"Do we have a choice?" he asked.

"Everyone always has a choice."

"Maybe in theory. Not in real life."

"So that's that, then. I wouldn't have pegged you for such a coward," she remarked in a deliberate attempt to provoke him, though she wasn't sure if it would make a difference. All he had to do was tell her that he loved her and that things would work out, and she'd happily give everything and anything up for him...

You're insane!

True. She was insane. Insanely emotional, painfully naïve. But what good was a fabulous job if she had to do it in a foreign country, a million miles away from everyone she loved?

"You don't know me, Rose, so cut the games. You're going to Frankfurt, basta."

"What if I don't want to?"

"That wouldn't change anything. I'm not cut out for relationships. Never have been, never will be."

"Oh, yeah? How do you know if you've never even tried? I thought you loved me."

"I was mistaken."

"Oh. You were mistaken. And you expect me to believe that."

"What do you want me to say, Rose? It won't work. Your friend was a hundred percent right: I'm a player. When I'm not at work, I'm hanging around a casino, occasionally drinking myself to oblivion. Stay away from me, or I'll drag you down with me." Jarred's eyes glittered with fury. He was obviously using every resource at his disposal to destroy the connection between them. Just like that, hm?

Rose scraped together the last remnants of her self-esteem. "I thought you were a grown man, not a marionette, but I was also mistaken. Have a great life." She stalked past him, holding her breath so she wouldn't catch a whiff of his scent, steeling herself against the overwhelming urge to grab him and kiss him until he couldn't see straight. Hormones in uproar, nerves shot. She willed herself not to cry, not to show weakness like that. She could cry at home. One day, he'd understand what a terrible mistake he'd made by letting her go.

Well, okay, then, she'd just have to bite the international-transfer bullet for a while, but her next order of business was to start looking for a different job. She had no desire to keep on working for Campbell Investments, pretending she didn't mind being treated like an object. She'd worked her ass off for that company for years, and now it was either move to Frankfurt or get out? What the hell kind of company policy was that? There had to be more to the story. She'd bet anything that Sean had somehow found out about her and Jarred. Apparently, Sean couldn't care less that she and Jarred actually had feelings for one another. Anything to avoid a scandal, anything to keep the shareholders satisfied. Rose was dispensable.

CHAPTER 31

JARRED

He'd gone back to talk to Sean one more time, but he remained as stubborn as ever. Even when Jarred told him that he loved Rose and didn't want to lose her, Sean had just stood there staring at him and shaking his head. Their dad refused to interfere with Sean's decisions; Marlene was the only one who took his side. But he didn't want her to start arguing with Sean or his dad.

Rose was avoiding him, and he could hardly blame her. His family were the ones making her life so hard. He could sense how much she disliked the prospect of moving away, and forcing her to choose between that or losing her job was pretty damn low... even for Sean.

Like it or not, Jarred had packed his bags. He'd found a fully furnished one-bedroom place in

Manchester for 1,300 pounds per month, not even a mile from the office. He'd been in Manchester for a week now, and was already counting the minutes until he could return to London.

Sean expected daily progress reports on all of Jarred's projects, though he knew perfectly well that hardly anything changed from one day to the next. Jarred had a large consulting firm on the hook, but unless and until they agreed to lease space in one of the new office towers, all he could do was keep casting his line. Jarred was stubborn, though. He just needed to land one big fish, and then the others would start biting.

Rose was probably already in Frankfurt. He hadn't spoken to her again. They'd already said everything there was to say. The only thing Jarred still had of hers was her notebook, which he'd apparently stuck in his jacket by mistake. She'd sketched a flower on the first page and written things that were important to her in the petals: *Being open to new love. Not telling my mom everything. Going dancing with Mandy. Planning a round-the-world trip. Spending more time with Ella. Finding a rowing club.*

It was harder than hell for him to wrap his mind around the idea that he was never going to see her again. He pretended like he was just on a short trip, and whenever he felt particularly lonely, he wrote her a letter.

Monday, February 4

Dear Rose,
I miss waking up next to you and getting your first smile of the day. I miss kissing you and showing you my love. I miss hearing your voice and getting lost in your stories. I miss admiring your drawings and wishing that they could make the whole world as happy as they make me. I could go on and on, because I miss everything about you. I miss you.

Love,
Jarred

Thursday, February 14

Dear Rose,
Happy Valentine's Day! I'd have liked to have given you a bouquet of your favorite sunflowers, but they aren't blooming yet. It was hard walking around Manchester, seeing all the romantic shop-window displays. The happy couples strolling hand in hand through the streets downtown, on their way to a romantic evening at a restaurant.

If you were here with me, we'd have been one of those couples. We'd have gone out to the best sushi place in the city. I'd have told you that an Australian owns it, and you'd have asked me to tell you about Australia. I wouldn't have had to think too hard, because I have a million stories I'd love to tell you. One of the funny ones is about the time I almost went to war with my GPS. You have no idea how dark the nights get Down Under—they don't have streetlamps everywhere like they do here. I was trying to get to Grampians, a national park near Melbourne. Well, I was enjoying the coastal road so much that I ended up turning inland way too late, and instead of sticking with one of the few main streets, the GPS sent me all over the damn map, on these tiny little dirt roads. I was just about having a heart attack, picturing the terrors that might be lurking around the next corner.

You'd have laughed and assured me that you were a much better GPS, and that I should take you along next time. You can't even imagine how much I'd love to. I'd never get lost if you were with me, because wherever you are is where I'd always want to be.

I love you, Valentine.
Jarred

Saturday, February 16

Dear Rose,
I was in London. I didn't really want to go, because I knew you wouldn't be waiting at the station. But Henry's back from Texas... I'd have loved to introduce you two. He was

in an unusually good mood. Maybe some Texan girl caught his eye? He wouldn't give me any details. He's going to help me with my mom's house. It seems to be empty, which won't make it any easier to locate the owner. I already know exactly how I want to decorate it. Cozy, colorful, with your paintings hanging everywhere. And all the way on the top floor is where your art studio will be, with a little dance floor beside it and a starry sky painted on the ceiling.
You're always with me in my dreams.

Love,
Jarred

Sunday, February 17

Dear Rose,
I wonder how you're doing every single day. Sometimes I pick up the phone and barely manage to stop myself from calling you. Hearing your voice would make me so happy. The urge was especially strong today, so I got in my car and drove to Cambridge. I found the old estate almost immediately. The snowdrops were blooming everywhere, just like you said. I'm not going back there without you.

I love you.
Jarred

Jarred stuck the letter in his desk drawer along with all the others. Today was an especially hard day... but this time, he wasn't going to surrender to the pain. No drinking himself into a stupor, no wasting hours at a casino, no drugs, no stumbling to a club and hooking up with whichever random woman threw herself at him. Rose would be disappointed, and he didn't want to disappoint her any more than he already had.

Jarred switched on his computer with a sigh. He hoped Henry really could help him out with his mom's house. The sooner he'd bought it, the sooner he could start spending his weekends fixing it up. Right now, every weekend seemed to stretch on forever, like chewing gum on his shoe. Any distraction would be more than welcome.

All at once, he had an idea. After a brief moment of hesitation, he dialed Vicky's number.

"Hey, baby, you calling to invite me out to dinner?" she purred in greeting.

"Since when do you eat anything but salad?" he retorted teasingly.

"True. Maybe we should make alternative plans."

"Me being in Manchester could make that a bit difficult, logistically speaking."

"Manchester? You're just telling me this now? The clubs in Manchester are legendary. Are you staying a while?"

"Looks that way."

"Perfect. I'll be there on Saturday. Can I stay at yours?"

"Of course. I have a guest room."

"I'd have slept in your bed if necessary." Vicky sounded amused.

"Best not."

"When did you get so boring, Jarred? Well, whatever, we'll find a way to entertain ourselves. Did you need something else, or were you just calling to tell me how fantastic I am?"

"I need your help."

"Okay."

"I'd like to purchase my mother's house, but I don't know who it belongs to. At least one of her mortgages was with your bank. Would you mind looking into that for me? Like, whether your bank repossessed the place after her death? It doesn't look occupied." Why hadn't he thought to ask Vicky before? Crazy. "You still there?"

"Oh, sure. I... um, so... you're looking to buy it, hm?"

"Yeah. Why, is that a problem?" He seemed to recall the deed situation being... knotty. Desperate for money, his mom had sold the land around the home and then leased it back; she'd struggled every month to scrape together payments on the two mortgages. She'd clung to that house until the very end.

"I wouldn't necessarily say 'problem.' I own the place, and it's not for sale."

CHAPTER 32

ROSE

She was sitting by the Main River. She had a thing for rivers, so that was one point in Frankfurt's favor, but it didn't change her desire to find a new job back in London. She'd been searching for weeks, in fact, but job-hunting was turning out to be easier said than done—especially since she was in another country now, so she couldn't exactly just pop over and meet a potential employer for coffee. Aaron kept offering to put in a good word for her at T&H, but Rose didn't want anyone else pulling strings for her. She wanted to land a job on her own merits. Of course, now that she'd been stranded in Frankfurt for nearly a month, she was starting to wonder whether she'd be better off accepting his help after all.

"Aaron's still trying to win you back? He's persistent, gotta give him that." Mandy looked perplexed. With Rose living so far away now, they communicated almost exclusively via Skype. Mandy was sitting at her dining table, and Rose could see that she'd already filled several pages of her notepad with random ideas—she always noted down every book idea she got, no matter how ridiculous. Too bad she kept getting distracted by a certain friend and her constant guy-drama.

"Yeah. Creative, too. I finally figured out how he got my cell number: he called a coworker of mine that knew him from before, and she was happy to help."

"Aaron, ever the charmer. Would working for him really be that bad? I mean, haven't a bunch of people from Campbell already moved to T&H already?"

"That would be, like, out of the frying pan, into the fire."

"I doubt the thought of having you as both a coworker and a girlfriend would bother Aaron too desperately."

"I'm not going back to Aaron. And I wouldn't want to manipulate him like that, to pretend I was interested in him just so he'd give me preferential treatment. That would be dishonest."

Mandy cackled. "Wait, you work in finance and you're worried about honesty?"

"Very funny, Mandy." Rose let her gaze wander. There weren't a lot of joggers out and about on this gloomy Saturday morning. She doubted she could take sitting around here much longer. She'd sketched the Frankfurt skyline a million times, but not a single portrait.

Her first instinct had been to throw the ones of Jarred away... but what good would that do her when she was still picturing his face all the time, as clearly as if he were standing in front of her? She hadn't deleted anything of his—not his number, not his messages. Sometimes, when she couldn't sleep, she'd reread them all. Which was pure masochism on her part, since she'd always end up a complete mess afterward. She just couldn't force herself to stop; she still hadn't given up hope.

"I've got an idea, Rose."

"For a book?"

"Yeah. For a really special book."

"Let's hear it."

Rose listened with growing enthusiasm as her best friend explained a plan she'd obviously been considering for a long time. Yeah, that could work. And if it did, they'd be accomplishing several things at once...

JARRED

Monday, February 25

Dear Rose,

I found a new tea shop today and stocked up on green tea. They had a few funny mugs, but I'd rather go out with you to pick out two new ones for the house. I can't stop thinking about you, about how happy I would be if you were here with me. I was hoping this would get easier with time. Doesn't everyone say time heals all wounds? I'm fairly sure I disagree, because the memories of you are getting more painful with every passing day.
I miss you more than I have words for.

Love,
Jarred

Another day done. Three weeks with no alcohol, no poker, no women. Just Jarred and his memories.

Alice had started calling every few days after he'd told her that Vicky had bought their mom's house. He couldn't believe Vicky was still hoping they'd get back together. How delusional could she be? He'd never given her any reason to think that! But he couldn't really warm up to the thought of buying a different house, either.

Marlene called quite a bit as well. Apparently chatting on the phone was the new source of distraction he'd been hoping to find. Marlene was happy to provide detailed reports on her new recipes, updates on their mutual acquaintances… she'd even recapped the last two episodes of her favorite soap opera for him. She was also in touch with Finn and Marie, who were still negotiating with the Rutherfords. Apparently Marie was pretty stubborn when it came to price.

"Who do you think we could rent Finn's place to?" Marlene mused aloud.

"The two bedrooms are the same size, so it'd be good for roommates." If Marlene wanted to play real estate agent, Jarred didn't see the harm. Probably helped her pass the time.

"A shared flat, yeah, not a bad idea. I'm sure I'll think of someone. When are you coming over for dinner?"

"Um, I'm in Manchester, remember?"

"You're not *exiled* to Manchester. How about Friday?"

"I don't think that's such a good idea. No offense."

"Oh, come on. Nobody said you had to live like a complete hermit. Have you forgotten how to have fun?"

Jarred only listened with half an ear. Well, a weekend in London would give him a chance to talk to Vicky in person, since her plans to visit Manchester had mysteriously failed to materialize.

ROSE

Late February already. Time was slipping through her fingers like sand. She spent every free moment working on Mandy's new book, and hoped to have her illustrations finished in the next few weeks. Mandy had most of the text finished, and a friend of Mandy's would be doing the edits; now all Mandy had to do was find a printer. They only needed one copy, but it had to be perfect. Keeping the final page blank had been Rose's spontaneous idea—the cherry on top, so to speak.

She drew whenever she had a chance: in her little one-room apartment near the train station, on the promenade along the Main River, at coffee shops. Rose's new German colleagues had taken it upon themselves to show her around Frankfurt and introduce her to local delicacies. She'd never known there were so many different varieties of sausage. Frankfurters, she knew, of course... but "zeppelin sausage?" And they put this strange green sauce on all of them...

Rose missed Sunday lunches with her family. She missed everything about England, actually. Especially Jarred. She was this close to accepting Aaron's offer —there were just so few jobs advertised that fit her profile. One of them was for a position managing projects in Africa and Southeast Asia, which made her wonder how much longer the company would even remain in London. Too risky. All the others wanted one to two years of job experience, which made Rose overqualified.

Maybe she ought to talk to Sean again? Surely he didn't mean to just write her off without a second thought? Rose told herself not to get worked up over it, since it wouldn't help anyway. She had a job, right? So she ought to be content. Ought to be. For the first time in her life, she felt like walking away from it all.

CHAPTER 33

JARRED

Wednesday, March 20

Dear Rose,
This will be my last letter to you. I have to let go sooner or later. Maybe telling you goodbye will make it easier.
I hope you find someone who deserves you. A kindred spirit that understands you without saying a word, someone who will give you the moon and the stars. I wanted to be that person, but it wasn't meant to be. Goodbye, Becka Pacino. I will always love you.

Jarred.

His final letter took Jarred over an hour and about ten drafts. It ended up being a lot shorter than he'd originally intended. Jarred took a deep breath. He didn't realize he was crying until his tears dripped onto the page. Whatever. He wasn't going to send this one, either.

Henry had talked him into spending the day on the Silverstone racetrack with him. Jarred headed out that very evening, a trip that took nearly four hours in evening-rush traffic. He needed to be at the track by seven the following morning, because he still had the usual paperwork to do, even though the only thing he was renting would be a helmet. Henry was bringing his Jag. Four hundred horsepower, not bad, but Jarred's Ferrari would leave it in the dust.

After an hour-long briefing on track safety and general regulations, the real fun began at nine-thirty. "Ready to stare at my exhaust pipe for the rest of the day?" Henry grinned at Jarred confidently. He always made the same joke every year, only to take his sweet time rounding the curves.

Just being on the Formula One track was a thrill in itself, of course. Even if he were there on a bicycle, he'd still probably get goosebumps as he passed the stands. They were empty today, of course, but he'd seen them packed with a hundred thousand people before, and this year they were planning for a hundred and fifty thousand. Crazy.

Even though he'd written that final letter to Rose, and even though he was in this incredible place, Jarred just wasn't getting that sense of closure he'd been hoping for. Henry had already hit the gas, and was now tootling past him at a comfortable pace. Maybe driving around and around in a circle for a few hours would help Jarred clear his head.

There were a handful of vintage cars on the track with them, including a 1950s roadster that still managed a pretty good clip. Jarred and his Ferrari glided effortlessly past. He loved the sound his car made when he sped up. Music to his little-boy heart. He went on accelerating, since the road in front of him was clear.

He did one lap after another. A spectacularly pointless activity. His thoughts shifted to the interminable loop that his life had become in the past several weeks. Vicky was tireless in her efforts to convince Jarred to give her another chance. Sean was as irritating as he'd ever been. At least Alice had finally found a good location for her beauty salon. In Shoreditch, not far from London City, sharing the ground floor of a warehouse with a photography and design school.

Maybe he ought to just turn in his resignation tomorrow and work as Alice's receptionist. As long as he kept his hair neatly combed and put on his nicest smile, he was bound to draw customers in, right? It was a crazy idea, but the look on Sean's face would be so priceless that it might be worth it.

The roadster came into view once again. How many times had Jarred lapped him already? Was the roadster really that slow, or had he sped up without realizing it? The distance between him and the roadster continued to close, but Jarred didn't slow down. Now a Mini was pushing in beside him as well. Pure megalomania, challenging Jarred like this here. Crap, this was going to be close. He'd have to speed up as much as possible and then hit the brakes as hard as he could—the curve coming up was tight, and he wasn't trying to spin out.

The Ferrari went off like a shot a second later—seven hundred horsepower, as it turned out, was really nothing to sneeze at. He slammed on the brakes and yanked the steering wheel to the left, which the car did not seem to appreciate one bit. Jarred's heart leapt into his throat. Was he going to roll the damn thing? When the car screeched to an abrupt halt, Jarred was frozen in shock. He was half-bracing himself for whoever was behind him to smash into him. But the track remained eerily silent.

Until someone began hammering on his door.

Henry.

"Jarred. You okay? Jarred! Jarred, open the fucking door, man."

Releasing his death grip on the steering wheel took Jarred a great deal of effort, but he eventually managed to kill the engine and open the door.

"What the hell is wrong with you? Idiot! Are you

trying to kill yourself?" Henry shook him by the shoulders until Jarred finally snapped out of it.

"No," he replied calmly. "I have to get to Frankfurt."

"The only thing you *have* to do is buy me a Scotch for giving me a heart attack."

They ducked into the first pub they found.

"You did scare the bejesus out of me, you know." Henry tossed back his first drink in one gulp and promptly signaled for another. "Drink. You still have that zombie look about you."

Jarred drained his own glass before telling Henry the whole story of the past two years. By the end, all he could talk about was Rose.

"I'll be damned. You really *are* in love with her." Henry looked astonished. "You weren't just saying that because you didn't feel like going to Manchester."

"Correct."

"Well, let's drink to that, then. Can't do anything about it tonight, anyway."

They drank to that and then went right on drinking for the rest of the evening, before finally staggering to a taxi and returning to the hotel. The next day was Friday; they both decided to call in sick.

. . .

When Jarred came down to check out, he was surprised to discover Alice waiting in the lobby. "Could have saved yourself a trip," he told her. "I'm not driving back to Manchester."

"Of course you're not. That's what I'm here to do."

"One, it'll be a cold day in hell before I let you drive my car. Two, I'm quitting my job and flying to Frankfurt."

"That was three things, not two." Alice rolled her eyes and murmured something that sounded an awful lot like *stubborn ass*.

It took several minutes of convincing, but Alice finally got Jarred to agree to wait until Monday to leave Manchester for good. He didn't really understand why he couldn't just spend the weekend in London, but his head hurt too much to continue arguing.

Luckily, he managed to sleep for most of the drive. When they arrived in Manchester, he peeled himself out of the passenger seat and shuffled, exhausted, to the apartment elevator. As he pressed the button, he heard Alice calling after him, and her heels clacking loudly on the white tile floor. Much, much too loudly. Aspirin, he needed aspirin.

"Hang on! You didn't even pick up your mail."

Mail? Why would he care about his mail?

"At least give me the damn mailbox key. Thank you. Now wait here."

Jarred did as he was told, and only moved when Alice returned and physically led him into the elevator. She also unlocked his apartment door for him, and then promptly opened every window in the place.

"Cleaning isn't your strong suit, I see." She shook her head wryly at the dozens of crumpled sheets of paper littering the dining table and the floors. "What are those?"

"What do they look like?" Jarred removed his jacket and tossed it on the couch before trudging to the bathroom. Surely there had to be painkillers around here somewhere.

Alice followed him like a shadow, waving a bundle of crumpled pages at him. "You two are so ridiculous. You're writing Rose letters and not sending them?"

"Maybe," he murmured between gulps of water.

"Well, she's obviously no better."

"What the hell is that supposed to mean?"

"Open your damn mail and find out." Alice turned away, still shaking her head, and returned to the living room.

Too dazed to object, Jarred followed. There were a couple of letters on the dining table, along with a flat package. "What's in there?"

"Open the damn thing and look."

Jarred retrieved a knife from the kitchen and cautiously opened the package. Inside was a book about Maisie, but one he'd never seen before. She was sitting on a wooden bench in a frilly dress, next to what looked like a bridal pair. *Maisie Wants To Be A Flower Girl,* the cover read.

Curious, Jarred opened the book. To his astonishment, the first page showed the London Eye, and a picture of him, Rose, and Ella-slash-Maisie. Each of the following pages featured a scene of Jarred and Rose: in the Campbell Investments cafeteria, at the charity fundraiser, in Verbier, even in Jarred's apartment.

Except the images weren't of real events—they showed what would have had to happen for Maisie's wish to come true. The charity fundraiser picture showed Jarred and Rose dancing while Maisie sang on stage... obviously love songs, judging by all the little hearts around the music notes. The ones of Jarred's apartment showed him and Rose cooking together and then kissing on a balcony that stretched up into the heavens. In Verbier, they were building a snowman shaped like Cupid. It went on like that throughout the whole book.

The final illustration showed him and Rose by the banks of the Thames, cheering on their teams at the Oxford-Cambridge boat race.

"But we never went to the race, it hasn't happened yet," Jarred told Alice, who had been perusing the book with him in silence. "And the last page is blank."

"When's the race?"

"April 7th."

"Well, then, maybe you're supposed to show up to

the race in two weeks, and the last page will fill itself."

"Did you have something to do with the book?"

"Rose called me because she didn't have your address. She sounded sad, but determined. We got to chatting. She never had any intention of giving up on you; she'd be back from Frankfurt already, but she hasn't found a new job in London yet. She misses her family and her friends... she's quitting whether you show up in April or not."

Jarred could only gape at Alice. Rose had done all of this just to win him back?

"I've gotta go."

He snatched his jacket and was halfway to the door before Alice had a chance to respond.

"Wait, go where?"

"Shopping." He'd already found the perfect ring for Rose. Not that he was going to propose to her today. Or tomorrow. But maybe the day after.

ROSE

Being back in London was incredible. And everything around her was in bloom, which made it even better. The sky was a brilliant blue, the birds were singing, the crocuses and daffodils were in full flower, and the first few cherry blossoms had started to open. Her mother would be weeding and raking, fully in her element.

Today was an extra-special day, because hopefully it was the day she would see Jarred again. Alice had written to say that he'd received the book and read it. She'd put a smiley at the end, which made Rose a tiny bit more optimistic that Jarred was coming.

She was standing on Chiswick Bridge near Kew Gardens, near the finish line of the boat race. The women's race was starting at four-thirty, and the men's at five-thirty. It was only three o'clock now; Rose was super early. She was trying to decide whether to kill time by calling Mandy… when she spotted him by the riverbank.

He stopped walking and glanced around. She was standing on the rise of the pedestrian bridge. Before she even had a chance to call out, he spotted her and waved to her. Rose sprinted down the stairs—wild horses couldn't have stopped her. Jarred met her halfway, and immediately swept her into a long kiss.

"I missed you so much," he told her, gazing deeply into her eyes. "I love you, Rose Murphy, and I'm never letting you go again."

"Well, I'd say that's quite convenient, because I love you too, Jarred Campbell, and I'm never letting you go either. Unless…"

"Unless?" Jarred flinched.

"Unless you've come up with some totally horrible punishment for if I lose the bet," Rose finished in a teasing voice.

"Is a month of breakfast duty too much?"

She shook her head, smiling.

"And I get the boss cup for the whole month?"

"I can handle that."

"Lucky me, then," Jarred laughed. He took her hand and started toward Kew Gardens.

"Wait, where are we going, and what do I get if I win?"

"We're going to the tea house in the Botanical Gardens, and... what do you want? You can have anything and everything." Jarred spread his arms wide.

"Anything and everything, you say?" Rose echoed with an impish wink.

He nodded silently, suddenly looking uneasy.

"Then I want to invite you out to Watford to meet my family." Rose watched his face, and was surprised to see that he looked a lot less horrified than she'd been expecting. Actually, he seemed completely delighted.

"I'd be glad to, even if I don't lose the bet. Which is good for you, because Oxford's clearly going to crush Cambridge today," he added.

"Dream on," Rose snorted.

"You'll see."

"Not gonna happen."

EPILOGUE

ROSE

"Happy birthday." Rose snuggled against Jarred, enjoying the first rays of morning sunshine on her skin. It was early July; they'd been officially together for two months, and had hardly spent a moment apart since the boat race. They'd talked for hours, celebrated Cambridge's victory together, and Rose had returned to Manchester with him for a few days… with a quick stop in Watford, of course. Jarred had given her his crumpled love letters; she'd cried like a baby reading them. They'd decided to fly to Australia together, but they hadn't picked the exact date. They'd moved into his mother's old house—after stalling for approximately forever, Victoria had finally agreed to sell the place to Jarred for an absurdly high price.

"Thanks," Jarred murmured sleepily. "What time is it?"

"Almost eight. Marlene should be here any minute."

The disadvantage of living in a house as they renovated it was that they couldn't use the upper floors at all, so they'd been forced to set up camp on the ground floor, in what would eventually be their living room. She and Jarred had decided to renovate the whole structure from top to bottom; when they were done, the repainted façade would be the only part of the house still remotely resembling the original.

Fortunately, Henry had a functional shower and a well-stocked kitchen, both of which they made regular use of. But Rose still preferred sleeping at their place, even though her back always hated her for it in the morning.

"Too bad, I wouldn't have minded having the wifey to myself for a little while longer." Jarred brushed a strand of hair out of her face with a loving smile.

"The *wifey*? Is that this week's nickname?" Jarred was always thinking up new nicknames for her, though she actually preferred it when he called her Rose—or Becka. Becka Pacino was still at it, working hard on new books with Mandy. The book they'd done for Jarred had given rise to a new business idea; Mandy's new website now offered customized books. Most of their orders were for wedding gifts.

Marlene was helping them with every aspect of their endeavors: she was now Rose and Mandy's manager, the lead architect on their new house, and a real estate agent for friends and family. Whatever came up, Marlene was on it. Rose liked Jarred's stepmother; she was a little ball of energy, and she was firmly convinced that she'd eventually manage to make a proper family out of the Campbells.

Jarred and Rose had both quit Campbell Investments, although Jarred had referred to his own resignation as "taking a break until Sean calls and begs for help." He was acting as Marlene's assistant these days, while Rose had found work teaching watercolor technique at the photography and design school next to Alice's beauty salon, where she also helped out at the front desk.

"Not exactly a nickname. I think we should get married."

Perplexed, Rose looked into Jarred's eyes, which had a provocative twinkle. He was joking, right? "What, did you have a dream about it or something?" Shaking her head, she turned away and started to get out of bed, but Jarred pulled her back.

"We could wait until the end of the year and then spend our honeymoon in Australia." Jarred fished a small box out from under the bed and presented Rose with the most perfect ring she'd ever seen. The rose-gold band had a pale orange citrine in the center, flanked by four diamonds on each side. "What do you say, wifey?"

"You mean it?" Rose whispered.

"Of course. Unless you think I should ask your father's permission first?"

"No, no. Just be aware that you can say goodbye to your quiet life after this. All of Watford will know who you are, because my mom will tell every single person in town."

"I can live with that, Mrs. Campbell."

"So can I, Mr. Murphy."

THE END

Thank you so much for reading **FORBIDDEN**! I hope you enjoyed Jarred and Rose's story. Curious about Alice and what she was up to while in Los Angeles? Read **DESTINED** now.

It would be great if you left a short review on Amazon, it helps other readers discover new books and it gives me feedback. Thanks! ♥

To make sure you don't miss the new release, please follow me on Amazon.

AFTERWORD

New year, new series!

With the Campbells we travel to one of my favorite European cities-London!

I worked there for seven years. Went in and out of the building I attribute to Campbell Investments.

I hope you feel the flair in my stories and take this quirky family to your heart as much as I do.

Five siblings, four mothers and a fast falling in love self-made billionaire father, that's the Campbells.

If you're in the mood for an exclusive short story between now and the next release, sign up for my newsletter and receive your exclusive gift. To sign up click here: https://dl.bookfunnel.com/1j5cq8ke8k

I'd further love to hear how you liked the book. You can reach me easily at books@gloriadaven.com and if you like also leave a review on Amazon, Goodreads, your blog ... and please recommend the book to others. Especially in self-publishing, we authors depend on it. Thank you from the bottom of my heart!

With love
    Gloria

ABOUT THE AUTHOR

Click "Follow" and never miss a new release!

Gloria lives with her husband and her ten-year-old son in beautiful Switzerland. When she's not reading, she's writing. And drinking Australian coconut cream coffee–her newest addiction!

Get in touch with Gloria:

Facebook: www.facebook.com/gloriadavenauthor
Instagram: https://www.instagram.com/gloriadaven_author
Website: www.gloriadaven.com
Bookbub: @gloriadaven
E-Mail: books(at)gloriadavon.com

ALL BOOKS BY GLORIA

The London Lawyer: A Second Chance Romance

The Fratelli Family Saga

Three siblings of a Roman gastronomic family are in search of their personal happiness. With humor and heartbreak to the happy end!

Unexpected Love: Opposites Attract Romance

My Forbidden Love: Boss Romance

Falling for the Italian: Enemies to Lovers Romance

The Campbell Family Saga

Five siblings, four mothers and a self-made billionaire father who quickly falls in love. Quick-witted, funny and with a guaranteed HAE!

Forbidden: A Billionaire Boss Romance

Copyright © 2021 by Gloria Daven and Rosenfeder AG

All rights reserved.

No part of this book may be reproduced in any form or by any electronic or mechanical means, including information storage and retrieval systems, without written permission from the author, except for the use of brief quotations in a book review.

This is a work of fiction.

Edited and translated into English: Jaime McGill

Cover design: Hippomonte Publishing e.K.

Cover photos: Background © by MPF_photography, www.depositphotos.com, Stockphoto-ID: 12762384; man © by ikostudio, www.depositphotos.com, Stockphoto-ID: 68909937; logo © by raftel, www.depositphotos.com, Stockphoto-ID: 84323896

Made in the USA
Middletown, DE
07 September 2022

73435799R00217